PAYBACK AIN'T ENOUGH

WAHIDA CLARK

CASH MONEY CONTENT

CASH MONEY CONTENT

First Trade Paperback Edition: April 2012

Book Layout: Peng Olaguera/ISPN

Cover Design: Nuance Art

For further information log onto www.CashMoneyContent.com

Library of Congress Control Number: 2011931198

ISBN: 978-1-936-39911-6 pbk
ISBN: 978-1-936-39912-3 ebook

10 9 8 7 6 5 4 3 2 1

Printed in the United States

To all my loyal readers. Love you much!

ACKNOWLEDGMENTS

All praise is due to the Creator. Wow! Book number eleven. Who would have thought it and where did the time go? I owe it to my readers, no doubt.

A special shout-out goes to all of you who made this book, *Payback Ain't Enough,* possible: Nuance Art, Al-Nisa, Hasana, Nobel, Maxine Thompson, Intelligent Allah, Keisha Caldwell (whose name was supposed to be in *Justify My Thug*), Molly Derse—thank you for your diligence, Linda Wilson, and Alanna Boutin. Everybody behind the scenes at S&S. Thank you. If I missed anyone, you know who you are.

Much love and thanks to the Cash Money Fam. Watch what I do in 2012!

Peace!

Wahida Clark

Follow me, the Official Queen of Street Literature at:
twitter.com@wahidaclark
facebook.com/wahidaclarkreadersclub
www.wclarkpublishing.com.

PAYBACK AIN'T ENOUGH

CHAPTER ONE

Fuck what you heard. Scratch all that shit that you was told before. This is the realest, slickest, illest shit right here.
—NICK

FOREVER

The only thing worse than being a prisoner in my own skin is the feeling of helplessness as I listen to the bloodcurdling screams echo from the next cell as a man gets another man's dick rammed up his ass.

Who would've thought that I, Forever Thompson, would be serving a life sentence confined to a fuckin' wheelchair and paralyzed from the waist down? I remembered it as if it was just yesterday, hearing my name followed by those six words, "You are hereby sentenced to LIFE." All of my dirt flashed across my mind after I heard those words. And to think that all this bad karma surrounding me started over some pussy and dough. A dangerous combination that will suck you in every time!

It all began with me using that bitch Shan to mule my dope into the prison. But no, I couldn't stop there. I had to fuck her and get her pregnant. Now, here I am again, for the thousandth time thinking about those I left behind: my brother, Briggen, by the same mother, my wife, Nyla, my daughter, Tameerah, and last but not least, my first cousin and partner-in-crime, Zeke.

"Bust cell 49!" I could hear the goon squad yelling into their radios and the sound of their boots hitting the cement steps. I knew shit was getting ready to get real ugly for at least one muthafucka. Forty-Nine was right next to me, and I could hear it in surround sound, the cat in the cell next to me screaming. It was the familiar sound of prison rape.

I sat in my wheelchair knowing what was getting ready to happen next. When the goons rushed past my cell I heard 49's door pop open. A few minutes later, they were dragging T-Bone, the punk-ass rapist, out. He didn't even bother to offer up any resistance. I watched as they stood him up and rested him against my cell with his hands cuffed behind him and a billy club to the throat.

The losing opponent was a new guy who had just come in yesterday. He came out wrapped in a sheet and limping slowly. He met eyes with me, and I could see the pain and fear peering through his tear-filled, red eyes. As the guards attempted to walk him past my cell, he lunged forward with a shiny object and stuck it into T-Bone's side about four or five times before the goons wrestled him to the ground. *Damn.* Old T wasn't the winner after all.

Bone slid down the bars of my cell and hit the floor. As

the blood trickled out of his mouth all I could say was, "You should have stayed true to the pussy."

DARK

"You ready?" I stood outside of Forever's cell and asked him for the hundredth time, as it was my courtesy to take him to make his regular Thursday pickups.

"Sheeeit. Nigga, you heard what happened up here earlier?" Forever asked as he maneuvered the remote on his wheelchair.

"I caught a little something," I told him.

"Yeah, that punk-ass rapist T-Bone finally got his ass handed to him trying to fuck one of them young boys who ended up guttin' his ass."

"Get the fuck outta here." I tried to act surprised. The young dude was Lenny. He was my homey Ray Ray's cousin, who had just went home. I tried to pull some strings and get him in another cell because I knew what he would be up against. But I couldn't swing it until next Monday and I'd already be gone. I gave him a shiv and schooled the young nigga. I told him to handle dude as soon as he stepped in the cell or get handled. I guess they both got handled, and I couldn't have cared less because I had much bigger fish to fry. "It's just another day in USP, Jonesboro," I said to Forever.

"Punk muthafuckas." Forever shook his head and wheeled himself out of his cell.

I got behind him and began to push him across the compound. As we passed the TV area, niggas were playing cards, chess, gambling, and talking shit. The shit reminded me of that HBO special *OZ*. Forever got his usual shout-outs since he still carried much weight in the Feds and he had much respect . . . wheelchair and all. And I had to admit I received plenty of benefits from being on his team.

"Yo, I need you to go pick up that weed from Shokkah," he told me.

"Aiight. I got you," I said as I continued to roll him down the corridor. After the first few stops I began to roll him in the opposite direction of Shokkah's cell.

"Hold up, where the fuck you going?" Forever snapped. Something I was used to.

"Nigga, Shokkah ain't going nowhere. They servin' that barnyard pimp today. You know everybody and they momma gonna be at chow. My man is gonna hook us up." I continued to roll him toward the chow hall.

"Word." Forever was in total agreement with me.

FOREVER

It was Thursday, and my man Dark was right. It was chicken day and every nigga in this bitch was rushing to the chow hall.

"What up, Moe?" I asked one of my newest customers.

"Forever, I gotta holla at you later."

"I'm sure you do, nigga. You know I got you," I told him. It was also payday for those niggas who worked in the Unicor factory. Payday was always a very busy day for me.

"Yo, where we going?" I asked Dark's black ass for the second time. Chow was to my right, but he was wheeling me to the left. My antenna went up. "Yo, nigga, what's up?" Dark wouldn't answer me. I looked back at him, and he was looking straight-ahead with this glassy look in his eyes. I saw that same look on him before. It was right before he took out King Bey. And I saw it again, right before he took out Big Will. Dark got off on taking niggas out. He was that one nigga who loved to put in work.

"Fuck!" I spat as I slapped the arm of my wheelchair. Dark laughed. He knew I had just caught on to what he was about to do. He picked a damn good day and time to do this. And the fucked-up thing was I didn't even see it coming.

I ignored my gut when it warned me that this mutha-fuckin' Dark was a snake! And as usual, my gut was right! I shouldn't have trusted him—let alone taken him under my wing. Youngins these days don't respect the code, and they damn sure don't respect one another. Shit . . . I should know. I used to be one of them grimy, backstabbing, lying, conniving muthafuckas. Here I done put the nigga up on game. I made him, gave him all the jewels and the word on any and everybody who thought that they were somebody, and now this dirty bastard was preparing to do me in. These new niggas got the game fucked up! How can I, a nigga in a wheelchair, be a threat to this muthafucka? I can't do shit for myself, let alone to him.

My wife, Nyla, made a huge attempt from day one to stay by my side and to do this bid with me. But every time she came to visit me, the look of pity and disgust on her face told it all, so I told the bitch to step. Fuck her. I couldn't stand for her to sit there and look at me like I was some fuckin' cripple. "Yo, anybody around? This Forever!" I yelled out.

"Chill out. Ain't nobody else down here, maine," Dark said as he looked back and forth down the hall before closing the double doors to the laundry room. He then wheeled me over to the far wall, snatched the remote off my chair, and hit the lock at the bottom so that I was parked.

"What's up? What's it gonna be?" I asked him.

"Forever, you a smart dude. I know you know what this is," Dark said as he pulled a cord out of his pockets and began tying my wrists behind my wheelchair.

I simply looked at this nigga and wished to have five minutes where my body was fully functional so I could stand up and rip this nigga's heart out of his chest. At that moment, it seemed that all of the washing machines started their spin cycle. Dark mumbled something, stepped away, and then grabbed some rubber gloves out of a bucket. My heart fell to my feet as he put them on, and as he was doing so the nigga had the nerve to be smiling. This nigga was crazy for real. I remember like it was yesterday, the day I took him under my wing.

I had been watching him the minute he arrived at the pen. Even though he was ruthless, he was a stand-up type of dude who wasn't on that homo-thuggin' shit. I got some niggas together, and we went to go see what he was made of. My crew cornered him up in the shower as I fell back in the cut.

"So you that nigga, Dark?" my dude Ronnie had asked him. No sooner than the words left his mouth, the other guys who were in the shower began to file out. They knew instantly what it was.

"You don't look like a man that would pick the wrong muthafucka. So do what you came for," I heard Dark say.

Okay cool. So the nigga wasn't backing down. He passed the first test.

Anxious, Ronnie was the first one to go at him, and they went at it. When the other niggas saw that Ronnie was being given a run for his money, they all jumped on him. Dark was swinging and tossing those niggas left and right. When they saw they had no wins, Gator pulled out a shank and started to swing. I sat amused, watching Dark duck and weave. Dark grabbed Ronnie and pulled him in front of him using him as a shield.

"Enough!" I screamed at them niggas. Immediately everyone started to stand down, but Dark was still holding on to Ronnie. He was breathing heavy and was ready to get it in. "Dark, let the muthafucka go," I told him.

Gator said, "You a lucky bitch today."

"You the lucky muthafucka," Dark spat, shoving Ronnie into Gator.

"I'll get with y'all later," I said. The four of them backed up slowly. Once they were all gone I moved closer to him.

"I don't owe you shit," he said right away in an attempt to let me know that he wasn't the type of nigga that was going to live his bid paying the next nigga back.

"I didn't say you owed me anything. And I don't owe you. But when shit wear off, come see me," I told him and then backed up and rolled out.

Once shit had time to cool down he came to see me and after that first conversation we became inseparable. Now here I was about to lose my life to the only nigga that I can say I trusted. Oh well, fuck it! It is what it is. Sometimes you the killah, sometimes you the prey.

I knew that Dark would kill a man for me at the blink of an eye and took pride in doing it! He had so much potential.

Niggas would tease him and tell him that he looked like that dude off of *Martin,* Brother-man from the fifth floor, and he would get pissed. He was just darker. Fuck that, the nigga was pitch black. Dark was a quiet dude, and at the same time he was gung ho. He had no qualms about puttin' in work, and he had lots of niggas shook because his hot temper was easy to set off.

"I appreciate how you put me on game and everything. It's mostly because of you that I'ma get out and get on top where I belong, real fast. And I'ma stay there," he told me.

The more I looked at him, the more he looked like the devil. That glazed look in his eyes grew more intense.

"See what happens when the student gets ahead of the teacher? You really think it's that easy, huh? You're gonna become the don overnight? You really think you're gonna come from behind these walls and take over? I created you with these hands, and by these hands I will destroy you." I spoke firmly like a father to his disobedient son or like Geppetto to ignorant-ass Pinocchio; this wood nigga thinks he's about to become a real boy.

"Show me a nigga that gets on top and stays on top and I'll kill myself and save you the trouble," I told him, at the same time wondering how I was going to die.

"It's my time to shine, Forever. I'ma get out and shake shit up! Too bad you won't be around to hear my name. And for the record, this shit right here is only business. It's not personal."

"Business for who? At least you can tell me that!" I needed to know. Only because I wanted to know how deep the saying "You reap what you sow" went. He ignored me and disappeared behind one of the industrial-sized washers. I heard him coughing. And then he reappeared, wearing a mask and carrying two thin plastic bottles.

"This bleach shit is strong," he said while coughing.

"Bleach? Nigga, why won't you just slit my throat and get it over with?"

"Nah, this is how they want it done. It's bleach and ammonia. And don't worry about for who. It don't matter nohow. You outta here."

"Fuck you, nigga. You doin' me a favor."

"Fuck me? Nah, fuck you, nigga," he said as he came toward me.

"Sheeeit . . . If you can earn stripes off of killing a handicap, then you deserve to be on top. I'll even give you my parking spot! Pussy-ass nigga!" He thought he was killing me? Sheeeit, I died the day that bitch Shan pulled the trigger and put me in this fuckin' wheelchair. Fuck the bullshit I ain't mad; I'm relieved. I laughed in that nigga's face, and if he was close enough I would spit in it. "My streets gon' eat yo' ass up," I said. "You young and you dumb."

"You watch. This time tomorrow, you'll be in the fridge and I'll be a free man preparing to claim my throne," Dark gloated. As his mouth twitched as if he were the joker.

Suddenly I began to laugh uncontrollably. "Throne? Who the fuck you think you is? There's a million-and-one hustlers just like you on the streets. I hope you got enough bullets!" I snapped. As I watched Dark adjust the mask over his nose.

DARK

I knew I shouldn't be doing this. Here I was getting out in about thirty-six hours and I gots to kill me a nigga one more time before I hit the bricks. Why did I have to do this? What stupid nigga would take this kind of chance? Why jeopardize my freedom like this? I could just walk away and chill out for the next thirty-six. Just as those thoughts ran through my mind, Forever looked over at me. And that look, the expression on his face, convinced me that I had to do this.

"I don't know why you playin'. You and all the rest of your Memphis muthafuckas around here don't know who the fuck I am and what the fuck I'm capable of. Y'all punks ain't the only ones who gets down and dirty. I'm from the 'D', and we gets it in too. D is also for Dark, muthafucka!" I said as I prepared myself to pour the strong-ass concoction down Forever's throat.

His ass being in a wheelchair made my deed much easier to carry out. With his wrists tied together behind his back, I put him in a chokehold. And since his mouth was open and he was talking smack, I shoved the opening of the bottle into his mouth, forcing him to swallow over half of the poisonous liquid. I stepped back and looked at him. Nothing was happening and then finally he started gagging. His body jerked and writhed uncontrollably. I was getting excited. The skin on his face turned yellow, and craters popped up. Blisters sprung up all around his lips. The whites of his eyes were now dark red, and tears streamed down his cheeks. His purple tongue now dangled out of his mouth. The shit was unreal. I'd never seen anything like it. He started puking yellow shit and shook his head violently from side to side. After a few more jerks, his body went still.

I snatched off the jumper I had on over my khaki uniform and balled it up. I took off the gloves and pulled off the mask that covered my nose and mouth so I wouldn't inhale the fumes. Unfortunately the mask wasn't helping. I couldn't stop coughing. I should have worn a pair of goggles because my eyes were stinging.

I threw everything in the trash bin, poured the remaining concoction over everything, and then wheeled Forever all the way to the back of the laundry room. Dude was fucked up. I went over my crime scene before opening the doors and peeking both ways. It was dead. I shut the doors and made my way back to my unit. My mentor was gone.

I couldn't get back to my dorm fast enough to jump in the shower, hoping that I didn't reek of that smell. I stripped and put all of my clothes in the washer. By now, my eyes were burning so bad I could hardly see. And that bleach shit was fucking with my breathing. I wished that I had taken Forever up on his offer and slit the nigga's throat and been done with it. But the reality was, slitting his throat would have been too messy, and this job had to be clean. Doing the deed damn sure was putting my release date on the line. Thirty-six more hours and I was a free, fuckin' man.

SHAN

When Briggen introduced me to Nick I could feel all of the color drain from my face. I was just hoping that he didn't notice. But he did, and he asked me, "Are you feeling sick again?"

"A little," I heard my voice squeak as I sat down on the lawn chair. We were chillin' in our backyard. It was almost seventy degrees. I hadn't seen or heard from my brother Peanut's road dawg and partner-in-crime in a couple of years. Nick showing up in my backyard threw me for a loop. He had a long history with my brother and I. He used to fuck with my best friend, Brianna. I had a hell of a crush on him while I was in high school and me and him held a secret that no one else knew.

"Let me get you a ginger ale. Nick, I'll be right back, and then we can make that run," Briggen said.

Nick waited patiently for Briggen to get out of earshot. I was so emotional I was trying not to cry. Nick was the only other family I had, and he just up and disappeared. Before I could get a word out, Nick beat me to it.

"You didn't think I would forget all about you?" he asked me. "Are you okay? And you're pregnant?"

"Nick! Oh my God! What are you doing here? Where have you been?"

"And who is this?" He got down on one knee and looked at my son. "He looks just like Peanut."

"That's exactly who he is," I said. "This is Li'l Peanut."

"Shan, are you alright? Sorry it took me so long to get to you. I promised your brother that no matter what happened I would watch over you. And I failed to keep that promise. How did you hook up with Brig? You were always against fucking with hustlers."

"Briggen ain't no hustler, Nick."

"Shan, you can't be that naïve. Why do you think I'm here? I only fucks with hustlers."

"Nick, I live with the man. I should know. He gave up that lifestyle a long time ago. He did that for me," I spoke in a hushed, angry tone. More angry that this is what he wanted to talk about instead of what the fuck, or should I say, where the fuck he had been. "Where have you been? What are you doing here? How did you end up in Detroit of all places?"

I didn't get any answers because Briggen was coming back into the yard.

"Brig, you all married up and shit. Got a son and one on the way. A playa like you got me baffled, dawg."

I watched as a wide-ass grin spread across my baby's face as he handed me the ginger ale he had poured over ice. Nick really shocked the hell out of me. What the fuck did he mean he only fucked with hustlers? What business did he and Briggen have together? My gut instinct told me to chill and act as if me and Nick just met.

NYLA

Somehow I knew the sound of my house phone ringing meant one of two things. A bill collector or bad news. I looked at the caller ID and was surprised to see that it read Bureau of Prisons. Forever had just called yesterday. He usually called only in the beginning of the week and at the end.

"Hello." I was expecting to hear the familiar recording, "You have a prepaid call."

But instead, there was a gentle voice that asked, "Good morning. Is this Nyla Thompson?"

I had to think about what he had just asked me. "Yes, it

is. Who may I ask is calling?" My defenses were climbing by the second.

"This is Chaplain Purnell from United States Penitentiary Jonesboro." He got quiet as if he was waiting for his words to sink in.

I finally asked, "How can I help you, Chaplain?" I was now breathing in spurts.

"Your husband, Forever Thompson. He passed away—"

"Excuse me?"

"I'm sorry, Mrs. Thompson but your husband passed—" My fingers went numb and I dropped the phone. What did he mean, Forever passed away? Did he know what he was implying?

"Noooo! God, no." I released a bloodcurdling scream. "Not now. Don't do this to me and my baby. Not now." I started praying. My knees buckled, and I went to grip the kitchen sink and missed it. I fell to the floor, flat on my face. "Not now, Lord. I need a little more time." I lay right there on the floor and began to cry. I cried until I couldn't cry anymore.

Mourning was strange because my level of sadness was damn near buried by my anger. I was angry because he left me, but more important, he left our daughter. I was angry because I didn't get the chance to show him that I was going to remain by his side regardless . . . through sickness and in health. Just because he was sentenced to life and had been in that wheelchair for the last two years, I wasn't going to divorce him or leave him there in that prison to rot. I still loved him and would always love him. I was angry because I tried to do my best by him and angry because I hadn't seen him in two hundred and twelve days—even though that was his fault.

He's the one who stopped me from coming to see him. Two hundred and twelve days. Yes, I was keeping count. And now I was angry that I'd never see him again. I was angry that our marriage ended up a total disaster. "What were the last seven years for?" I screamed as I pounded the floor.

Shit started going downhill as soon as he started fucking that prison teacher bitch, Shan, and getting the home wrecker pregnant. Then when he was released he couldn't leave the bitch alone. Whatever the bitch was doing must have been good. The nigga went after her and ended up shooting her brother, the same brother who I was creeping with. She was the one who ended up shooting Forever. Why wasn't she in prison instead of my Forever? Why does she get to live happily ever after with her man, Briggen? And me, why do I have to be all alone? I never could figure that out.

The longer I lay on the cold floor, the more questions swirled around in my head. What happened to my husband? Chaplain Purnell didn't say he was killed but I know that's what happened. Who did this to him? Why did they do this to him? He was in a wheelchair for God's sake! How can you be in a wheelchair and paralyzed and make enemies? That shit made no sense to me, which definitely supported my theory that this vendetta had to be over some old shit, and it had Briggen and Shan's names all over it.

Oh my God! I jumped up and began pacing the floor. I snatched up the phone off the floor from me not hanging up and dialed my sister.

"Lisha?"

"What's up, Nyla? Why are you sounding sooooooo funny?"

"Forever," I whispered his name.

"What? Forever what?"

"I got a call from the prison. He's dead, Lisha. He's gone."

"Oh God, no, Nyla." I could hear her scrambling around. "Give me twenty minutes. I'll be right there."

"No!" I stopped her.

"What do you mean no?"

"I'm on my way out."

"Out where? Where's Tameerah? How are you going to tell her?"

"She's in school. But I'm on my way over to give the news to Briggen."

"To Briggen?" she snapped.

"Lisha, I'll swing by your house when I'm done." I hung up and couldn't find my keys fast enough. The walls were crashing down around me. I rushed out the front door, jumped in my car and sped off.

BRIGGEN

"Who the fuck is that banging on the door like that?" I rushed to my bedroom window, looking down on my freshly manicured front lawn, but didn't see anyone.

"I'll get it," Shan yelled from the living room.

It was almost noon, and I was getting my little two-year-old Peanut dressed. He and I was about to hit the streets. We had our new True Religion outfits laid out. It was warm and sunny outside, and I needed to go see a few people. That was when I heard all of the rumbling. I put Li'l Peanut in his playpen and dashed downstairs into the living room. Nyla and Shan were going at it. Nyla was on top of Shan, trying to punch her in the face. Shan was try-ing to block the punches. She was four months pregnant so I had to move quickly before she jeopardized my seed. I snatched a kicking and screaming Nyla up off Shan. I had her in a chokehold.

"Get off of me, Briggen!" Nyla foamed at the mouth, fight-ing me as if I was her number-one enemy. "I know this bitch was in on it, wasn't she? You probably was in on it too. What role did you play, Briggen? Huh? The both of you mutha-fuckas was in on it! I know it!" she screamed as I tossed her down onto the sofa.

"Nyla, what the fuck is you talking about?" I asked.

"You know darn well what I'm talking about," she snapped, popping back up and rushing at me.

Shan was up off the floor coming for Nyla. She had her brother's old football trophy in her hand and was looking like a raging bull. I could tell she was getting ready to go all in on her.

"Shan, back the fuck up! You pregnant, remember?" I shouted.

"Fuck that! This bitch jumped on me first!" Shan yelled, though she did stop gripping the trophy so firmly.

"Forever's gone, Briggen! Your brother is gone! But then again, you already knew that, didn't you? You probably arranged the hit!" she screamed.

I froze in place, and Nyla slid out of my arms and fell to the floor. Frantic, she turned and looked up at me. She was trying to read me.

"He's gone, Briggen," she sobbed. "He's no longer a part of our lives."

"What do you mean *gone*?" I knew she wasn't saying what I thought she was saying. My little brother couldn't be dead.

"I got the call earlier this morning. They killed him. Briggen, I'm telling you this bitch had something to do with it. You can't trust her," Nyla said, still trying to catch her breath. She sounded crazy. One minute she was blaming Shan, the next minute she was blaming me. Then she blamed both of us.

"I'm not gon' be too many more of your bitches!" Shan said, coming toward us.

"You gon' be whatever I call you, bitch!" Nyla yelled jumping up off the floor.

They started spitting profanity and name-calling back and forth while trying to get at each other.

"Both of y'all shut the fuck up!" I yelled as I stood between them. I turned my gaze on Shan first. "Take yo' ass upstairs. Now!" I said between gritted teeth. Then I turned my attention back to Nyla.

"First of all, you know as well as I do that Forever had enemies," I said as I gave her the grittiest stare that I could. I actually wanted her to keep it in her mind that, yes, I could have done it.

"You love that bitch more than you love your own brother? Your blood?" she asked with her eyes squinted. At the same time she was breathing hard, as if she were possessed. I'd never seen her like this before.

"Let me share something with you. That nigga, my brother, Forever, who I used to know and love, has been dead to me for years. So this little so-called bad news you call yourself delivering doesn't affect me one way or the other. So, I suggest you take the blame game somewhere else because if I would have done it, you wouldn't be here guessing. You'd know."

Obviously that shocked her because it took a minute for her to speak. "You're a coldhearted muthafucka, Briggen. That was your brother."

"Yeah, and you're a piece of pussy that my brother and Shan's brother, Peanut, passed back and forth like a Dutch. So don't act like you care all of a sudden. Scandalous-ass ho. Get the fuck outta my house before they end up burying you next to him!"

Her mouth hung open. I could tell that those words cut deep. "How could you disrespect me like that, Briggen? You know me better than that."

Eavesdropping, Shan charged down the stairs. "Oh, we *know* you alright."

Nyla laughed. "So, you conveniently forgot all about how your woman was being passed around from brother to brother? You and Forever both was diggin' in this ho's pussy. We was just one big ole happy fuckin' family, wasn't we? Oh, that don't count? Brig, watch what I tell you. You better get rid of this plastic bitch! She ain't all about you, the way she claim to be. She don't mean you no good."

"That's it, bitch!" Shan stormed up to her, grabbed her by the throat, and pushed her out the front door and slammed it shut. I didn't know she was that strong and could move that fast.

A few seconds later I heard glass shatter. Nyla had thrown a brick through the window.

"You and that bitch will pay! Mark my words!" Nyla yelled, and then gave the door one last pound before storming off the porch, jumping in her car and tearing out of the driveway.

SHAN

As I stood by the window watching Nyla storm off and peel out of our driveway, I couldn't help but conjure up a smile. I was sure I wasn't the only one who wanted that nigga Forever dead, and if he suffered any, that would be the icing on the cake. But the news that he died alone actually tickled me. Words could not explain the humiliation I felt when he used me to bring in his dope, fucked me, and when I got pregnant, wanted me to get an abortion, making it clear that I was just a fuck and a sucka.

The thought crossed my mind to go to the funeral, but I quickly brushed that off. For one, if I saw Nyla again, it would be on. And two, I would end up spitting in Forever's cold face. That would cause too much drama for Briggen. I was gloating that Forever was gone. However, my moment came to a screeching halt when Briggen stormed out of the house without saying a word.

CHAPTER TWO

DARK

It was Monday afternoon, and I was amped. I was free! I was relieved that there were three killings and a wounded guard the same day I killed him. They didn't even get a chance to question me about Forever's death. It didn't matter now. I was gone. And I had just taken two flights from Virginia to Detroit. I ate a hot dog and cheese fries from Nathan's, a burger from Johnny Rockets and had ice cream from Baskin Robbins. It was a step up from the usual prison cuisine. But I had to admit, the airports were intimidating to a killer like me. I was getting lost and feeling like everyone knew I was lost and had just stepped out of prison.

"I'ma freeeee man!" I sang out loud as I leaned over and kissed my cousin and partner-in-crime, Sharia, on the cheek. She picked me up in a black Porsche SUV, with the peanut butter seats. I didn't even know there was such a thing.

"Nigga, I don't know where your lips been!" she said as she wiped my kiss off her cheek. "And fasten your seat belt."

"Girl, you betta stop playin' and recognize. I'm about to make you rich!" I told her.

"Negro, please! We about to make each other rich. You need me—remember? Plus, I'ma be puttin' in work, too," Sharia proclaimed proudly, wheeling her smooth ride through the airport traffic.

"Giving me info and gettin' all pretty to sit up at the bar ain't puttin' in work," I teased.

Yeah, I was only teasing. And she was right. I needed her. Even though Forever put me up on game, he wasn't out here on the streets with up-to-date intel. I needed real, live info on the new players. Those on top and the ones tryna get there. I needed to get close to somebody high up on the food chain and for what I needed done, only a chick could do. And who better than a bad-ass bitch like Sharia and someone close to me that I could trust.

Sharia was that bitch that made it possible for all them pole-dancing hoes to have those big asses. Her shit was illegal. She learned from a plastic surgeon that she used to work for and took what he was doing and made it her own hustle. Now for 3 Gs a cheek she would inject anything that she thought would plump those asses up. She worked out of hotel rooms keeping her hustle on the move. The best part was the main bitches that could afford her ass injections were those that worked the poles for their pimp daddies, and those hoes that fucked around with and chased them hustlers. Those very same bitches told all of their business. And those were the niggas that we were after. My plan wasn't to rob them. Hell no! I just needed to be put on, introduced to all the key players, and then make my move.

SHARIA

I had been waiting on this day for damn near a year and a half. I needed to show all them muthafuckas around here who really had the last laugh. And, for all who didn't know, that would be me.

Niggas thought it was funny when I lost my club for a measly fucking two dollars. Actually, I didn't lose my club. Briggen stole it from right under me. That was followed up by me losing him to some off-brand bitch who was fucking both, Briggen and his brother, Forever. That nigga, my ex, Briggen, don't respect nothing. The sad part was he fucked over everybody who cared about him. That's why I was now in the fast lane headed for Payback. Thanks to my hungry cousin, Mills aka Dark, my day was coming soon. But first things first. I had to stay focused. I had to hook this nigga up with some gear. He needed an outfit to wear to the funeral I was sure that Forever's people were going to have and to a couple of big parties they had been promoting the shit out of the last few months. If we couldn't get the leads we needed from the funeral of a former baller and some parties, then we were some sorry-ass muthafuckas that didn't deserve to come up.

BRIGGEN

I was driving around the city, veered off and ended up in front of Mia's. I hadn't been back home since Nyla came by and told me that Forever was gone, and that was three days ago. I gotta admit I was feeling some kinda way since I cut him off. After all, he was my brother, even though he did do some stupid shit. But hell, who didn't? Even though I was mad at him, I didn't want him to die, especially not the way he did, bound to a wheelchair and I got word that he was drowned in bleach.

Shan had been blowin' up my phone with texts asking when I was coming home. "I'll be there when I get there," I texted her back. Right then, I just needed to clear my head. Partly because she was a big part of this picture. He was fucking her at one time, and then I took her. And plus, I was busy pulling strings to get Forever's body from the prison in record time. My moms wasn't having it any other way. She said fuck all of the Bureau of Prison's red tape.

I rang the bell and Mia opened up. She and I used to kick it heavy, that is, until Shan came along. Shan showed up right when I thought I was ready to purge myself of anything and anybody that had to do with the streets. That included hustling, Mia, Sharia and Tami. My plan was to go one-hundred percent legit. That notion, however, didn't last for long. Shan and I had been together for the last two years, but I got bored, living the square life. In less than six months I craved the action of the streets.

Finally, Mia appeared in the doorway sporting a sheer nightie and not a damn thing else, saving me from my thoughts of one sin while replacing them with another.

"Damn, girl! Can't you put on a robe or something?" I inquired, not that I minded her little show.

"Last time I checked, this was *my* house. It's 2 A.M., and

besides, it ain't like I'm showing you something you ain't seen before," she said as she slammed the door behind me.

"What's up, Mia?"

"For what it's worth, sorry about Forever."

"What else is up, Mia? You called me over here," I asked, exhausted and exasperated at the same time.

"And just like the obedient nigga you are, you came running, didn't you?" she gloated.

This chick was still bitter because she could no longer get the dick. I stopped blessing her a little over two years ago, but she refused to let what we had in the past go. "I don't have time for this shit," I said as I turned and headed for the door.

"Briggen, stop it with the attitude. I'm serious." She paused for a moment. "Demetria got busted," she told me.

I stopped in midstep and stood there hoping I heard her wrong.

"She got busted last night."

Demetria was my main mule and had been running my dope for a little over a year. She only got busted once before and kept her mouth shut. *So what happened?* I wondered.

"And you just telling me now?" I bellowed as I turned and got up in her face.

"I tried sending you messages, but they said nobody could find you! I told them you was playing house and for them to go by and let you know that it was an emergency. But them niggas was scared and on that, 'nobody goes to Brig's crib' bullshit. I would have come myself, but that ho you shackin' up with probably would've come slick out of her mouth, and then you would've been bailing both me and Demetria out," Mia explained.

"Where was she?"

"I think she was coming through Arkansas. The same place she got popped before."

"Fuck!" I gritted. "What did she say?"

"She hasn't called me yet!" Mia blurted.

"What the fuck you mean she hasn't called you yet?" I looked at her like she was crazy.

"She called her sister!"

"Sharia? She called Sharia?"

"Yeah, it's odd to me too. And I only found that out because of Melky." Mia's voice sounded suspicious. Melky was one of my most trusted workers.

Damn! I knew she had twelve keys a piece of both raw and dope. And Sharia? Hell, she couldn't stand her damn sister and wouldn't extend a rope to Demetria if the bitch was stuck in a ditch. I could understand why Mia was skeptical. The shit ain't adding up. I needed some answers and I needed them fast. I stood there, trying to run what little details I knew of the scenario through my head but kept coming up empty. First Forever, and now this? Shit wasn't right; that's all I knew. I sat down on the sofa, not sure what moves I was going to make next. I lived for these moments. That shit was like a live chess game.

"So what are you going to do?" Mia asked as she sat down next to me.

"The first thing you need to do is call Rudy," I told her. Rudy had been my attorney ever since I got in the game.

"What do you think about her calling Sharia and not head-quarters?" Mia inquired.

I lay my head back and thought about her questions.

Demetria's actions definitely raised a red flag. She was in total violation. We have rules, and she had just broke a cardinal one. That's not a good sign in the game. I planned to have Rudy look into the root of her deviation. Everybody knew those two sisters didn't get along, and Demetria can't stand Sharia, which made it all the more suspect.

"Let Rudy do the diggin'. In the meantime, keep your eyes open and your mouth shut. I want niggas to stay asleep," I ordered.

"If you say so," Mia said sarcastically sweet. She was the one who told me not to use Demetria, and if I did, it was going to come back to haunt me. I hated to admit it, but by the looks of things, she just might turn out to be right.

"You damn right, *if I say so*," I glared at her. "Right now, we don't know shit. We can only speculate, and I'm not one for speculation." Mia folded her arms across her chest, sat back and clammed up. I took that as my cue to leave. I stood up, and she grabbed my hand.

"Briggen, don't leave," she pleaded.

"I gotta go," I stated sternly.

"Answer me this. You don't find me sexy anymore?" she asked as she took her finger, circled her nipple, and then ran it down her stomach.

"Mia, don't start that bullshit. You know I got shit to take care of right now." She was turning me on, but it was not the time.

"Briggen, she will never love you the way I love you," she professed as she moved closer to me. "I don't know why you can't see that. And she will never have your back the way I do. You do know that, right?"

"Mia, it's over between us." I looked her right in the eyes.

"Just remember those words when she shows you her true colors," she warned.

"Mia, let it go, aiight?"

"Well, answer me this, Briggen. Why did it stop working between us? Because at one time, I was all you needed. What does she have that I don't? She has nothing, Briggen, nothing."

"Mia, just do what I told you. I'll talk to you later," I said as I turned and walked out.

What the fuck was going on? She was the second bitch in less than a week to tell me to watch my wife and that she was a fake.

MIA

And just like that he was gone. I swore to myself the last time that I saw him, I was not going to let him see me sweat. But just like the last time, I caved. "Damn it!" I said as I locked my front door. "Damn it, Mia!" I fumed again.

Whenever Briggen came around, it was still a struggle for me. And he could lie to himself all he wanted, but I knew that he still loved me. And I wasn't buying that good-wife-at-home-I'ma-have-your-kids bullshit. To this day, I haven't been able to put my finger on it, but I do know that bitch Shan is not for real, and he better hope that when he finds out I'll still be here for him.

SHAN

Since Forever's death, Briggen had been acting like an entirely different person. He'd been standoffish, real short with his words and had been trying to stay out of the house. So now I was sitting here watching him get dressed to go to Forever's funeral, and the way he was taking his time, it was obvious that he didn't want to go.

"Is there something you want to talk to me about?" I asked him as he adjusted his tie. That was my first time seeing him wear a tie.

"What made you ask me that?" Briggen replied.

I chuckled. "You know what? If you have to ask me that, then forget it," I snapped.

"What's that supposed to mean?" he hollered at my back because I had left his ass standing there. I had my purse, keys and my son, and I was out the door.

BRIGGEN

I dreaded the day. I always wondered which one of us the streets would take first. Even though I was mad enough to hate and stop speaking to Forever, he was still my flesh and blood. If it wasn't for my mother, I would not be attending my brother's funeral. I tried to get out of it by paying for everything and saying that I did my part, but my moms wasn't having it. Ever since his death, I've been on edge, and Shan has been picking up on my mood swings and has been trying to trip. But the one thing she does not know about was that my mule got busted. Okay, well, she didn't even know that I had a mule. As far as she's concerned, I no longer hustled, and I wanted to keep it like that. But I kept feeling like any day now the Feds were going to put those iron bracelets on me.

I stepped outside and every cloud in the sky was dark . . . just like my mood.

By the time I pulled up in front of the funeral home it was drizzling. My family was mad because I chose to ride solo. I wasn't up for being around my family showboating and fighting over who rides in the first car and all that silly bullshit. My moms was rolling with her two sisters, Aunt Jane and Thelma, their daughters, Tanisha and Jeanette, and I can't leave out their henpecked husbands, Paul and Tony, who were there to sniff up their asses. Keeta, my uncle Bill's daughter, was in the mix. My uncle Bill was my mom's only brother. He died one year ago to this day. That's why my moms was hell-bent on having Forever buried today. My plan for real was to arrive when shit was almost over.

Before I could get out of the car good, I spotted Mia coming my way. I got out and said, "Not now, Mia."

"What do you mean 'not now', Briggen? There's a place and time for everything, and even I know that."

"I'll get with you later," I said, my eyes fixed on the New Day Baptist Church awning.

"I think you want to hear what I got to say right now. Word is Sharia talked Demetria into giving you up to the Feds," Mia revealed.

"What?" I snapped incredulously.

"I told you something was up. And Rudy said to come see him as soon as possible," Mia informed me. The day couldn't get any better.

CHAPTER THREE

DARK

Whoa. It was my first time in a church in seven years. I was surprised when I saw that the casket was open. I was sure the nigga was going to have a closed casket send-off. The last time I saw Forever, his face was yellow looking and he had craters all over it. Obviously, nothing a skilled makeup artist couldn't handle.

We had arrived early, and the church was packed. You would have thought that the president of the United States was up in that casket. Sharia ran off to the bathroom, so I quickly found myself a corner to stand in so that I could observe. I had to admit, they had laid him out real nice. There was a thick, red carpet that led to his solid gold coffin which sat at the end of the middle aisle. On both sides of the coffin were over a hundred bouquets of flowers that consisted of mostly black and red roses. In the background I was surprised to hear a CD playing a variety of sad songs. I had to ask myself, "When the fuck did a funeral come with a mixtape?"

The ushers were dressed in all-black and strategically placed around the church to assist the family. And there was security out the ass. His family had spared no expense. As I looked around I didn't know whether I was at a club or a funeral procession. Niggas were gathered in different groups talking, and bitches had on short dresses, ass and tits everywhere, weaves lookin' tight, wearing hooker heels and were competing for seats up front. This was definitely an experience to remember.

People were pouring in like it was open bar up until 12:00 A.M. I looked around for Sharia and thought to myself, she better hurry up before we be standing in this bitch. I started to go see what was taking her so long when I honed in on a conversation between what appeared to be two hoes that Forever used to fuck with. I thought one looked familiar.

"Look, Tracey, I don't give a fuck if Forever was fucking you on the side and you got a kid with him. He ain't never told me shit. As a matter of fact, I don't even know why you are bringing it up. The nigga is dead, so I really don't give a damn," the pretty one said.

"I'm just saying, you wasn't the only bitch that Forever was fucking and got pregnant. But why do the children have to suffer? I want Mercedes to know . . . her other family members." Tears welled up in the woman's eyes as her voice squeaked, barely able to form the words.

"Bitch, please. Call it what you want to. But you ain't flaunting your illegitimate child in my face," the pretty one snarled. And just as shit was getting ready to get hot, two older women came over and calmed things down.

"Look, both of you need to be ashamed of yourselves talking this way inside the house of the Lord. Forever would not want this. Now let's take our seats and act civil," the older woman said looking back and forth between the two women who didn't want to back down.

"Damn, you nosy," Sharia said as she approached me.

"Sheeiit . . . It was getting ready to turn into *Jerry Springer* up in this piece," I chuckled.

"Well, come on. I see two empty seats. Let's get them before somebody else does."

I WAS STRUGGLING NOT to laugh at Sharia because she was trying to be inconspicuous. But in doing so, she became anything but that. She had on big, black round sunglasses that damn near covered her entire face, with an oversized droopy black hat. Under that she wore a scarf over her head that covered her cheeks and tied under her chin. Then she had the nerve to tell me to call her "Rhonda." I said, "This is your town. These people know you." I had to laugh to myself. Since no one had acknowledged her, maybe they didn't recognize her.

She leaned over and rested her head on my shoulder. I put my arm around her, and she whispered, "See him sitting down? They call him Mo' Betta. He tryna come up, but he don't have enough muscle. Remember, I told you it's all about the muscle in the 'D'. Now, the wheelchair punk over there, that's Melky. His brother Skye used to be real big until they murdered him. Melky has been real quiet, which don't mean nothing. He's somebody to watch. Wheelchair and all. Because I know he's keeping shit under the radar. Don't let the scooter fool you."

"Who put him in the wheelchair?" I was curious. He made me think about Forever. Plus Forever had already told me about Melky. I just wanted to see what or how much Sharia knew.

"Him and his brother Skye used to jack all the big hustlers. They from New York. They jacked this one nigga and Melky got shot in the back. You know the story," she said.

I couldn't get a clear view of Melky's face. But it didn't matter. The nigga was in a wheelchair. How could I forget that?

"Okay, pay attention," Sharia instructed. "This is a crew that you gotta watch. Terany, Slim, JoJo and Kay-Gee. Them niggas there are wild and unpredictable, but they get money. Lots of it. They once kidnapped a man and his family who owned several banks in the city. They had him empty each of the vaults. Word was they got away with at least three million. Oh yes, they do get their money."

"I remember Forever talking about that."

As my cousin told me who was who, and some more of their history, my mouth was salivating. After all, I was hungry, and these niggas had my food.

"Yo, there go Six-Nine. Niggas behind the wall got mad respect for him. I saw his flicks several times. That nigga gettin' lots of clean money; see, he was smart. Once he got his first big score, he invested it. Dude got stocks, bonds and shit. He's just too nice and trusting. He's like Robin Hood on his side of town. He makes sure everybody eats. At least that's what they say."

"They're right," Sharia confirmed. "He runs a food bank, he does clothes drives, he pays the electric bills of seniors, and he buys their medicine. So if you fuck with him, it better be on the DL because you fuck with his whole hood. Them niggas will come after you."

"Who does that shit?" I mumbled.

"Okay, now we talking. This bald-headed nigga right there, that's Cisco," she said pointing with her eyes.

I glanced to my left and checked out the flashy nigga with the bling who was flanked by two bodyguards. His grill had to cost every bit of six stacks.

"Now, that nigga there, he's gettin' money and wants everybody to know it. He even got some cops on his payroll. I'm assuming that's why he's so flashy," Sharia sang, all into it and shit.

She had me all hyped up as I scanned the room.

"Stay with me now. The brother with the light eyes, that's Born Mathematics. He's the opposite of Cisco. He's low-key, ruthless and will be much harder to get to. He screens everybody in his camp, and he digs more into your background than a mortgage underwriter. He got mad bodies under his belt. Cisco may be the nigga we go after first. I think he's gonna be real easy. All you gotta do is feed his already big-ass ego."

Then my cousin's head popped up, and she snatched off her shades. "Oh shit! Oh shit!" she kept saying.

"What?" I asked, noticing that several people were squirming in their seats just like Sharia was.

"I don't believe this," she said as she hurried and put her shades back on. "Where the fuck did Boomer come from? If he's here, then where is Big Choppa? Word on the street was Born killed him," she added in a little over a whisper.

Suddenly, a titter rippled and roared through the church. There was now lots of mumbling going on among Detroit's underworld.

"Why is everyone trippin'? And who is this big, black, fat

nigga that got all of y'all in here all squeamish and shit?" I begged her to tell me. I needed to know the nigga causing all of this commotion.

"Boy, that's Big Boomer. Big Choppa's muscle. Oh . . . my . . . God. I thought he was dead. So, where is Choppa? This is gonna be good," she squealed, sounding like all she needed was some popcorn and a soda so that she could watch her favorite movie.

I watched him go up to the casket, toss a black rose on top of it and just like that, his big, fat ass was gone. *Real smooth*, I thought to myself.

"There's Briggen. That's Forever's brother," she said and damn near broke my rib with her elbow.

Yeah, that was him. Forever talked about him a lot. I used to tell him that I couldn't get with two brothers falling out over the same pussy. That shit made no damn sense to me. The code is supposed to be MOB: Money Over Bitches. I had to crane my neck because people were all around him. I felt like I knew him already. He was the dude I saw in the pictures which were obviously outdated. This guy looked like a much-older, sterner and darker Forever. He turned and looked directly at me as if he knew who I was and what I did to his brother. *Damn.* That shit creeped me out and caused the hairs on my neck to stand up. I felt that I saw all that I needed to see for the day. I was ready to bounce.

BRIGGEN

When I entered the church I was instantly turned off. All these niggas we hadn't seen in years were packed in here like sardines. It's funny how when a nigga is out on these streets you can hardly find a loyal nigga. But drop dead and everybody is your best friend.

I wiped my feet on the rug and proceeded forward. All I could hear were voices coming at me saying, "Sorry for your loss," "Hang in there, soldier." And the most famous of them all, "He's in a better place." How the fuck is dead a better place?

People were patting my back and rubbing my arm. I didn't even stop. I kept my cold demeanor and kept it moving. I looked around to pinpoint where the family was sitting. I saw my mom being comforted by my little cousin.

I began walking down the plush red carpet to make my way to the casket when I became overwhelmed with grief. Each step became a struggle. My heart sank into my stomach at the thought of the figure that lay before me being my little brother, the same one I taught to ride a bike and to tie his shoes. I flashed back to the last civil conversation we had in which we promised to never let any of this hustling shit come between us. A promise neither one of us kept. The same game that had given us so much had taken everything back.

When I reached the casket and peered down at him, a lump formed in my throat and all that tough shit went right out the window. My soul began to ache as tears formed in my eyes, threatening to run down, ignoring the dark shades I had on. I grabbed the handkerchief from my pocket and caught them just as they were about to fall. I took a deep breath before I attempted to make my peace.

"You free now, little bruh." I put my hand on top of his. "On my son, the nigga who did this to you won't live." I said a quick silent prayer. When I turned around, all eyes were on me like I was going to go off. I headed toward my mother and sat down. It was almost time to start the services, or as I like to call them, "the theatrics." Here you had a so-called man of God about to speak good over a man who never stepped foot in a church, killed niggas as if it was legal and sold more dope than a little bit. A bunch of bullshit if you asked me. But hey, it's the American way. My mother clutched my hand tight as the organ started to play.

SHARIA

I was not expecting a jaw-dropping moment at Forever's funeral. But instead of one moment, I got two. When Boomer walked in, that was my first moment. Him and Big Choppa ran Memphis and the surrounding cities, and they were working on taking over the 'D'. But the Feds finally ran down on them a few years earlier. They even rounded up Choppa's two daughters. Everybody thought that Boomer and Choppa got taken out by Born, but now that Boomer was around, I'm sure Big Choppa had to be somewhere nearby. Where there's smoke there's fire. Boomer showing up at Forever's funeral? I can only attribute that to one thing. He wanted niggas to know that the HNIC was alive and well, and was getting ready to do business as usual. I had to find that out for sure before we moved in on Cisco, because if Choppa was back, that was our man. Hell, that would be a dream come true. From what I knew, Cisco was peanuts compared to Big Choppa.

Seeing Briggen for that brief moment was my second jaw-dropping moment. I couldn't remember the last time I saw him. When he looked over in our direction for that brief moment, I felt totally naked. I couldn't tell if he recognized me or not. He was that good at wearing a poker face and having a poker game attitude, if there was such a thing. However, seeing him only magnified the love-hate thing I had for him. We had a little history.

Calvin, whose street name was "Briggen," was a ladies' man—more like a ladies' magnet. Once you start fucking with him you get pulled in . . . for life. I don't know any other way to explain it, or rather, him. Don't get me wrong. He was a good-hearted person, and he definitely looked out when you were on his team. But being on his team came at a price. It was all about business, and you had to get in line with the many ladies. He didn't keep a lady; he had ladies. Briggen couldn't just have one lady. Like most sorry-ass Negroes, he had to have several at a time, whether you liked it or not. When he was done with you or felt the relationship served its purpose, he turned into a different person. I thought I could be the one to change him, but instead, he ended up fucking me right out of my livelihood and destroyed my life in the process. He took my club, the one thing that I built from the ground up with my very own sweat and blood and dared me to do something about it. But I promise you, when it comes to Briggen, *Payback Ain't Enough.*

"Let's go, Dark. You movin' too slow," I snapped at my cousin.

"Why you buggin' out all of a sudden?" he asked. "Oh, I know. Seeing your ex stirred up some old feelings, huh? I told you he still had you open."

"Fuck you, Dark. Ain't nobody got me open, but the dolla dolla bill."

"Yeah, right. If that nigga would have come over to you and said let's go, you would have left me in the dust."

I didn't have a snappy comeback for my cousin's remark. Simply because if that would have happened, I don't know what I would have done.

JANAY

"Carter, get dressed. You're going to court. I'll be back in ten minutes," Pittman, the guard, announced.

I pulled the blanket off my head and looked at the green fluorescent numbers on my clock. It said 2:07 A.M. I stuck my head over the side of the bunk and looked down at my cellie, Esther.

"Esther," I whispered.

"What, Janay?" she whispered back.

"Did she say for me to get up and get ready for court?" I asked as if it were a dream.

"Yes!" she snapped, which also meant, leave her the hell alone.

I sat up, snatched the blanket off me, swung my legs around and jumped off the top bunk. My feet hit the cold concrete, and I quickly stepped in my bunkie's flip-flops and sat on the cold, steel toilet. I was warm and toasty under my blanket and didn't want to get up and pee in the middle of the night. Now my bladder felt as if it was about to burst. After I relieved myself, I hit the silver flush button on the loud toilet and then went to my cell door. Something I did countless times here in the Fed's holding facility in Detroit.

"Crystal!" I yelled for my sister. Her cell was on the same tier but all the way at the opposite end.

"Shut the fuck up!" some unknown voice yelled back.

"Disrespectful bitch! It's two in the damn morning. Folks got to work in the morning." I recognized Miss Anthony's voice.

"Fuck y'all! Y'all do the same shit!" I yelled right back at them bitches. "Crystal! They woke me up for court!" I announced.

"Me too. Do you know what for?" she asked.

"Naw, man," I told her, but as I started getting ready, I said to myself, "It's probably to slap some new charges on us." But I couldn't tell her that because she was just adjusting to the fact that we were in here. She was such a wimp.

Later on, we rode about thirty minutes to the Jackson courthouse, hands and feet shackled. We both were on pins and needles from the moment we got dressed and stepped on the bus. "Nay, what do you think they are going to do to us?" my sister asked me.

"How would I know, Crystal? I know just as much as you." And that was the truth. When the Feds ran down on us a little over two years back, we had a dead body lying on my living-room floor and were the daughters of Kingpin Big Choppa, who was on top of the FBI's most wanted list but was nowhere to be found. And because of that, they held us as bait. They were still holding us, thinking it would bring him out of hiding, or we would give them all of the information they needed to put a tight seal on the case that they built around him. But we didn't know shit. Hell, he hadn't even sent us a letter. When my daddy up and disappeared, he did so without a trace. My thoughts were that they were getting desperate and frustrated and now I was sure they were bringing us to court to slap more charges on us.

"I swear, Nay, I can't take this. If they throw more charges on us, I don't know what I'm gonna do. We already don't know if we ever gettin' out of this bitch."

I understood where my sister was coming from.

When we arrived at the courthouse, they unchained every one of us that was on that prison transport bus. Men and women. My sister and I were put in a holding cell with six other ladies. We remained in the freezing cell until after lunch. By that time I was mentally drained and way beyond aggravated.

When they finally escorted us into the courtroom, it was as if I walked into a different world. It was soundproof, quiet and plush. I saw our attorney Jack Brunswick and then did a double take. I had to be hallucinating. My father stood there in a navy blue pin-striped suit, and a shiny bald head with a tan. When Crystal started screaming I knew that my daddy was real.

"Daddy!" we screamed as my sister and I started to dash toward him, but the marshals grabbed us both as if we were about to shoot the place up. "Please, let me speak to my father," I begged. A marshal grabbed us by each arm, lifted us up and took us to the opposite side of the room.

"Nay and Crystal, it's okay," my daddy said. It sounded so good to hear my daddy say my name.

"Daddy?" was the only word that I could babble. I still couldn't believe it was him. My dad looked as if he had lost a hundred pounds. I knew he had cancer, but would he be dying within the next month or so? I thought as every scenario ran through my brain.

"Your Honor, I need to have a word with my clients. Please, consider that this was all done in haste and at the request of the government. They wanted to get this over with as soon as possible. Especially since, you, the presiding judge on this case will be going on vacation," Jack, my daddy's attorney and friend of over thirteen years, said.

"Five minutes, Mr. Brunswick," Judge Silverstein said as she banged her gavel. Her bright red hair was piled high on top of her head and wrapped in a bun. She looked to be around fifty as she peered over the top of her wire-rimmed glasses at me and my sister. I had heard that for a white judge she tried not to be an asshole. "Your clients can have a reunion outside of this courtroom on your own time. Not the court's time."

The second she said that Crystal and I jumped up and made a mad dash over to our father. He grabbed us both and all three of us were crying. I missed my pops so much and always prayed that I would be able to see him again.

"Okay," Jack said interrupting our family reunion, "let me bring the girls up to speed."

As Jack ran down all that was going on, my mind began to run wild. I was right. The Feds didn't want us; they wanted my dad. They had been watching his operation for years. So now here he was turning himself in, in exchange for freeing us. I wasn't comfortable with that at all.

"Daddy, are you sure?" I asked him. "What if it's a trick? And what about your health?"

"Yes, he's sure, Janay," my weak-ass sister snapped at me. No one paid her any mind though.

"I'll be fine. Hell, I'm damn near sixty-eight. I ain't got much time left. I lived my life, and for that I'm grateful. I can't be selfish. Y'all are young and damn sure don't need to be sitting in some damn jail cell for the next twenty years." He moved in closer and put his lips to my ear. "I just want you to carry on the legacy. I owned the game, and I want my baby girl to remind them niggas out there of that. You hear me?" His words resonated in my head.

So that's what this is all about. My daddy wants me to take over that which he built. *Damn.* I just can't get out from under his wing. Ever since I was seventeen, I knew how to cut, cook and serve dope. Even though I was thrilled at the possibility of getting out of prison, I wasn't saying to myself, "Hooray! I am so looking forward to getting back into the dope game." I was tired of the shit. We had our run. So much for not being selfish. If at age sixty-eight he was on his way to prison, then what's the point of me carrying on his legacy?

CHAPTER FOUR

BRIGGEN

"I know that this is a lot to have come down on you all at once, but Calvin, it is what it is," Rudy, my attorney said, as he sat across from me. A week has passed since Forever's funeral, and I had finally made it to his office.

"So, what are my options?" I asked, as if I had many to choose from.

"The indictment is definitely coming down. She's a snitch for crying out loud," he proclaimed as he took the stack of papers fanning them in my face.

"Then why haven't the muthafuckas locked my ass up?" I challenged Rudy.

"Trust me, it's coming. Plus, remember, you pay me to prolong some things as long as I can."

"I understand that. However, can you assure me that I can get a bond? If not, I'm telling you, me and my family are out of here," I promised him.

"I don't see any reason why they shouldn't grant you a bond," he assured me. "Look, Calvin, you're worried about the wrong thing. That's my job. And after careful scrutiny of the indictment, I do think we can find some holes in it. But that's my job. Let me do what you pay me to do."

I got up and walked out of the office, mad as fuck. I worked at keeping myself out of all equations, then all of a sudden, I was at the top of the list on an indictment. I didn't know how I was going to tell Shan, or if I should tell her at all.

SHAN

I looked over at my son taking a nap on the couch. Anthony was only eighteen months, and here I was pregnant again. If Briggen didn't get anyone to help me, I was going to have to walk away from overseeing our day-care center and the motel. Shit, he could sell them both for all I cared. Well, not the day care, because I did drop off Anthony sometimes. But having a child was like having three businesses. Add that to having a husband and taking care of the house, and that shit was overwhelming. I was tired simply at the thought of it all. I already didn't have a life. Outside of Briggen, and with this new baby on the way, combined with him and his mood swings and Nick telling me that Briggen was out there hustling hard, I couldn't see any relief.

"Shan, the boy is asleep. Go!" Keeta, Briggen's cousin, hissed as she was pushing me out the door. Her daughter was babysitting while she and I went out. I was on my way home to get my shoes and matching bag.

"I'm going, damn," I said as I got shoved. Who pushes a pregnant lady?

"Then hurry up. And don't get all the way home only to call me up to say you aren't going. I didn't do all that work on you for my damn health," Keeta warned.

I laughed. "You call this work? I look like a damn clown," I teased her. My nose was starting to spread across my puffy, pregnant face.

"Bitch, please. You ready for a cover shoot. Just pick the magazine and I'll make it happen," she bragged.

Earlier we went to Neiman Marcus and I found this cute little short trench dress by Gaultier. I got it for $2,700. I had to have it because I had the perfect platform bootie sandals and Céline bag already at home to match. I brought the sandals, and Briggen had given me the bag last summer.

I already had the dress on, Keeta did my makeup, which I don't even wear, and I put on these long-ass, thick, fake eye-lashes which had me looking like Betty Boop. I didn't even recognize myself. Briggen talked me into cutting off my locks, so I was wearing my hair short and permed and Keeta had just styled the hell out of it.

"Shan, I'm not playing with you!" Keeta yelled out the door.

"Girl, just keep an eye on my son. I'll be back," I said, jumping into my whip.

Twenty minutes later I was in my house, had used the bathroom, slid on my bootie sandals and was ready to paint the town. When I got to the back door, Briggen was coming in. He had a bouquet of roses and from what I could see, about three gift-wrapped presents. He set them on the kitchen counter, and I walked right past him and his phony-ass gifts as if they weren't there.

"Hey, hey. Hold up. What's up?" he asked, looking shocked and confused. I'm sure it was because I didn't go anywhere and there I was all dressed up and on my way out. "Where's my son?"

"*Our son* is at Keeta's. I'm on my way over there now," I answered flatly.

"To do what? Why are you all dressed up?"

"Why do you think I'm dressed up? I'm going out, that's why," I said and walked out the door.

"Shan, why are you trying to leave?" He came rushing after me.

"I told you, I'm going out, Briggen." I continued my strut.

"So, you were just going to go out without letting me know?" he asked as if he couldn't believe it.

"Briggen, please. You are not my father, plus, you haven't been concerned about me or your son for the past few weeks." I pushed past him.

"Shan, I'm not in the mood for your bullshit. You need to come sit down so we can talk." He grabbed my hand as I kindly snatched it away.

"I have been trying to talk to you for weeks, and you ain't have shit to say then, so act like you ain't got shit to say now. Like I said, I'm on my way out," I stated defiantly, hitting the alarm to my car. He snatched the keys out of my hand, taking me completely by surprise.

"Come back in the house so we can talk," Briggen demanded.

"I'm not going in the house. Now give me my keys so that I can leave. Keeta is waiting for me," I snapped, hoping that I could get out of there without having to talk to him.

"Fuck Keeta. Who's more important? Me or her?" He came at me with that sorry and old-ass line.

"No, you didn't just go there. You know what? Keep them. I'm not going back and forth with you. I got a set of spare keys in the house." I started to walk past him but stopped. "I will tell you one thing. I ain't got shit to say to you right now, Briggen, and I think it's best that way because I may say something I just might regret." I was fuming as I stormed up the backstairs and turned the knob, but unfortunately, the door was locked.

BRIGGEN

As Shan ran to try to get into the house, I sat down at our patio table and knew that she was pissed. I had her car keys, her house keys, and if she stepped off the back porch, she was going to get wet because it was beginning to drizzle.

My wife had on all this makeup, including them fake-ass lashes that all the chicks were wearing and a sexy little trench coat dress. Still with all that, she looked uptight as hell. It's because I've been preoccupied with all of this other shit and haven't been giving her any attention or dick. Hell, I hadn't fucked her in weeks, and with her being pregnant, I knew that her emotions were all over the place. I was watching her as she stormed down the steps heading for her car, hoping that it was open.

After yanking on the door, she snapped, "Briggen, open the damn door." I just stared at her and smiled, which pissed her off more. "Open it now," she huffed.

"I will. Once you talk to me," I said.

"Briggen, you know what? Fuck you! You had the last two weeks to talk, but you didn't, so fuck you. We ain't talking until I'm ready to talk," she said, arms waving around frantically.

Well, damn! My baby was really upset. "I told you I was going through some things," I responded. It was no longer drizzling; it was full-tilt raining.

"So you couldn't talk to me?" she asked pausing. "Who am I to you, Briggen? I mean, you've been gone most of the time and when you do come home, you act like I'm not even here."

I just sat there looking at her.

"Exactly. Now give me my keys so I can go out," she ordered.

"C'mon, Shan. For real. When have you known me to talk when I'm stressin'? Give a nigga a break," I started to plead my case.

Shan laughed. "That's the best you can do? That's your best apology?" She rushed me and was actually swinging at me. I grabbed the back of her thighs so she couldn't move, holding her in place. I then bit her nipple through that cute little trench dress.

"Briggen! Stop! Get off me!" she yelled and tried to push me back. "I still can't believe that you just tried to spit that tired-ass game. It's been over three weeks that you haven't had shit to say to me, and now, all of a sudden, you want to talk. Well, guess what, nigga? I'm good now. So let me go!" Just then, the thunder made it sound as if the sky opened up and downpoured buckets of water. I didn't let that stop me. I slid my hands up to her ass cheeks, glad that she had a thong on that plump, pregnant ass.

After a few minutes of squirming and struggling, I think she had given up the fight. "It's raining on my outfit." Shan started crying. I continued to nibble on her nipple through her dress. "I don't believe you. Get off me. Stop it. I'm getting all wet."

"I like it when you're all wet," I said as I moved to the other nipple to give it the same attention.

"Briggen, let me go." She was still crying, and we were both now soaked from the rain. I eased my hand between her inner thighs. It was hot and moist. I rubbed her pussy and slid a finger inside her. "Yeah, you're wet, alright," I told her as my dick jumped. I was ready to put in some work.

"Briggen, my hair, my dress, my makeup. I wanted to go out. Now, I'm all wwweeeet!" she cried. "Briggen! We are ooooutside!" she moaned, unable to ignore my two fingers all up in her. I plunged deeper, and she spread her legs wider. She moaned again as she gripped my shoulders.

SHAN

As Briggen flicked across my G-spot, my head fell back, allowing the warm rain to mix with my tears. Hell, I had been pissed at him for a while. But getting my coochie finger fucked and enjoying his head game during a thunderstorm had me on fire and caused me to forget why I was angry at him in the first damn place. Thank God for high fences because I didn't want nothing to stop him from whizzing me to cloud nine. "Don't stop," I moaned. But he did, and when he stood, he took me with him and lifted me onto the wet patio table. I wasted no time wrapping my legs around his back while he unzipped his pants.

"Grab 'em," Briggen directed. His voice was hoarse and raspy, which meant that he was ready to do some serious fucking, and that made my pussy that much hotter and wetter.

I heard and obeyed. I grabbed his dick, and it was just as I liked it—long, hard and thick. I ran the head back and forth, up and down and over my wet pussy. I could feel the head soaking up my juices. The nigga started groaning. Then he began to babble. "I'm sorry, baby." His lips found mine and as he kissed me, I kept rubbing my pussy and clit with the head of his dick. I hadn't left cloud nine. Our kiss was mixed with the warm rain that was falling from the sky.

My three thousand dollar dress, thousand dollar sandals and twenty-two hundred dollar handbag were probably ruined. I couldn't even buy them again. Nor could I recall exactly at what point it came off of my arm. But at that moment, I didn't give a damn. My baby could no longer take my teasing and pushed me back onto the table. My eyes were shut tight as the rain beat down on me, stimulating my nipples. I anticipated his dick. He then pushed himself deep inside me. I'm glad it was thundering because when he got all the way in we both got loud moaning and groaning. He put each one of my legs over his shoulders and began to stroke, hitting my pussy from all angles, not missing a spot. It felt as if his dick had gotten fatter and longer since the last time we fucked.

"Brig—" I moaned. Yup, this nigga was Brig in the bed, because he was *that* nigga when he fucked me. But I married Calvin. "Brig," I moaned again as I felt tingly sensations from my toes up to my pussy, and then my muscles started clamping around his thick dick and I began to cum. "Oooooohhhh, Briggen, damn," I heard myself scream.

"This is what you wanted, right?" he asked me as he kept his hard dick deep inside of me. I was spent and could only nod my head yes. "This is what I wanted too." He grabbed my ass so he could get in deeper. He hit the bottom about three times, and that's all he could take, and he started cumming and beating the shit outta my pussy.

I lay there spent, my legs still up on his shoulders. We both were trying to catch our breath. I was praying that the table wouldn't collapse under our serious fucking and come crashing to the ground.

We finally made it into the house, soaking wet, and finished what we started outside. What a way to argue and talk. If that's how we would be conversing, then I didn't mind him not speaking to me for weeks.

A few hours later, even though Keeta was pissed off at me, she still brought Li'l Peanut home and didn't sweat me about why I didn't come and get him.

I THOUGHT I WAS dreaming when I looked at the clock. It was ten minutes to five in the morning, and we were awakened by banging on the door. To my surprise, Briggen got up and started getting dressed, as if he was expecting whoever was banging wildly on our door. I looked out the window and much to my dismay it looked like the Feds and every other law enforcement agency in Detroit surrounded our house. The white with blue striped Detroit police cars, narc vehicles with tinted windows. The white men emerging from the vehicles wore dark jackets with FBI, DEA, and ATF printed on them. This was definitely a raid.

"What the fuck is going on, Briggen?" I asked.

"Just throw a robe on. They are here for me, not you."

"Here for you? What did you do? Kill somebody?" I questioned.

"Naw, I ain't kill nobody."

"What, you robbed a bank?"

"Shan, chill out. You know damn well I didn't rob no bank." He handed me a card. "Call my attorney and let him know they got me."

I tossed the card onto the dresser yelling, "Nigga, I know your ass is not still hustling!"

"Somebody mentioned my name on some shit. It ain't nothin'," he said, cool as a cucumber.

"Nothing, Briggen? Nothing? The Feds are outside! They don't just come to your house at five o'clock in the morning for *nothing*," I screamed.

"I'll tell you about it later," he said, as if he was talking about the fuckin' movie of the week.

"Later? Later, Briggen? You better pray that there is a fuckin' later, nigga! What is happening to you? I swear I don't know what is up with your ass anymore," I hollered as I hugged myself and tried to stop the tears from rolling down my face. Why does every person I care about get taken away from me? "Why all of a sudden it looks like you have all of these secrets? What's happening with us?"

He started to answer but the banging sounded as if the walls were about to come down. He turned and walked out of the bedroom. "I'm coming. Don't break down my fucking door!"

he yelled as he raced down the steps. I stood at the top of the stairs watching as he opened the door and was tackled to the floor. They swarmed in like roaches with weapons drawn.

"All of this ain't necessary. I'm dressed and ready to go," he yelled at them as they put him in handcuffs. "My attorney already told me that you were coming. All y'all had to do was tell me to come turn myself in. Y'all ain't gotta go through all of these theatrics," I heard Briggen say.

"Who else is here?" one of the agents asked, ignoring what he had just said.

"Just my wife and eighteen-month-old son. But you already know that. Y'all been watching the house for the past month."

"When were you going to tell me, Briggen?" I screamed.

"Shut up, ma'am, and stay there!" The officer directed his order at me. He had the nerve to have his gun pointed in my direction.

"You shut up!" I snapped. "You're in my house!" I didn't care about his gun. I then turned on my husband. "Briggen, you knew this shit. When were you going to tell me?" I kept the answers and questions flowing.

"Is the house clean, Mr. Thompson?" the agent asked as per protocol.

"C'mon now. Y'all know it is," Briggen said, as if it were a silly question.

"Briggen!" I stammered.

"Shan, not now. Calm down and go check on the baby," he yelled just as our son started to cry.

"Then when?" I shot back.

"After he gets out in twenty," a female agent said, coming up the steps.

CHAPTER FIVE

SHAN

I had Li'l Peanut with me and was now banging on Keeta's front door. As soon as she opened it, I barged in.

"Well, damn. Good morning to you, too," she said snidely.

"It is not a good morning," I snapped.

"Why? You and Brig having a lover's spat?" she giggled.

"He's locked up, Keeta. They came and got him this morning." I stormed by her and headed for the living room.

"What do you mean they came and got him? Who? For what?" she asked as she followed behind me.

I sat Li'l Peanut down. "You tell me. And don't act like you don't know what I'm talking about, Keeta! The fucking Feds." I glared at her with my hands on my hips, waiting for a response.

"So what did they say?" she asked dumbly.

"Nothing to me other than shut up and he will see me in twenty years."

Keeta waved that off. "Girl, don't pay that shit no mind. They always tryna scare somebody. He ain't gettin' no twenty years." She said as if she really knew what she was talking about.

I looked at her nonchalant attitude and went off. "You know what? All y'all are a fucking trip. You sat in my face knowing the whole time what he was doing. All that bullshit about let's get out, and you need to do some shit for yourself. Bitch, you phony as hell." I looked at her with disgust.

"What the fuck you expect me to do? That's you and Briggen's business. Don't get mad at me. You the one fucking him. You should have more answers than I do," she replied, trying to turn the shit on me, then sat down.

I wanted to curse her ass out, but she had a point. Here I was, standing in the middle of her living room going off about my man. I was disgusted with myself.

"So what's your next move? Did you call his lawyer?" she asked leisurely as if this shit was normal.

"I left a message," I told her.

"Aiight then. Rudy will handle it," she said with confidence, then got up and walked into the kitchen.

I watched this bitch calmly go into the refrigerator and get an orange. "You want one?" I glared at her while she stood there and started peeling it.

That was the last straw. "So everyone knows but my dumb ass? This nigga doing dirt right under my nose, and I don't even know it. Everybody looking at me as the poor little dumb bitch he playing house with." I chuckled and shook my head. "So this means he still got all of them hoes still working for him? Sharia, Mia and God only knows who the fuck else! I'm so fuckin' dumb!"

"Shan, you know I don't get into my cousin's business like that. To be honest with you, I thought you knew." She held her arms and shrugged, and I wanted to hawk and spit in her face.

"The only thing I do know is y'all muthafuckas are crooked as hell. C'mon, Anthony, Mommy gotta go." I was sorry for coming out of character like that in front of my son. Even if he was only eighteen months, I shouldn't have been cussing in front of him like that. I couldn't even look at that bitch. I had to get out of there before they ended up hauling my ass to jail.

I grabbed my baby and left. I had to finish mapping out my game plan. I did know that I was sick and tired of being played as some dumb, stupid, naïve, stay-at-home goody-two-shoes broad, while everybody around me was doing dirt behind my back as well as right under my nose.

I needed to go by this bitch Mia's house. I didn't have reason enough before, but I damn sure had reason enough now. It was still early in the morning so I knew the ho would still be home. I knew that she'd be surprised that I knew where she lived, I felt like I needed to shake things up, use this opportunity to let this bitch know who the boss was. I'd tell her I came to pick up some money. How she responds will let me know if Calvin is still fuckin' with her and if he is still out here living foul, despite the fact that he told me he wasn't. I drove to her house taking the scenic route so I could get my mind right. But that ended up taking me damn near an hour.

I pulled up into her driveway and got out. I opened the backdoor, unstrapped Li'l Peanut from his car seat and marched up her driveway to her door. I knocked, then rang the doorbell twice. After a few seconds, I finally heard her.

"Who is it?" Mia called out.

"Shan."

She was quiet. I knew she was wondering why I was at her front door. The curtain moved which confirmed that she saw me, and having the baby on my hip, I'm sure, let her know that I was not here on no whip-her-ass bullshit.

MIA

Why was this bitch at my front door? And with the baby on her hip to boot. Briggen had not called me to say that he was sending her over, and I didn't fuck with her like that, so what could she possibly want? I decided to make her wait, so I took my time going upstairs and threw on some clothes. Then I changed my mind and decided to fuck with her. I took off my clothes and put on a robe.

I went downstairs and unlocked the door and stood in the doorway. I couldn't help but stare at that baby. He looked more like Forever than he did Briggen. He had Forever's complexion, nose and lips. I had been trying to have Briggen's baby, but he was always so extra careful not to let that happen, as if I wasn't good enough. Then she pops up out of nowhere and he wifes her all up and now here she is pregnant with child number two.

"What's up?" I asked her.

"Can I come in?"

Little Miss Prissy was more street than I thought she was. I didn't think she even knew where I lived, and now she wanted to bring her ass inside my house. The curiosity was killing me. I opened the door, and she stepped inside.

"Can you take off your shoes, please?" I offered ever so sweetly.

She paused and looked at me as if to say, "Are you fuckin' serious?" Damn right I was. I had cocaine white suede carpeting. Even Briggen knew to take off his shoes. She finally did.

I led her into the den. "You can have a seat," I said, still staring at the baby. "You just missed Briggen. He left a couple of hours ago," I stated, trying to throw salt in the game while tightening the belt on my robe.

"Bitch, please. You wish," she said, laughing. "Actually, Briggen, my husband, you know, the one that you can't seem to let go? Well, he was home all night eating pussy and getting his dick wet. Then the Feds came and got him at five o'clock this morning. But nice try." She had the nerve to pause and smirk.

"Look, no hard feelings. I'm just here to pick up any monies that you are holding for him," she said, bursting my bubble.

"Money?" I said, indignant. My blood was boiling over and I wanted to stab this bitch.

"Yes, money. He left me with a list of things I need to take care of immediately, and collecting his money, that's one of them."

"Well, I have no clue what you are talking about," I told her. Shit, Briggen hadn't called me and neither had the attorney, so I wasn't giving this bitch shit. I didn't even know who sent her. It could have been the Feds for all I knew. And I damn sure wasn't taking any chances.

"So what do you want me to tell Briggen? That I came

way over here to get his money and you said you don't
have it?"

"You can tell him whatever the fuck you want because
like I said, I don't know what you're talking about," I said as
I stood up, letting this 'bama bitch know that she had just
worn out her welcome. It was time for her to go, but the
bitch had the nerve to keep sitting there. I was praying she
would do something to make me kick her ass out.

She must have seen the look on my face. "Okay. It's your
call," she said, standing up and picking up her son. I led her
ass to her shoes and the front door.

SHAN

He left a few hours ago. Mmmhumm. I thought to myself.
That bitch don't know who the hell she's fucking with. The
one thing I was sure about was that the bitch was holding
his money. The look on her face told it all. I should have
known that Briggen had this bitch trained well. Just like I'm
now seeing that he had me well-trained, too. So as far as I'm
concerned, it's confirmed. This nigga was still in the streets.

On my way back to my house, the sounds of tires screeching caused me to swerve over. I looked in my rearview mirror and two unmarked cars whizzed past me chasing a silver
pickup and a black Nissan. *Damn! A real-live police chase.*
I was amused. They had to be doing eighty to a hundred
miles per hour. I wondered where they were going because it
was barely ten in the morning. And why did the police have
their sirens off? I knew it wasn't because they were trying to
be courteous.

I sat there; it took me a few minutes to get my bearings straight. I finally pulled off and got a couple of blocks away only to hear the tires screeching again. I couldn't tell from what direction they were coming and I didn't know whether to hurry and turn left or turn right or just park the damn car.

I figured the best thing for me to do would be to turn right onto the side street and get the hell out of their way because it was sounding as if it was about to be on, so I did.

Why did I do that? I heard the tires screech loud and clear. Out of nowhere that same silver truck jumped the curb and crashed right into me, spinning my car halfway around so I was now facing the opposite direction. Li'l Peanut started crying. I almost swallowed my tongue, and my hands were shaking like a leaf. I looked in the back at my son and thanked God that he was still secure in his car seat and unharmed. I got out to get my baby out of the backseat so I could calm him down and check my car.

A guy with a hood over his head jumped out of the driver's side of the truck and started limping away as fast as he possibly could. He didn't even look back. I put my son back in his seat, strapped him in and shut the door. I eased over to the truck to get a better look, and the passenger door popped open. A head dipped out the door as its body slumped across the seat. I moved in closer to see if the victim was still breathing. He looked up at me and struggled to speak. He was holding onto a duffel bag while lying on top of another one. I knew what kind of bags those were. Blood was all over his face, and he started mumbling, but I didn't understand him. I wasn't trying to hear what he was saying.

I heard tires screeching again in the distance, and this time, they were blazing. I grabbed the bags and when I did, dude grabbed my wrist. Our eyes met, and again, he tried to speak, blood bubbles forming on his lips and I quickly pulled away. I grabbed one bag and then the other. One was much heavier than the other. Struggling, I rushed back to my car. I threw the bags in my front seat, jumped in the car and sped off. My poor baby was screaming at the top of his lungs.

The sirens were getting closer, and I was doing damn near fifty in a residential area. Then out of the blue the black Nissan was behind me and two Detroit police cars and a state trooper vehicle were behind him. I pulled over to the side, and once again my heart was pounding a mile a minute. I struggled to catch my breath as I gripped the steering wheel tighter and they flew right by me. *What were the odds of this happening?* Only on T.V. do you see the old white lady who finds a bag of money and turns it over to the police. That wasn't going to be me. I exhaled slowly and pulled off while praying all the way.

Finally I pulled up into my garage and didn't get out of the car until the door was closed. I jumped out and unbuckled Li'l Peanut from out of the car seat to calm him down. While I was holding him and bouncing him I looked at my wrist and saw blood. I went into the house to wash my shaking hands. I sat Anthony in his high chair with some juice and crackers and headed back to the garage to go see what exactly was in those bags.

I grabbed them and carried them into the kitchen. After placing them onto the counter I unzipped them both and looked inside. Just as I hoped, money in one and dope in the other. But at that same moment, what I had just done hit me like a ton of bricks. I quickly zipped the bags up and stepped back with my hands over my chest. My heart was pounding a mile a minute. *Oh . . . my . . . God! Whose fuckin' package did I just jack?* I unzipped both bags and again looked at my new stash, wondering what I had just gotten myself into.

I went back to the garage to check out my car. I walked around it to see the damage, and yes, the rear driver's side was banged up. "Damn," I said, following the long dent and scratch. When I got to the back, my knees buckled when I saw that the license plate was gone.

"Shit! Fuck!" I said, starting to panic. I paced back and forth wondering what to do. Snatching up Li'l Peanut, we went looking in front of the house. Nothing. I started walking down the block. Still nothing. I couldn't get back to the house quick enough to dash upstairs and get Briggen's keys to his Benz. We jumped in the car and drove around in an attempt to backtrack. I had to go find that plate.

SHARIA

"You mean to tell me, you left my shit and my money in the truck?" I overheard him say to the poor soul on the other end of the line.

My head was underneath the sheet, but I peeked out, trying to see Cisco's facial expression. He looked as if he wanted to cry. I could hardly contain myself. For this nigga to be ballin' the way he was, turning out to be too easy of a mark. I was able, in just two nights, to bed this nigga, make him fall hard and was positive I was about to get him to start giving up valuable info. It had to be all that soaking wet, slip and slide I was giving the nigga. They kill me. They get a few connections, stack some dough, get a little bit of muscle and immediately begin to believe that they are invincible. Puhleeze, Negro. Every man's downfall is pussy. I put that nigga to the back of my throat, and his punk ass damn near gave up his momma. Now look at him, over there about to cry. After talking a few more minutes, he hurled the phone at the wall.

I snatched the covers off my head and acted as if I just woke up. "Is everything okay?" I asked him as I stretched.

"Yeah. Get dressed. You gotta go," he snapped. I tried to look disappointed, but this nigga didn't know that he did me a favor because I definitely didn't feel like fucking him again. Because from what I could gather, and from those few minutes of ear hustlin', I figured that he just lost some workers, dope, and some cash, which would definitely be in our favor. This nigga was gonna need some muscle, and that is where Dark would come in. That's when the whole plan would begin to unfold. I couldn't wait to spill this shit to Dark.

"Are you sure, Daddy? Is there anything I can do before I leave?" I asked, already up putting on my panties and bra.

"Nah, I gotta make a run," he said, sounding all depressed.

"Okay," I said as I hurried and got dressed. I was ready to follow his ass to wherever it was he was going.

CHAPTER SIX

SHAN

Here I was at the house, on the phone, not wanting to believe or hear what Briggen was telling me. This nigga was a professional liar. What he didn't know was that I had already talked to the lawyer and knew the jam he was in. He had been locked up now, going on a week. I thought he would have been home by now, but he had some old warrants, and therefore, the judge thought he was a flight risk and denied him bail.

"So when can I see you?" I asked.

"Just hold up. The old warrants should be taken care of in a few days, and I'll be out of here."

"Why don't you want me to come see you?" I wanted to know. After all, we did miss him.

"Shan, there's no need for you to come down here. Stay home with my son."

I couldn't believe I had to beg this nigga to come and see him. God forbid he had to go away and do a bid, he'd then be on the phone crying like a bitch, begging and pleading with me to come visit him.

"Stay home? That's all you ever say is I should stay home. Stay home? I'm sure you ain't tell that bitch Mia to stay home. You want me to stay home so I won't know all the shit you into. You—"

"Shan!" he shouted, interrupting my rant.

"Briggen, it's not fair. I don't even know why you're in there. Plus, I need to talk to you." I needed him to sense the urgency in my words, and I needed to tell him about the dope and cash I found. Something I couldn't do over the phone. I needed a face to face. But more important, I needed to tell him about my missing license plate. If the niggas whose stash I took had my tag, I was in deep shit.

"I'll get back to you later," he told me.

"When, Briggen?"

"Later," was the last word he said to me.

He hung up. I couldn't believe it. I looked at the phone, thinking, "I *know* he didn't just hang up on me." Who was this nigga? He had done a full 180 on me. I didn't even know who he was anymore.

JANAY

I cried like a baby the other night. I cried for my daddy because he was getting ready to spend the rest of his life in prison. I cried tears of joy because me and my sister were free. I cried tears of anger and confusion toward God because I didn't understand why I couldn't have both. Why couldn't we be free and all be together? Even though I knew deep down inside that you can't do dirt and expect it not to come back on you in some form or fashion, karma doesn't take as long as it used to. The life my family chose to live was dirty.

We were standing on the steps of the Memphis courthouse as a wide grin spread across my face when I saw Boomer get out of his ride. Crystal and I ran and jumped in his arms, just like we did when we were kids, and he picked us up and swung us around just like he used to do.

"Yo' daddy just hung up. Y'all just missed him. He said he ain't gonna be able to relax until he's sure that y'all are out. He said he was gonna call back in fifteen minutes. Y'all hungry? Yeah, y'all hungry."

"I sure am," Crystal said.

"I can't wait to see Marquis," I gushed. I needed to see my son who was now seven years old.

"He's with Ida. They won't be home until later on. He ain't going nowhere," Boomer assured me. We loaded into Boomer's extended Escalade SUV, just like old times, and drove off. I looked out the window as we drove around the city. It was amazing to me how shit can change but yet remain the same in just two short years. I saw a few familiar faces that were sitting in the exact same spot the last time I saw them.

"Take me by the house," I instructed, wanting to see something comforting and familiar.

"You ain't got that house no more, Nay. Y'all gotta start over." I could hear the regret in my uncle's voice.

"I know, Boom. But I still want to ride past it. Is someone living in it?"

"No," he replied.

"Well, we can get it back then, Boomer. That's our house."

I was feeling hopeful. Shit, I was out of prison, so I knew that anything was possible.

"Nay, once the Feds took the house and had it all boarded up, you know how the feens do. They broke in, started using it as a crackhouse and then ended up burning it down to the ground," Boomer told me.

"What?" Crystal and I shrieked.

"They burned down yours and the Middeltons, right next door to it," he said. "The Middletons lost their house to foreclosure."

"So where are we going to live?" Crystal always asked the dumbest questions.

"Now what kind of question is that? Y'all comin' to Detroit."

"Detroit!" we said at the same time.

"That's where the family is now. You know yo' daddy already made arrangements for y'all. What? You thought me and yo' daddy was gonna just let you roam around homeless?" he joked.

Detroit? "So, Ida don't mind you living in Detroit?" I asked him.

"I goes back and forth. Hell, all these Memphis niggas done set up shop out there. It's a hell of a lot of money out there. Niggas have been gettin' filthy rich for years. But since they are so divided out there we were able to step right on in and set up shop and now we basically run shit. You'll see."

Just then we were coming up on a Burger King and Crystal lost it. "Oh my God! I've been dying to have a Whopper with everything on it! Please, can we pull over? I wanna go to this

Burger King." Crystal begged Boomer, sounding just as she did when we were kids.

"Are you sure? After two years of eating prison food, that's all you can think about is a Whopper?" he joked halfheartedly.

"That's the first thing, Boomer. Every time I think about a Whopper with cheese, my mouth starts to water." Crystal grinned from ear to ear.

Boomer pulled over and parked in the Burger King parking lot. He went into the glove compartment and pulled out two envelopes. He handed Crystal one and me the other. I sat mine in my lap. Crystal ripped hers open, took out a fifty and jumped out of the car.

"I'll be right back," she called out, jogging toward Burger King.

"You want something outta here?" he asked me.

"Nah. I need a home cooked meal. Especially your chicken and dumplings or Ida's meatloaf and gravy. Hint, hint," I responded, knowing he never could deny my meal requests. I lay my head back onto the headrest and folded my hands.

Boomer laughed that big, hearty laugh of his and it was so good to hear it. And then it got silent.

"Boom, tell me something. Is my dad okay? Is the cancer spreading faster? Does he have a certain amount of time to live? Why has he lost so much weight?" I asked, not sure if I wanted to know the answer.

Boomer looked at me through the rearview mirror. "You'll have to ask him that when you talk to him again."

I thought about what he said and understood that to mean that my pop's health was taking a turn for the worse.

"What he did want you to know is, he don't want you out

of the game. And, Nay, you know I ain't gonna bullshit you. You know your father needs you back out here. He won't let nobody else take his throne but you. Crystal . . . well, she's sweet, bless her heart, but she has shown us that she ain't that bright. You have what it takes. Besides, he said he made this city and he wants you to carry on his legacy, not Crystal. She weak. Always has been. He said that's why he made the sacrifice. He made the sacrifice for his name and the game." Boom unloaded that on me.

I sat there, staring at the back of Boomer's bald head. What Boomer just said was a hard pill to swallow. What uncle would tell their niece that her father said to be the best drug dealer she can be? Odd to some but this didn't come as a surprise. My family was full of murderers, drug dealers, pimps—you name it, and we have one.

But, sitting in that cell for the last twenty-two months had me looking at the game with a different eye. Especially knowing and realizing that there's only two ways out: a cell or a coffin. I composed myself enough to ask him, "Boomer, what do you have to say about all this?"

"Your daddy wants you back in, and the streets need some new blood out here. You have to carry out your father's wishes. Everybody is depending on you. Plus, he told you he sacrificed so we all could be out here. I'm here for you, at your disposal. Just like I was there for yo' daddy. The real question is, how do you feel about all this? If your heart and mind ain't in the right place, I have my own instructions to follow."

"What are those? To kill me?" I squeaked out. I said it as a joke, but one could never know with my father.

"Of course not! However, I have my own opinion which

ain't important. But I practically raised you. I know you, Nay. Even though you a girl and all, yo' daddy built you like a fine car; mean, clean, made of steel, sharp, sleek and dangerous." He rattled off those adjectives as if he was the brand-new owner of a car just like the one he just described.

So there it was. Boomer had laid it all out for me. I was only freed because my daddy wanted me to rule the streets in his name. I wasn't given the option to choose. The choice had been made for me. And it's just like my daddy to choose the game over his family.

"We get started tonight. I gotta introduce you to some people and reintroduce you to the old heads. Just about all of them left Memphis and set up shop in Detroit. Them niggas up there so divided that we were able to slide right on in," he said, sounding just like my dad. Neither one of them taking no for an answer. Our motto was: *Money never sleeps.*

SHAN

I waited around for two days, hoping that Briggen would get out on bond or at the very least send for me. When he didn't, I dropped Anthony off at Keeta's and marched my ass right down to the Federal Detention Center where they were holding him. Those corny bastards processed me, and I sat in the visitation room only to be informed that he was no longer being housed there. He was being extradited to Miami on some old state charges he had neglected to address.

As soon as I got to my locker to pick up my handbag and phone, I called Rudy.

When he picked up I asked, "Rudy, this is Shan, why didn't you tell me they moved him?"

"They moved Calvin?" he asked, sounding surprised.

"Uh, yeah. They moved him today. I think he's on his way to Miami," I regretted to inform him.

"Shit! How do you know?"

"I'm down here at the jail. They just told me."

"Hell, they obviously packed him up and wouldn't allow him to use the phone. I'll call you later with an update."

"That would be nice, Rudy," I said sarcastically before hitting the end button on my cell.

As soon as I got in the house, I fed Anthony and laid him down so he could take a nap. I went and got both of Briggen's cell phones, took my time and went through them. I took a deep breath before I dialed Nick's number. No one answered. I hit send and tried him again.

"Brig, what's up?"

"It's not Briggen, Nick. It's me, Shan," I told him.

"Li'l sis, you alright? What's up?" he asked, concerned.

"I need to see you. Briggen is locked up. Can you come by?"

"When?"

"Now! It's important."

"No problem. I'll be there in a few hours."

Those few hours felt like a few days. I paced nervously back and forth and kept looking out the window. I redusted the furniture and wiped down the already spotless kitchen counter. Finally, I saw a black Hummer whip into the driveway and park. I watched Nick as he got out and rushed up the driveway and onto the porch. I opened the door. When he stepped inside the house, I looked at him and started crying.

"Shan, what's going on? Did he hurt you?" he asked, sounding like a worried father.

I shook my head no.

"Then what's the matter?"

"I'm trippin', that's all. And seeing you reminds me a lot of my brother and Brianna, reminds me too much of the past that I miss so much. Sorry about that," I said and left to go get some tissue.

When I came back into the living room Nick grabbed me in a bear hug. "I'm glad I found you," he exhaled.

"Where have you been, Nick? My brother—" I wanted to tell him what I had been thinking, but he stopped me.

"Shan, I know. You don't have—" he paused. "There's not a day that goes by that I don't think about how I wasn't there for you and Peanut."

"Where were you, Nick? I mean, you just up and disappeared."

"Trinidad. My father lost his sight. He went blind. He refused to come over here and let me care for him. He suffered for almost a year before he died of natural causes. I have to believe it when they say, 'death comes in threes.' First Brianna, then Peanut and then my dad. I'm sorry Shan. You know if I could have been there I would have been," he explained.

Even though I didn't know his father, I was sorry to hear that he had passed away. That didn't stop me, however, from being angry at him for not being there for my brother who was the only person in the world, other than my son and Briggen that mattered to me. Before I knew it, tears were once again streaming down my cheeks.

"I miss him so much, Nick. You don't understand." My stomach knotted up at the thought.

"Shan, I know. I miss him too, and he made me promise that if anything happened to him I would look after you. I'm sorry. Once I found out where you were, I came to check on you. I'm kicking myself because I feel like I came too late, and the worst part is, you were right here under my nose all of this time."

"But how did you find me?"

"That's a long story, and it doesn't matter now," Nick said. "All that matters is, I found you."

"So now what?" I asked, smiling through my tears. "You are going to pick me up and take me away? Did you even know that I had a baby?"

"Yeah I heard. And looks just like Peanut. I had to contain myself when I saw it was you in the backyard. They said you was all wifed up with Brig. I said they had the wrong Shan."

"I know. So now what? We gotta lot of catching up to do." I whispered as if Briggen were in the next room and Nick was going to sneak me out of the house. I was trippin'.

"When do you want to do that? You have to let me know when you are ready," he replied.

"What makes you think I ain't ready now?"

"Because you're just calling me. I came by here a couple of weeks ago. Did Briggen tell you to call me?" he asked me.

I shook my head no. "I told you he's locked up. I called you because I need to show you something." And with those words a bit of weight seemed to lift up off me. I grabbed his hand and led him to the garage. I flipped on the light, and he followed down the steps. I lifted the drop cloth off the two duffel bags. "Open them up," I directed.

Nick knelt down and unzipped the first bag and saw the cash. He let out a whistle as he thumbed through the stacks of dough. He zipped the money bag back up and unzipped the other one. He whistled again. He saw the keys of dope, took them out and separated them.

He stood up, looked at me and shook his head in disgust. "Why would that nigga, Briggen, try his hand with you? And you're pregnant with his seed! That is fucked up. I expected more from him. I'm all for ride-or-die broads, but this is on some other shit," he spat.

"Nick, no. Calm down. For starters, I am not a little girl anymore. I'm a grown-ass woman. And Briggen doesn't even know anything about these two bags. That's why I called you. I stumbled across them a couple of days ago," I explained.

"Whoa. Come again?" he asked confused.

"See, look at the side of my car. Some niggas in a pickup hit me. I jumped out ready to curse out whoever it was and call 911, but instead, I stumbled across this shit." I pointed at the bags.

"Awww, fuck, Shan! You know somebody is looking for this, right? Whoever shit this is, is going to want it! Who all was with you? What did the nigga look like? How did you just take their shit? Who saw you?" He rambled off so many questions I didn't know where to start. "And they fucked up your car. Your tag. Where's your tag? Please don't tell me you lost your damn tag. You got the tag, right?"

I bit my bottom lip and said, "My tag fell off." The way he looked at me when I said that had me shook and feeling like I should have left the shit right there. "I went back for it, and it was gone," I told him that part under my breath.

"Damn, Shan!" he mumbled. I could hear the disappointment in his voice.

"What was I supposed to do, Nick? The shit fell right into my lap. I wasn't going to leave it. Would you have left it? Can you help me or not? I need your help," I pleaded after just showing him all of my cards.

CHAPTER SEVEN

DARK

It took me a few days, but I finally got put on. I didn't meet with Cisco himself, but with one of his lieutenants named Dreamer. I bought a key of coke and told him I needed to speak to Cisco because I heard that he was hurtin' 'em out here.

"Hurtin'? Hurtin', muthafucka? Who the fuck is you? Looks like you the one hurtin' if all you can afford is one key! And you wanna talk to the boss? You better get yo' broke ass the fuck outta here with that bullshit." Dreamer gritted his teeth, pushing me like I was some feen who just sucked his dick for a rock. I stumbled back, but as soon as I caught my ground, I pulled out my burner and shot him in the leg.

"Ouch, muthafucka! Owwwshit!" he hollered and groaned as he fell to the ground. "What the fuck is the matter with you?"

"Your ignorant ass must be tired of living!" I snapped as I stood over him and grinded my boot into the fresh bullet wound. I wanted to torture this muthafucka but had to remind myself to chill. I was on an important mission and couldn't allow my temper to fuck it up.

"AAAAH!" he let out a painful scream as I snatched the pouch that held the loot I had just used to cop the key. "Oh, so now you gonna rob me? You's a dead nigga!" he yelled at me.

Before he could say another word I applied more pressure to his leg.

"AAAAH, shit, man! What the fuck?"

"You must be the dumbest dope dealer in the 'D'. Your bitch ass don't even have a burner or a lookout. I could kill you right now! Get your boss on the phone. Tell him I want to give him his money personally," I commanded.

"Is you the police?" he asked.

"Hell no, I ain't the muthafuckin' police. My ass just got done finishing up a bid," I told this stupid muthafucka.

"Well, I can tell you right now, he ain't coming down here to see you."

"Nigga, you got two choices. I'll shoot you again and let you lay here and bleed to death, or you can get him down here. It's up to you."

We were in the back of a storefront, and it wasn't even eleven o'clock in the morning. This clown was all by himself, and somebody was ringing the buzzer, probably another customer trying to get some dope.

"Yo, hit the buzzer and tell them to come back later," this clown had the nerve to tell me.

"Later?" I could only laugh to myself at this fool. I went to the wall and hit the silver button. "Come back later!" I roared into it. Whoever was there buzzed again. "I said come back later! Damn," I roared again, hoping that whoever it was got the message.

Dreamer had taken off his white tee and wrapped it around his wound. "I'm fuckin' bleeding, yo!" he bawled out.

"What the fuck do you think you should be doing? Get Cisco down here. Tell him to come alone. Now, muthafucka!" I instructed.

He started laughing as he took his cell out and pressed a button. "He ain't gonna come here, and if he do, he damn sure ain't gonna come alone," he said with confidence.

"Just get the nigga on the phone." He was really starting to piss me off.

"Ay, I need you to come to the store. This nigga here say he took your money. He said if you want it come and—"

I snatched the phone from this bitch-ass faggot. "Look, dawg, I ain't trying to beef with you. I'm trying to eat with you. I just came off a seven-year stretch. And once you hear what I have to say, you won't be mad. Plus, I got your bread and I ain't giving it to this pussy." Dude was quiet on the other end. I wasn't sure if he had hung up or what.

"So you thinkin' you just gonna take my shit?" he asked me.

"Nah, playboy. I told you it ain't like that."

"He shot me!" Dreamer yelled in the background like a bitch in a bedroom.

"I'm here, solo. I got yo' money. You can either come get it, or I can drop if off to you. You da man. It's your call."

"He shot me!" Dreamer yelled out again. "I'm shot!"

"Did he say you shot him? Is that what I keep hearing him say?" he questioned.

"Yeah, that's what he said. Ya man needed to learn some respect, so I taught him some. He better be glad I needed to holla at you or he wouldn't be breathing."

Cisco burst out laughing and asked, "You shot him? Hey, Mook, some nigga shot Dreamer!" he told another dude.

I refused to laugh with him because this nigga was definitely a clown.

"Just to show him how shit is done," I reiterated.

"Aww, man! I gots to see this! Since you got my attention I'ma check you out," Cisco said.

That was exactly what I needed to hear so I hung up.

"Nigga, you watch. He ain't gonna give you no job. Only thing you gonna get is a bullet through your head," Dreamer called out warning me.

"Man, shut the fuck up before I tape yo' mouth shut!" I threatened.

"Fuck you, nigga," he said in his best tough guy voice. So I got up and shot him in the other leg just in case he was thinking about trying something. I found some black electrical tape and some cords. I tied his hands behind his back and taped up his mouth. He was screaming at me as the buzzer and his cell kept ringing. I knew I would have to kill this nigga.

Finally, after about an hour of waiting on "tha boss," the back door opened and a nigga with dreads stepped in, burners waving in each hand.

"Eat the floor, muthafucka!" he yelled at me.

"Naw, my man. I ain't the laying-down type nigga. I will

lay my gun down, but that's about it," I said standing my ground.

"I said eat the floor, muthafucka!" he spat, and I heard one slip into the chamber.

I slowly slid my gat on the desk. "It's only peace with me, man. I just want to pay the man what I owe him," I explained and got on the floor. I would get with this nigga another time.

"I said eat it!" he exclaimed furiously.

As I lay thinking about my face touching this dirty-ass floor, I heard the laugh. I recognized it to be Cisco's. He was over by Dreamer and pulling the tape off his mouth. Dreamer wasted no time giving his half-assed version of why he was lying on the floor, both legs shot up. I got a little shook when I realized Cisco was no longer laughing. And I no longer had my burner. I had made myself a sitting duck.

The dude with the dreads came over to me, kicked my foot and told me to get up. I did and he frisked me and told me to get against the wall. Out the corner of my eye I saw Cisco approaching wearing a shiny platinum and diamond necklace. He walked over, bent down and got my gat.

The silence in the room was thick until Cisco spoke. "You know what? The only thing worse than a nigga is an incompetent mutherfucker." Then he walked back over to Dreamer and shot him once in his dome. His brains splattered against the wall.

Point taken.

"The nigga recently made me lose some money," Cisco said before turning his attention my way. "My man, what's your story?" he asked me.

"I've been home for almost three weeks. I just did seven in

the Feds for trafficking and possession, and I have no time to waste. As you can see with that muthafucka over there. Your money for the key is sitting right there. That's it, and that's all," I explained.

"A key, huh? Who you work for?" Cisco asked.

"I don't work for anybody. I'm hungry out here," I told him.

Then after about a half hour of him grillin' me about what hood I was from, what I did time for, where I did time, who I ran with, he finally got down to business. But not before he had the dread get on the phone and check me out some more.

"Where you set up at?" he asked.

"Nowhere yet."

"Then how you gonna move a key?"

"I got soldiers waitin' on this. As a matter a fact, I can come see you in a couple of days. From what I can see, you short on muscle and brains. That cat over there shouldn't have been here by himself," I informed him.

"This my spot. I run this all up and down here," Cisco said, waving his hand as if it were a magic wand referring to the block.

"That's what's up. I wouldn't mind getting in on the action. Plus, word on this same street here is you just suffered a major loss and you know that should have never happened," I said.

The way Cisco was looking at me, I wasn't sure if he was going to take me out or what. But I had to put it out there.

Finally he said to his dread, "Yo, Dread! Call Duke and y'all get this nigga's shit cleaned up." He pointed to the mess he made from blowing Dreamer's brains out. "Me and this hungry nigga here gonna make a run."

My key was in a box inside of a brown shopping bag. I

pointed to it. "That's mine, and the money is right there," I had to remind this nigga.

Cisco headed for the door and said to me, "Leave that shit there. It ain't going nowhere. I damn sure ain't gonna be ridin' around dirty. And for the record, I'm only giving you a pass this once for shooting a team member. So, today is your lucky day, hungry man."

SHARIA

My plan was falling into place perfectly. Dark hadn't been out a month, and he was already on Cisco's team. It was on and poppin'. Hooking them two niggas up was like me creating my own Frankenstein monster. Dark had it fixed in his mind that it was going to be a slow grind where he would be moving a key here and there. But hell no! Once Cisco saw how fearless he really was, the shit was over. Cisco kept Dark with him, but they were making things hot because now Cisco felt even more invincible now that the whole Eastside was his. He took over every nigga's block. The dread who ran the weed spot . . . dead. Papi who was selling E and coke out of the back of the bodega . . . dead. The niggas who had the clothes and bootleg DVD's, CD's and crack spot were the only ones who bowed down and joined his team. Cisco wanted all the business and all the money. He was greedy. He had Dark working night and day, putting the fear in niggas and putting his own people up in those same spots.

Dark was bringing me bags of cash every single day. He tried to bring me dope, but I told him 'no thanks'. Then that nigga dropped off a license plate and told me to find out who it belonged to. I told him I ain't no damn Department of Motor Vehicles employee and tossed that shit in the garage somewhere.

DARK

As I walked up to the door that I had not visited in over seven years I tried to run through my mind how I was going to deal with the woman that would be on the other side. Each step reminded me of the pain that rested behind these walls. My mom, Sandra, was the type of woman that could push 'em out and then kick 'em out in one breath. I love my mom no doubt, but she ain't shit. I seen more niggas go in and out of this door than go through a prison reception area, and each one of them either beat on us, tried to fuck one of us or just held her attention and distracted her to the point where she neglected to feed and clothe us. No matter what, all five of us still loved and respected her. Now here I was, getting ready to pay my respects. As I walked up the steps I took a deep breath and prepared my mind and my heart.

Buzz. Buzz. I rang the bell as I stood there with a knot in my stomach and throat.

"Who is it?" I heard the familiar scratchy voice yell from the other side.

"It's me, Ma," I answered.

I heard the door opening and then I saw her standing there with one hand on the doorknob and the other up to her mouth as she pulled hard on a Newport long.

"You just coming by here to see me?" She blew the cancerous smoke in my face. I put my head down and prepared for the bullshit she was getting ready to take me through.

"I just got out. I had to get right before I came to see you."

"Mmmmmhmmm," she mumbled as if she didn't believe me. "Who did you kill *right before* you came to see me?"

"Nobody, Ma."

"Mmmmhmmm. Didn't I tell you that temper of yours was gonna land you in somebody's jail?" She took another drag of her cancer stick. I stared at my moms who looked like she had aged an extra ten years. When I last saw her, she had a few strands of gray hair. Now she had a whole head of gray. "Well, come in, I ain't trying to cool the whole damn block."

I stepped up into the house and she closed the door behind me. She turned and headed for the kitchen. I followed as she went to her favorite spot, the same raggedy, cheap, black kitchen table we had since before I could remember. I sat in the chair across from her.

"So what's up? What you got for me?" she sat and continued to smoke her cigarette as she took a mug to her lips that I was sure was filled with vodka and no frills coffee. I reached into the inside pocket of my jacket and pulled the envelope of money out and slid it across the table.

I watched her take it and look through it with her nose turned up. "This will do for now."

I had just given her fifteen stacks and here she was acting like I had handed her a fifty dollar bill.

"You know I got you, Ma." I continued to look down.

"Well I hope so. And I hope that you can stay your ass home this time. I ain't raise you muthafuckas to be a paycheck for the Department of Corrections. You gotta control that temper, boy. I don't know how you got your Uncle Norman's temper, he ain't yo' damn daddy. But you sure inherited it. Have you seen your brothers?"

I sat there feeing like I was nine years old. I fucking hated it but there wasn't shit I could do about it. "I ain't seen 'em. No, not yet."

"Well, they sorry asses is around here somewhere. When am I going to see you again?"

"I'm not sure, but if you need anything let me know."

"Sheeit. I'm not going to be looking for you. That's for those bitches you fuck with. You come check on your momma in two weeks. In case you ain't noticed, I don't get around the way I used to."

"Alright." I rose to my feet.

"Don't walk out my house without kissing me," she said, looking at me with her eyes wide and lips twisted. I leaned in and could smell the vodka and coffee combination and cigarettes coming from her pores. It made me sick to my stomach. I kissed her on the cheek, then stood and turned to walk away. I needed to get out there as quick as possible.

"I saw yo daddy yesterday. That sorry bastard," I heard her yell out and laugh as I headed for the door. My temper flared immediately, so I didn't respond. I refused to give my moms the satisfaction. Here it was, my dad was living with one leg and a shit-bag because he stood in the way of her getting her wig split for stealing from the local dealer. I knew that if I didn't get out of there quick I was going to do something I would regret.

SHAN

Okay. I know everyone is dying to know why Nick showed up in my backyard and why we acted as if we didn't know each other. Actually he shocked the hell out of me. I didn't know how or why he showed up. I didn't know how to react and simply ended up following his lead.

Nick and my brother Peanut were best friends since junior high. Just like my best friend Brianna had a major crush on my brother, I had a major crush on Nick. I talked him into taking my virginity. Yes, he was my first, second, and third, but because of my brother he wouldn't continue to fuck with me like that. The most memorable thing about him was something I didn't learn to appreciate until I got with other niggas. Nick's dick had a slight curve to it—talkin' about a good fuck! The curve of his dick would rub up against my walls and hit my spot every time. Just the thought of it still makes my knees buckle. Woohoo! Let me stop that shit right there before I'm all wet up.

Anyway, Nick ended up fucking with Brianna. He was gone over that ho. I never could figure out what she had in between her legs, but she turned his ass out. But my crush on him was never revealed to Brianna or my brother, and now they both are gone.

There were still many questions that Nick had not yet answered. The question of why he disappeared when Peanut got locked up? How did he end up in Detroit at Briggen's of all places? He said they told him I was with Briggen. Who in the hell is *they*? How did he even know Brig? What was Nick into? What business did he and Briggen have together? I didn't even know where to start in order to put those pieces together.

In any event, when I asked Nick to help me move the dope, he seemed hesitant. Hell, I had no one else to ask, and I needed to get rid of the shit, like yesterday, before Briggen came home. I wasn't thinking about the Feds coming back, I was more scared of what Briggen would do. Other than Briggen, Nick was the only other person I could trust. He told me he would get back to me in a couple of days. The strange thing was, his visit didn't feel awkward until he was leaving and Briggen called. It was as if Briggen knew that something was up. I was even feeling guilty, as if I was caught cheating or some shit like that. As I spoke to my husband, Nick kissed me on the cheek and quietly left.

JANAY

Just that quick, Boomer had me leaving Memphis and on to our new playground, The Motor City. We drove two-and-a-half hours from the Detroit airport to the outskirts of the city to have a meeting at a lodge called Benny Thrillz. We had checked into the Radisson where I only had about two hours to enjoy the plush suite, shower and change clothes. My uncle Boomer got out, adjusted his shoulder holster and came around to the passenger side and opened my door. As I stood up and inhaled, I caught the brisk air and remnants of baked rolls or bread. My stomach growled. We walked up the gravel-filled driveway to the main entrance of the lodge. We walked through the lobby and went straight to the elevators in the back that opened up on the second floor in front of the dining area. I followed Boomer outside onto a deck. It felt good to be wearing stilettos and a pair of Seven body-hugging jeans. I was glad that my hair and nails were done because I noticed that I was the only female present and was now in a room full of men.

Boomer held out my chair while all of the men at the round table stood up except, of course, the one in the wheelchair. I sat down, surprised that a bunch of street niggas acted as if they had some home training.

Born Mathematics then introduced everybody at the table, starting with myself as Choppa's replacement. The room was full of Detroit's most notorious drug dealers. BMF wasn't the only crime mob family in this city. Every corner of the city was covered. Even the three cities outside of the city were being represented.

Then he introduced Six-Nine, who ran an international counterfeiting organization duplicating credit cards and cash. He once made a million dollars disappear from a dirty politician's bank account with no paper trail. The twins from the North End. Tommy from the Number Streets. Rich from the Zone. Silk also known as Zeus was the God of Trap Cars. His company Full City Motor, Inc., specialized in custom-made trap cars. His work was so good that one time it took the DEA three months to figure out how to chop his cars up without destroying the evidence. Tareek from the Southside, and his drug of trade, dope. Then Cisco and his sidekick Dark were in the cut. They had been wreaking havoc all over town and their names had been ringing real heavy. Kay-Gee had every pizza and chicken spot on lock. But looks are deceiving to the average joe. Selling food was just a front. A lot of them chicken boxes held ounces of dope. Word on the street was he even put raw in the food to get the people hooked.

Melky was a handicap nigga getting bread, living off of his rep from when he was able to walk.

Six-Nine stood up, came over to me and grabbed my hand and lightly kissed my wrist. "Welcome home, sis. I'm going to miss your father. He's a good man, and he taught me a lot about this game. If you have any problems or need anything, call me."

Like he said, my father taught him a lot. I'm glad he said it loud enough for all of those other niggas to hear. I knew Six-Nine better than I knew everyone else. He was from Memphis. I knew Kay-Gee and Tareek vaguely; Silk, I knew *of* him, but the Cisco and Dark cats I knew nothing about. Born, of course, was family, since my ex was his uncle. The dude in the wheelchair looked familiar, and he was a little stiff. I didn't get a good vibe from him at all.

"Excuse me," I smiled at the dude in the wheelchair. "Did he introduce you as Milky or Melky?" I asked as I kept studying his face. I knew this could not have been who I was thinking it was.

Born leaned over and said, "I'm sorry if I wasn't clear enough. Naw, that's Melky."

"You look familiar. What side of town are you from? Do you have any brothers?" I asked him.

"You may know his brother," Born interrupted again, not giving Melky a chance to talk. "Skye *was* his brother. Light skinned, one of them pretty niggas," Born joked.

"Born, I can speak to the lady myself," Melky finally spoke.

I heard what Melky said, but I was more focused on what Born said. *Skye.* Skye was Melky's big brother. That light-skinned pretty nigga. The same nigga that was all up in my house and who tried to kidnap me. That's the nigga who Crystal bodied.

DARK

Shit was going smooth, and I was happy as fuck to be here in the midst of those that held the keys to this grimy-ass city. A couple of these cats were muthafuckin' legends. And here I was, straight out of the joint and sitting right smack-dab in the midst of it all.

Before I could fully enjoy the moment, Shorty had grabbed the bottle of Goose and hit the nigga in the wheelchair across the head. It stunned everybody. The shit happened so fast that by the time anybody reacted, she had hit dude in the throat two times with the broken bottle. Just that quick, shit turned from serenity to chaos. At first, I thought that maybe she used to fuck with dude. But then I heard her say, "These niggas tried to kidnap and rob me!" She kept screaming it out and shit.

Half the table was pulling the girl off of Melky, whose wheelchair had tipped backward. The other half was sitting him upright and trying to stop the blood from gushing out of his neck.

"Can we get some fuckin' order out here?" Born had the nerve to yell out after he had just instigated that shit by making sure he made Melky known. He had to keep banging on the table. "I don't know why y'all niggas acting all startled and shit. Each and every one of y'all muthafuckas seen and did much worse."

"You gonna just let him bleed to death?" Tareek snapped.

"And look at this muthafucka. All of a sudden he got a conscience," Born said as he glared at Tareek. I was loving every bit of the drama.

"Hell yeah, let him bleed to death," Boomer yelled. "You forgot the rules? You against one, you against all."

"Boom, with all due respect, that beef is old, man," Kay-Gee countered. "And plus, we all did some grimy shit on our way up. Hell, some of us still are."

I sat back and took note. Big Boomer made a call and sure enough, a few minutes hadn't passed when two niggas came out on deck and wheeled him outta there. Boom must have had muscle waiting downstairs for him. The chick was covered in blood so she disappeared. The waiters reappeared and reset the table and refilled the drinks, acting as if they were used to niggas acting like this.

Born lit a blunt and began to pass it around. He then announced, "So, now, we got some new business to handle."

JANAY

I can admit it. I fuckin' lost it. I knew that Skye had a brother in a wheelchair, even though I didn't learn that until after I got locked up. Skye and Melky were the local jack boys. They also had a cousin on their team from New York that they would send for to help them do their dirt.

Skye was so slick with his shit that he was setting me and my sister up at the same time. She knew him as Skye, and I knew him as New York. If she wasn't there at the house and I hadn't recognized his voice I wouldn't be alive today. I had hung out with him a couple of times, and he even helped me to get revenge on some punk who had slapped me. He was smart because he was patient enough to build up my trust. And as a result, I got caught slippin' and allowed the nigga into my home. Before I saw it coming, he had pulled out a rope and some duct tape and then punched me dead in the mouth, knocking me backward. Then he jumped on me and tied me up. Where he fucked up was, he didn't bother to check to see who else was in the house with me. Crystal had been upstairs asleep. When she heard me scream from being punched, she had eased downstairs, and I can still hear the sound of the .380 going off. Skye was alive until he grabbed Crystal's leg. She then panicked and shot him two more times by mistake.

"Nay, you alright?" Boomer was on the other side of the bathroom door. I washed my hands a few more times. "Nay!" he called out to me.

"I'll be right out, Boomer." I looked at myself in the mirror and then tried to wipe most of the blood off my shirt. My jeans were ruined. I looked at myself good. Not my outer self, but I was trying to look into my soul, and I found nothing. I opened the bathroom door.

"You alright?" he asked as he kept looking me over.

"I'm fine," I said and gave him a hug.

He took my hand. "Let's finish up the last of this business so that I can get you home."

When we made it back onto the deck, I sat down. Boomer remained standing. I looked at each of the men's faces and saw smirks, smiles and a stone-faced Dark.

"So, do y'all niggas think my niece can handle this shit? Did she pass the test?"

I looked at my uncle in disbelief. This shit was planned well beforehand.

"Before, some of you were saying that a woman does not need to be at the top." Everyone started talking at the same time. "Hold up now. Let me finish," his voice boomed. Everyone calmed down, and it got quiet. "She handled her business and she passed the most important test. She knows how to keep her mouth shut." When no one commented, he said, "My thoughts exactly. Now I make a motion for the dead man's territory to be turned over to my family. Anybody oppose?"

Dead man? Shit. They must have killed his ass because he was still breathing when I left.

There was a new face at the table, his name was Nick. From what I gathered he was there to fill in for Briggen. Boomer sat down, and the men talked as if I wasn't there for almost another hour. So just like that, I inherited more territory.

I was supposed to be in charge, but no one asked me shit. If everything was already decided for me, then what the fuck did they need me for?

DARK

Cisco and I drove back to the city in silence. We were both lost in our own thoughts. Cisco ran his mouth all the time. This was his worst flaw. So I knew that when he wasn't talking, I needed to be quiet. I couldn't stop thinking about ol' girl. Sharia had told me that she was gangsta but I didn't know she was carrying it like that. I wouldn't mind fucking her.

Of course, The Consortium wanted me and Cisco to tone our shit down. They said we were making it hot. Cisco didn't have anything to say, but I knew he was thinking, "Fuck all of them old niggas." I know that's what I was thinking. We thought alike. We wanted it all. Life was too short to be eating only a slice of the pie, when you could eat the whole thing.

No sooner had those thoughts left my mind than Cisco said we needed to have a meeting in the morning. "Get word to everybody to be on standby for the time and place."

"Aiight. I gotchu."

He dropped me off, and I chilled for the rest of the night.

CHAPTER EIGHT

JANAY

Boomer and I met up at the Original House of Pancakes in Southfield. The night before he had put me in a separate car when we left the lodge. I assumed he wanted to oversee the handling of Melky. In any event, I was anxious to hear his thoughts about the night before. I knew that every move I made was critical to the impression I needed to put in the minds of all these powerful muthafuckas that was now watching me.

Uncle Boomer had the nerve to be straight 'D' boy style. He was wearing a Dickie work suit and a pair of Timberland work boots. He was looking as if he had been working under a car all morning.

"Sheeit. Upon setting eyes on that nigga, you wasn't supposed to ask that nigga for a hug. You should have slit his throat," he stated, then chuckled. He was making a point to highlight one of the monumental moments from the meeting.

After waiting in line for about ten minutes we were finally led to our table and sat down. I picked up the menu and scanned it for my favorite things. My stomach started to growl. I was ready to lick the pages. Boomer wasted no time telling the waitress that he wanted a ham and cheese omelet. I ordered the popular apple pancakes. *Damn, it is good to be free.*

We sat talking and laughing about old times until the food came. Our waitress placed everything on the table, asked if there was anything else, then disappeared. Once she was out of earshot, Boomer, while digging into the stinky hog omelet, said, "Nay, you did good last night."

"But?" I quickly shot back while cutting into my hot buttery pancakes. "I knew there was a 'but' coming, so let me hear it. And you better not say shit about them seeing me sweat. I still can't believe that you set that up like that."

"Girl, that was a good test. Your uncle Boomer still got it," he said proudly. "I needed to see how you would handle it, and The Consortium needed to see it as well. Sheeit, I need to pat myself on the back for setting that up. Here's a nigga who was down with robbing and kidnapping you, so what else was you supposed to do? Like I said earlier, why give him a hug? You shoulda killed his ass. He's a fool for even showing up. Ain't no way in hell I would have came to no shit like that knowing that you were going to be there. He failed. These young niggas don't think."

"So let's get back to the 'but'."

"You was too quiet when we were discussing the business."

"Boomer, I've only been home for a few days. I don't know what the fuck is going on out here. But I bet you I can tell you everything that was said."

"Alright, then, tell me." He pushed his plate forward, sat back and folded his arms across his big belly. I pushed my plate aside, leaned forward and by the time I finished recapping the entire meeting and ending with, "My daddy taught me that if I keep my mouth closed, I'll hear better," Boomer was clapping.

"You ready, baby girl! Run yo' daddy's bizness!"

Just then, Born Mathematics and one of his henchmen came and invited themselves to our table, interrupting our conversation. I wanted to spend more quality time with my uncle. His henchman waved the waitress down and ordered a vegetarian omelet for Born and steak and eggs for himself.

I caught Born looking at me as if I was on the menu.

"Y'all youngins just can't be on time, can you?" Boomer looked from Born to his partner.

Born simply turned to me. "So you had some questions for me, I'm told?"

"For the record, don't be looking at me like that. You are way too young for me, and plus, I have a son by your uncle," I told him.

"Whatever, Ma. Now, what's up?" he asked, getting right down to business.

"Cisco. His beef was that everyone wanted him to tone down his guerilla tactics, but at the same time you and him are running neck and neck." I tried to be as diplomatic as possible.

"So what's your point?" Born had the nerve to ask.

"My point is, what's good for the goose is good for the gander. Fair is fair. Everyone should be subject to the same rules."

"I understand that. What else?"

"Nick. What's up with him?"

"What else?"

"Briggen. Why wasn't he at the meeting? And back to Nick, what's his story?" Listening to everything that was said at the roundtable, those were the only things that kept popping up in my mind.

"One of Briggen's workers got popped and started singing. When they snatched him up they were able to hold him, only because he had some old warrants. So he's off the scene for a minute. As far as Nick is concerned, we didn't want to put all of our eggs in one basket. We still have Mr. G, whose product is the best, Nick's product ain't grade-A but his prices are much much lower. So for now, he holds the key to our profit margins and with one word he can cause The Consortium to split. That shit would be bad for business right now."

All of us at the table let his words marinate.

"Can I ask you something personal?"

"What's up?"

I leaned over and whispered in his ear, "Why did you kill Shadee?"

He looked at me and then looked over at Boomer. I watched him as he took a swallow of his orange juice.

"You can tell me. I can handle it."

He leaned over and whispered in my ear, "You know I did you a favor. You know I loved my uncle, but he disgraced our family."

DARK

After meeting with Cisco, I had to drive around and clear my head. This nigga wanted me to relocate to Bumblefuck

Tennessee and set up shop. I told him the 'D' was my home. And plus, I was on paper. I couldn't just get up and go. But mainly I needed to be around and up on everything when it was time to make my move on him. When I discussed it with Sharia, she said it may be beneficial to set up shop for him and for me to think about it. I figured that we could weigh our options.

I was nursing a bottle of Guinness Stout in my ride on some chill shit, bending corners from one side of Seven Mile to the other. I sat at the corner of Mack and Warren, when my eyes settled on the roundest ass in history. It was jiggling just right. I had to be staring hard because I didn't even notice the light change. The horns blowing snapped me out of my lustful daze. I followed, enjoying the visual as she continued to get her jog on. When she slowed down to look before crossing the street, I was stunned when I saw her face. It was my lost love, Lisha, in the flesh, the woman who I allowed to get away.

I followed her for another block and a half, and she finally stopped in front of a brick house with gray stairs and started stretching. I pulled over and parked. It had been seven years since I'd seen her, and she looked as if she hadn't aged a day.

Lisha was a good girl. I turned her out, and had her nose wide open; therefore, she ignored my fucking around and all I did was dog her out. Because of all the shit I took her through, word on the street was she didn't fuck with dudes no more. If I had it to do all over again, I wouldn't have fucked that up.

I got out of my ride and closed the door. As I approached her, I saw her glance over at me and we locked gazes. She kept stretching, opening up her legs and bending over and shit.

I slowed my pace when I noticed the front door open and this peanut butter toned chick came out. She rushed down the stairs and slapped Lisha on the ass. Lisha straightened up, and the chick moved in and got her a kiss. She slapped Lisha again and rushed to jump inside the navy blue Beamer parked in the driveway.

As soon as she pulled off I made my way across the street. Lisha went back to stretching, and this time she gave me more of a show. I remembered how teasing me was always her thing. I told myself, fuck it, being that she's bent over advertising the ass, I'll go ahead and get up on it.

"You give your neighbors a show like this every day?"

She looked back at me smiling as she slowly rubbed her ass back and forth on my dick. She bounced, backing that ass up closer to me. The thin tightness of her stretch pants allowed me to feel her every move.

"Only if they are watching."

"You really think they can help it?" I shot back enjoying the feel of her soft ass pressing against my now semihard dick.

"I don't know and really don't care. But it feels like you can't help it," she stated seductively as she jiggled her cheeks, causing my dick to jump. I know she felt it.

"Yeah, you right, I can't help it." I grabbed one of her hips and guided that ass where it needed to be. I swear if she had on a skirt I would have pulled my dick out and went up in her raw. We were damn near dry fucking right there on the walkway.

"Can you feel what you've been missing and what you can no longer have?" she asked me.

"What you mean what I can no longer have?"

She was still bent over so I grabbed onto her other hip and held her firmly in place. When I grew to full potential she stood straight up and looked me in my eyes.

"You been shaking my ass in front of niggas?"

"Your ass? This stopped being your ass a long time ago."

"I can't tell."

"Same old Dark." She smirked, then broke away and sashayed up the stairs. Then she turned and asked, "How long have you been home? You look good." Not waiting for an answer, she turned and headed toward the front door.

"Not long." I came up the stairs. "You look even better. Can I get a hug? It won't hurt," I said as I followed right behind her.

"Sorry, Dark. I just got finished running. I'm all wet and sweaty," she said as she opened her front door.

"I like wet and sweaty," I told her.

She turned and gave me a hug. She couldn't help but to plant her pussy right on my dick because it was hard and sticking out. I grabbed two handfuls of her ass as she wrapped her arms around my neck.

"What are you doing around here, Dark?" Her voice trembled as she got ready to break our embrace, but I held her tighter causing her to stay there.

"You want me to leave?"

"My girl said she'll be back in an hour." She began grinding on my dick, and my shit was rock.

"Then we wasting time," I told her as I backed her up into the house. I kicked the door shut with my foot. She eased my jacket off my shoulders. It fell to the floor. I pulled her T-shirt up over her head, and she pulled my tee up over mine.

I unbuckled my belt and took off my jeans and sneaks. She wiggled out of her sneakers and sweats. I stood there buck naked as she peeled off her wet panties.

She turned around, spread her legs and bent over. I eased up behind her and made the head of my dick slide across her wet pussy and then eased inside. I stroked in and out as she moaned and backed that pussy up on my dick. Her shit was tight, wet and hot.

"Damn, baby, when was the last time you had some penetration? You don't make that bitch strap on or nothing?"

"Oh my God, Dark . . . this feels so good. Fuck me, baby. Fuck this pussy real good. Who's in charge, big daddy? My bitch or your dick?"

"My dick." I hit her pussy harder. "My dick." I started stroking faster and just as that shit was getting good she pulled forward causing me to slide out.

"Let's go upstairs." She led the way. I followed behind her, dick sticking straight out.

We got to her bedroom, and she yanked the covers off her king sized bed. "Lie down," she told me. I did what I was told, and she climbed on top, straddled my waist grabbed my joint and slid down on it.

She closed her eyes and started riding me fast and hard. She had the prettiest 38 Ds I had seen in a long time. I wanted to suck on them, but I couldn't interrupt her or stop her from getting her fuck on.

"Oh, this dick is good. Oh my God, it feels so good. I missed you. Oh, it's good." She was moaning and groaning. Then her facial expression twisted all up and she started cumming. I grabbed onto her hips and pumped as deep as

I could get. When her pussy stopped jerking, she slid off me and started sucking my dick. She hungrily sucked me, sliding me in and out of her wet mouth as she moaned and slurped. The work she was putting in was so good I grabbed her ponytail and pushed myself to the back of her throat. I thought I was gonna knock her tonsils out. She swallowed all of my cum and didn't stop until there wasn't anything left.

It turned out to be a good day. After Lisha drained a nigga, we both lay sprawled out in the bed breathing heavy and staring at the ceiling. She sat up and smiled at me. I smiled back, and then remembered her saying that her bitch would be back in an hour. I got up, and we both hit the bathroom. She jumped in the shower and I headed downstairs to get my clothes. As I was putting them on I heard the keys turning the lock to the front door. *Aww fuck!*

In walked the chick who slapped Lisha on the ass earlier. Homegirl was about five foot six, Gabrielle Union-looking chick. She and Lisha could have passed for twins except Lisha had long hair. I wouldn't mind fucking her, too.

She stepped into the house, looked at me half-dressed, noticed Lisha's pile of clothes on the floor and asked, "What the fuck are you doing in my house?" She gave me a death stare. "Lisha, who the fuck is this, and why is this nigga in my house?" she yelled as she walked through the house looking for Lisha. She turned her attention back to me and asked, "Who the fuck are you?"

"I'm Dark. What's up?" I said as I zipped up my jeans.

Lisha came rushing down the steps in her robe.

"Lisha, who the fuck is this? What the fuck is this black nigga doing in *my* house?"

"Chill out. He was just leaving."

"What the fuck is going on?"

"This is Damon's father, Tiffany. Calm down, damn."

Damon's father?

"Calm down? Calm down? Bitch, you got me fucked up!" Her chick was so mad, tears were running down her cheeks.

"Dark, you need to leave," Lisha told me.

"Yes, you better get the fuck out of here because I don't give a fuck who he is. This is my fuckin' house!" She went to the door and snatched it open. "How dare you bring your baby's daddy up in my house when I'm not home." She glared at Lisha.

"Hold up. Baby's daddy?" Was I hearing this bitch right?

"Dark, thanks for stopping by. I'll call you later." Lisha had her hand on my chest and was pushing me toward the door. She was giving me that look that said go ahead, we'll talk later.

"Hold up, Lisha. Who is Damon?"

"Lisha, you ain't tell this nigga?" She looked from her to me and back to Lisha. "You fucked the nigga and didn't have the decency to tell him?" Tiffany was screaming. She took off running for the stairs. I knew she was headed up to the bedroom to confirm that we had been fucking.

"Dark, go. Now. Please."

"Not until you tell me who Damon is."

She shoved me onto the porch. Tiffany was coming down the steps screaming, "You fucked this hoodlum raw?" I know this bitch didn't go check the sheets and shit.

"He's your son, Dark. His name is Damon, and he's your

son. Now go! I promise we'll talk later." She slammed the door in my face.

I stood there stunned. *A son?* I knocked on the door again. I could hear them in there arguing.

"Get the fuck off of my door!" Tiffany screamed.

Damn.

CHAPTER NINE

NICK

I didn't plan on finding Shan like this, shacked up with one of my main buyers. I imagined her having a nine to five, married to some government worker, not mixing with the likes of me and my kind.

I was still trippin' over what she had stumbled up on. That girl always did have the strangest luck. I remembered one time . when she found a package and gave it to Peanut, thus jump-starting his career of hustling. I supply the majority of dope to the city of Detroit. And if it had been anybody else I would have made it my business to put whoever up on who had their package. I know the feeling of taking "L." But I damn sure wasn't going to turn my fam into one of my customers.

Shan opened the door and let me in. "I bought a new car," she announced, wearing a big Kool-Aid smile.

"You did what?"

"I traded the other one in. I couldn't be riding around in

the same car with the big dent in the back. What if they are looking for the car?"

"Shan, I told you to lay low."

"Nick, I was calling you. You never called back."

"What else have you been buying?"

"Some clothes and a new dining room set."

"Shan, you got to stop spending."

"Okay, I will," she reluctantly responded.

"I'm serious, Shan."

"I heard you. What about the dope? If Briggen knew I had this shit in my house he'd kill me." She sounded like a nervous child.

"I'm here to pick that up now."

"How soon can you flip it?" she asked, carrying the heavy duffel bag into the living room.

"I meet with some people tomorrow night."

"How much can I expect?"

"I'll let you know in a few days. In the meantime, chill the fuck out." I picked up the bag and threw it over my shoulder.

"Promise me you'll keep this between me and you. Briggen *cannot*—and I mean *cannot*—find out about this."

"I got you."

No sooner than I got in my ride, my man was calling me to tell me that it was Cisco's package that Shan stumbled upon. He assured me that Cisco had no idea who had it.

BRIGGEN

I'm standing in line, scratching my head, waiting to get on the phone because my sources had just told me that Nick had been going in and out of my house and Shan had been spending money like it's water.

"Yo, Briggen. My man Ace said you ain't got to use that phone. Come see him and he gotchu."

I looked at dude. I didn't know him or his dude Ace from a can of paint. "I'm good, homie. Tell him I'm good. Gotta get my thoughts together while I'm waiting."

"Aiight. I'll tell Ace you turned down his offer." He stepped away.

Damn right I turned it down. I didn't need to be owing nobody shit. Especially muthafuckas I didn't know.

After damn near half an hour I finally got a phone and dialed Shan. When she answered I said, "Hey, what's up?"

"Baby, I miss you."

"I miss you too. What's going on? Everything alright?"

"Nothing is going on around here," she said, sounding strange. She definitely wasn't sounding like a bitch who missed her man. "What's going on with you? Any word on when you coming home?"

"Rudy is trying to get another court date. He's working on it. I should be out of here soon. So ain't nothing going on?"

"Nothing, baby. Just missing you, that's all."

"Bullshit. Come see me right away." I didn't give a fuck that I was all the way in Miami.

"Come see you?" she stammered.

"Yeah, come see me. You was just bitchin' about not being able to come see me; now I say come on and you offering resistance? You coming or not?"

SHAN

Oh shit. No, he did not just order me to come see him. He must have heard something. But . . . No, he couldn't have. Fuckin' bigmouth Nick! I knew Briggen. He knew if he got me in front of him he'd be able to get me to tell him everything.

"Shan! You coming or what?"

"When do you want me to come?"

"As soon as possible. Visits are seven days a week."

"I don't feel like dragging Anthony with me."

"Get Keeta to keep him for a couple of days."

"Okay, baby. I'll get right on it."

Click.

He hung up.

I had already called the holding facility there in Miami. They only allowed them four hours a month and one hour a day. I was not flying way to Miami by myself to sit on a visit for one measly hour to be interrogated. And leave my son? I don't think so.

I knew Briggen would be calling back. He only hung up to get my blood boiling. Sure enough, fifteen minutes later, the phone rang.

"Shan, I want you down here as soon as possible."

"Briggen, I said I was coming. You only hung up fifteen minutes ago."

"When are you coming, Shan?"

"Call back in an hour. I need to make a reservation, hotel, babysitter, all of that, Briggen. When I was trying to see you, you didn't want me to come. It wasn't necessary, you told me. Now all of a sudden it's urgent."

"You damn right it's urgent. So why are you bullshittin' around?"

"I'm not bullshittin', Briggen. Anthony's crying, I gotta go." I hung up before he could say another word. I'm a grown-ass woman and he ain't my muthafuckin' daddy.

As I was online going through the motions of finding a travel agency and looking for flights and hotel deals, just doing what I was told, it hit me. Something came over me like I was possessed by the spirit of my girl Brianna and her *fuck it* attitude. I was fed up with second-guessing myself and putting everyone else before me. I had been doing that shit since high school. I was fed up with always doing everything Briggen wanted me to do and when he wanted me to do it. Even if I didn't feel like it. But not this time. I was not up for going to Miami for no damn one-hour visit. For what? For him to lie to my face about how he was one-hundred percent legit or lie about how he didn't fuck with Mia no more? Fuck that! I had a shitload of money stashed in my garage, and it was mine, all mine. And once Nick moved that other dope I would have another shitload of money coming in. So I decided, "Fuck it!" I knew I could get Miss Carrol who ran the day care to keep Anthony. She loved him to death. I had it all mapped out. I was going shopping, getting my hair done, and then I was packing my bag and going to Vegas.

FIVE DAYS LATER . . .

BRIGGEN

I was on pins and needles as I waited for the guards to tell me I had a visit. But Shan's ass never bothered to show up, which only confirmed the rumors my sources had been pullin' my ear to. On top of that, every time I dialed her number it would shoot straight to voicemail. Her ass thinks she slick, but I ain't gonna sweat it because I told her once they straightened out those old warrants I would be out and she and I would be face to face.

And here I was, fresh out, back on the street and locked out of my own damn house. Shan was still refusing to answer her phone, and I hadn't heard from Keeta. My cell was in the house and I just wanted to get inside.

I went next door to my neighbor's house and asked to use their phone. I called Keeta, and, of course, she was running the streets. I told her to run her ass by her house and get my keys that I had stashed there.

"Boy, what else you stashed in my house without me knowing?"

"Just bring me my damn keys so that I can get inside," I told her and hung up. I thanked Billy, my neighbor, and went back and sat on my front porch.

Shan's sudden behavior had definitely raised a red flag. I had no clue what she was up to, and I didn't even have a clue as to where she was. I was trying to figure out why she didn't tell Keeta where she was going and why she wasn't answering her phone. The more I thought about her, the more I started buggin'. What if someone kidnapped her and my son? I damn sure didn't want to get the fucking pigs involved. This was not like her. On top of that, I'd been hearing that Nick had been over here several times. What if she was with him? My mind was swimming in the questions that I had no answers to. I sat on my porch ready to lose it.

Finally Keeta pulled up, jumping the curb, damn near missing my fence by a thread. I stood up and waited for her to get out of the car.

"What's up, jailbird?" she teased me.

"Just give me my damn keys, Keeta. You haven't heard from Shan at all?"

"Not at all, I already told you that." She came up on the porch and gave me my keys.

"I got it from here," I told her. I needed to get inside and focus.

"You don't need my help?"

"I said I'm good, Keeta."

"Damn, you don't have to snap. I guess you don't need to know that Miss Carrol has the baby. Oh, that's right! You don't need me. I'm outta here." She turned and started for the stairs pulling out her phone and went to dialing.

"When did you find that out?" Miss Carrol had been a friend of our family's ever since I could remember. She had been helping with the running of the day care since it opened.

"On my way over here." I followed behind her bombarding her with questions. She held up her finger to shut me up. "Miss Carrol, hi. This is Keeta again. Anthony's father just made it to the house. He wants to talk to you."

She handed me the phone. "Hello, Miss Carrol." I was glad to know that my son was fine.

"Hi, baby. Your li'l man is fine. I don't have a problem keeping him for another two days until his mama comes back. Y'all know he's a good baby."

"I know. But I'm just getting back. Have you talked to his mother today?"

"She calls every day. She's in Vegas winning all types of money! That girl got good luck."

"I need to come pick up my son. I'll be there in a half hour."

"Okay, you know I'll have him ready."

She hung up, and I gave Keeta her phone back.

"You want me to get him?"

"Nah, I'll go. Thanks, Keeta."

"Boy, you know I got you. What about your car keys?"

"I got an extra set in the house."

"Alrighty then, if you need me, call me."

She left and I went into my house. I needed to shower, shave and call Nick. As I got dressed, I put together my plans and then thought I better take Keeta up on her offer. I grabbed the house phone and told her to go pick up Anthony and to tell Miss Carrol not to tell Shan I was home. She said something slick and hung up on me.

The next thing I did was go through my house. I had to get a feel for whatever Shan was up to. I saw the new Mercedes GL450 in the garage. I found my cell and called Nick.

"Nick, what's good?"

"Briggen, what's up with you? Where you at?"

"I'm at the crib."

"Oh shit, you out?"

"For now, yeah," I said.

"Fuck that for now shit. Money talks, nigga. You forgot? You want me to swing by? I gotta run something by you."

"Yeah, come on through."

CHAPTER TEN

JANAY

Boomer and I were waiting at the Detroit Science Center for this Nick character. We were just told that our shipment was dropped off already and being distributed. "Why do you think he's giving us such a good price, Boomer? I mean, he's practically giving it away."

"Here he comes, you can ask him yourself."

"Boomer, what's up? Glad you are back out on the battle-field." He embraced my uncle, and then turned to me. "And this must be Janay."

"Yeah. This is my niece."

"It's cool to finally meet you. I didn't get an opportunity to speak with you at the round table. What did you want to ask me?"

Nick was such a pretty boy, looking around my age, thirty-one. He was staring at me, waiting for my response.

"Why are you giving us such a good price?" I asked focusing on the business at hand.

He smiled. "That's an easy one to answer. For one, it's out of respect. And two, I want to contribute to the family that should be at the top of this food chain. Y'all know how to treat your people and run your business. Makes my job that much easier."

"If that's the case, then how long can we get it at this low price?"

"That depends."

"Depends on what?"

"That depends on you."

NICK

I'm not one to mix business with pleasure, but damn. Seeing Janay up close and personal I wasn't expecting her to be supermodel sexy and so damn feminine. She had on a pair of black stilettos, black tight-fitting jeans that showed off each and every one of her curves and a simple but expensive white blouse. She was dressed like a woman with class. I didn't want to take my eyes off her, and had to remind myself that I was here on business. The ball was in my court, and it was time for me to make that move.

"I'm listening," Janay responded.

"Make me your main connect and I can guarantee that the price will stay the same. I'm confident that you can't get a lower offer than mine nowhere."

Janay's expression remained blank. Boomer glanced over at her, then back at me. He then reached into his pocket and pulled out a pen and paper. I watched as he jotted something down and passed the note to Janay. I kept my game face on as

I waited for a reply. I knew the outcome because like I told her, she wouldn't find shit lower or better than what I was offering.

After a long silence, Janay extended her hand for me to shake it. "We have a deal." Once our hands locked, she pulled me close for an embrace. "Don't fuck us over, baby boy," and with that, she pinched my cheek.

Boomer thought that was funny.

"Boomer, our business is concluded here with Mr. Nick. I'll be in the car."

I watched her hips sway as she walked away. *Damn, she's a bad bitch!* I thought.

Boomer obviously read the expression on my face because out of the blue he said, "You ain't her type, youngin."

"What's her type?" I asked him.

"Trust me. You ain't her type. But I'll be in touch. Let me catch up with my niece."

He left me standing there, and I left and headed over to see Briggen.

WHEN BRIGGEN OPENED THE front door, I stepped into a tension-filled atmosphere. I could feel it. He was carrying Li'l Peanut and had his cell glued to his ear. He waved me inside and pointed to the sofa. I sat down, and he disappeared upstairs. I heard him arguing with whoever it was he was talking to, and then his voice trailed off.

I sat there and waited for him to come downstairs, deciding how much I was going to tell him. I knew a nigga of his caliber didn't leave his castle without anybody watching it. I wasn't going to show my hand; I was going to feel my way through this. I knew I had to be careful and needed to call his bluff.

When he came back into the room, he said, "Nick, when they say 'when it rains it pours', whoever said that shit wasn't lying."

"What's been up with you, man? Don't tell me your ghost walking ass finally caught a case."

"Man, I don't even want to talk about that. But there a few things I do want to talk about. Why have you been stopping by my crib?"

"You don't know?"

"If I did, do you think I'd be asking you?"

"Shan told me she got my number from your cell. She called me because she found a package and she needed help."

"She found a package of what?"

"A key of dope." There I was calling his bluff. I wasn't sure what or how much he knew. "She took me to the garage and showed me a bag that had a key of dope in it. She said she didn't know who else to call and asked me to move it for her. I had heard that you was locked up, but she confirmed it that day. I took the dope so you wouldn't have it sitting around in your crib."

"What the fuck?" He looked confused and shocked as he tried to process what I had just told him.

"I know, man."

"How she just gonna call you outta the blue?"

"She called me. She said she found my number in your phone."

"Nick, stop bullshittin'. You know it's MOB . . . *Money Over Bitches*. What's the real deal, nigga?"

"I ain't bullshittin'. But your concern should be that who-ever she took it from crashed into her, and as she was leaving, her tag fell off the back of the car. She said she went back for it, and it was gone. She don't know who has it."

"Fuck! And just a key?"

"Yeah. One key," I lied.

Brig looked at me as if he knew I was lying. But what could I say? I glanced at my watch. I didn't have any more time to waste sitting here playing twenty-one questions. "What else is up?"

"Big Choppa's peoples were at the last roundtable."

I had to laugh. Choppa was a rare breed. Here he disappeared only to resurface to make sure his daughter sat on his throne. "I'm not surprised. Choppa is from the old school. He rides until he dies."

"Yeah, that's true. But at the same meeting they took Melky out. He was one of my key players. How they gonna do that without my vote?"

I could hear in his voice that he had major problems with that move. "Man, you know you can't be attached. When niggas fuck up and have to pay the cost ain't shit you can do about it."

Brig's face was all contorted the fuck up. I didn't know why he was surprised. He knew better than me how the game was played. "Him and Skye were the ones who tried to kidnap Choppa's daughter, remember? You know Chop wasn't gonna let that shit slide."

"Yeah, but they took Skye out. That beef was supposed to be squashed."

I shrugged his comment off. My mind wandered off to Shan. I wanted to ask him about her but at the same time, I didn't want him to become more suspicious than he already was. If he didn't have anything else for me, it was time for me to leave. He seemed as if he was ready to start trippin'. I was glad when I heard his son, my nephew, crying.

JANAY

I couldn't believe that Nick had the audacity to try to hit on me. Didn't he know who I was? And Boomer had the nerve to tell me to use it to my advantage. That shit was old as hell and I told him how insulted I was that he would even say that to me.

"What? You think I'm talking about pussy?"

"Of course. What else could you be referring to?"

"Nah, baby girl. I'm talking about his mind. His knowledge. What he knows. His information." Boomer poked the side of his head. "How did he get to be the consultant to eighty percent of the drug families in Detroit? He's slowly becoming the only supplier. He almost controls the supply and demand. The boy is smart, Janay."

I laughed, "Boomer, y'all force me to run the family business. Now y'all gonna tell me who to fuck?"

"Janay, you know you have to be ready for whatever the game throws at you. You backing out on the family?"

Why did my uncle just call me out? Boomer told me that if my heart wasn't one-hundred percent in this, then I would need to make a decision.

Needless to say, I ended up on the phone with Nick and we talked for damn near four hours . . . This was some bullshit!

SHAN

When Briggen first called with that visit shit, I admit, I did panic. And most of the time when I panic, dumb ideas come to mind. Vegas being one of them. I booked a trip to Vegas, first-class everything. I stayed at a new boutique hotel called The Atria. My timing was perfect. Floyd Mayweather was fighting, and I was making it my business to be there. At the fight I bumped into some fly bitches from Jersey, and we made plans to hook up right after. And it was on.

But when I spoke to Miss Carrol and she said that Briggen came and picked up Li'l Anthony, I could have died. I immediately came down off of my "freedom fun" high. And talk about fun? After I hooked up with the two Jersey chicks, we got it in. We gambled, we swam, we went to the shows, gambled and partied some more. I won $27,000, but only had fourteen of that left and decided to quit while I was ahead.

My new friends, Courtney and Michelle, were disappointed that I had to leave and cut my trip short by two days. It was time for me to go home and face the music. So, here I was pulling up into my driveway.

I paid the cabbie, and he got out to get my bags. I was anxious to see my baby, but I had mixed emotions about seeing Briggen. I missed him, yes, but at the same time, I knew to be prepared for battle since I did not come and see him like he instructed me to. I put the key into the lock and before I could turn it, Briggen snatched the door open holding our son.

"Anthony!" I couldn't help but smile and take my baby into my arms. This was the longest I had ever been away from him. Briggen stood there looking me up and down before grabbing my bags from the cabbie. My son was so glad to see me, and I was so glad to see him. He wouldn't stop bouncing up and down.

"Shan, what the fuck has gotten into you?" Briggen snapped before he even got into the house good. "I can't wait to hear what you got to say, and you better hope I like what you tell me."

I looked at this nigga as if he was crazy, held my son tighter and headed for the stairs.

"Shan!" he yelled so loud he startled me, and I froze in place. "Where the fuck have you been?"

"Briggen, I am grown. I took a vacation and went to Vegas by myself. I met two ladies from New Jersey, and we hung out together, and we enjoyed ourselves. That's it; that's all."

"What made you decide to leave our son with the daycare worker? When I asked you to come see me, you bitched about how you wasn't leaving our son with no stranger for days at a time, but you go and pull this shit!"

"Daycare worker? Briggen, you have known Miss Carrol for how long? Hell, you are the one who introduced me to her. You forgot she used to be the nanny? I needed to get away from everything that was going on."

"Everything going on? What the fuck, Shan? A little bit of pressure and you just cave in like a spineless bitch?"

"Briggen, if I'm not stuck in this house, I'm running your fuckin' businesses. I never do anything for me. I needed to do this for me. I was beginning to feel as if I was going to have a nervous breakdown. Yes, I feel like everything around me is caving the fuck in! I'm glad you fuckin' noticed," I screamed. "And as you can see, our son is fine. If I didn't trust Miss Carrol, do you think I would have left my baby with her? You asshole!"

"That's not the only thing I'm pointing out, Shan. I told you to come see me, and you didn't. Then I'm hearing some shit about you spending money like it's water and you got niggas running in and out of my house."

"What?" I got indignant. "What about me hearing that you still hustling? And what about me hearing that you still fuckin' with all of them bitches you had when I first met you? You wanna get shit out in the open, let's get it out. From what I'm hearing you *big*." I put lots of emphasis on big. "Larger than you were when I first met you. I never say shit when you go see them bitches to take care of your business. I called Nick because I had no one else to call. He came, and I'm sure he told you why he came. Now what?" I was screaming at the top of my lungs, and it was feeling damn good to let it all out.

Briggen hauled off and punched the wall right on the side of my head while I was holding Anthony. "That's what. You better watch how the fuck you talk to me. I ain't some lame-ass nigga off the streets."

Startled and dazed, I held Anthony tighter as I leaned against the wall. "You wasn't here to help me, Briggen. So I did the best I could. You wasn't here. Now you are, so make shit right, if you are so concerned." I began to walk up the stairs. I was scared. I honestly didn't know what to do.

He came following behind me. "As far as them bitches are concerned, you knew what was up when you started fuckin' with me, Shan. You chose me, remember? You know how many bitches wish they were in your spot? And don't you ever call some other nigga over to my home. I don't give a fuck what you need. As a matter of fact, get your shit and get the fuck out. I'll be damned if you gonna disrespect me in my own house as if I'm some fuckin' chump and talk shit about it. How am I supposed to trust you, Shan? I can't."

I stood there looking at him as if he had lost his fuckin' mind. "What? You gonna put me and your son out in the streets?"

"No, not my son. Just his momma."

"Nigga, you must be crazy. I got your son and I'm carrying another one. I think you are the one who needs to be packing, not me." I went into our bedroom, slammed the door and locked it.

CHAPTER ELEVEN

MIA

Briggen and I pulled up in front of my house at the same time. Around 6:00 I decided to go to the gym, and then I stopped by the Super Walmart out in Livonia to pick up a few things.

The last time I saw him was at Forever's funeral. I had only spoken to him a couple of times while he was locked up.

His trunk popped open, and I watched him as he got out of the truck and walked back to the trunk. He grabbed a duffel bag and shut it. My heart fluttered as I turned away to grab my gym bag and the bags from Walmart. I didn't want him to see me watching him.

"Are you going to open the door or what?" he asked me as he stood in the driveway.

"Are you going to help with these groceries or what?" I shot back at him.

"You ain't got but three bags," he snapped, but still came over to my car.

"I don't care. Come grab these three bags." When he got to my trunk, I gave him four bags and I held onto the rest. "Thank you. Now was that so hard?"

"Just come on and let me in the damn house."

I closed the trunk and went into the house, still curious as to what Briggen was up to. I kicked off my sneaks and he did the same. He headed for the kitchen. "You want these in here, right?"

"Yes." I followed him and watched as he sat the bags on the counter and left. I stood there waiting to see what he was going to do next. Usually, when he came into my house he would sit on the couch, state his business and leave. If he had something to drop off, he would drop it and be gone.

He went upstairs, and my heart did the flutter thing again. I thought about the duffel bag he was carrying and got excited. I tiptoed to the bottom of the stairwell to see if I could hear something that would tell me what he was up to. When I heard the shower come on I grabbed my chest. I didn't know what was going on, but my kitty who had been hiding under her covers since God knows when, had stretched. I felt a tingle down there and rushed back to the kitchen. I quickly put the perishables away and went upstairs.

When I walked into my bedroom the duffel bag he had was unzipped and I could see the clothes. I came out of my workout gear thinking, if this nigga thought he was only going to sleep, eat and shit in my house he had another thing coming. He was definitely giving up some dick. We hadn't fucked in almost eleven months.

I went to join him in the shower. His back was to me as he had both hands against the wall, leaning over as if he was being frisked as the water rushed over his head and the rest of his body. He obviously was deep in thought because he didn't move. I grabbed an extra sponge, soaped it up and began to gently massage his back, shoulders, arms, butt and legs. Getting impatient, I motioned for him to turn around. I washed and massaged the front of his arms, chest abs and legs and obviously was doing a good job because his dick was sticking straight out and was rock-solid. It was beautiful. I savored the view and figured I'd save that for last, massaging first his balls, gliding gradually back and forth, making them nice and soapy. When he seductively gazed at me licking his lips, I began soaping and stroking that rod, going over the head, then back down the shaft causing him to grow longer, fatter and harder.

I became so aroused that I found myself getting on my knees. He may have belonged to Shan, but right now, he was all mine. I craved him. I needed him. I wanted to taste him. I wanted his hardness to fill my mouth. I ran my tongue across the head as I gently massaged his balls. I then licked his dick long and slow, teasing the base of the head. His dick jumped. He grabbed my hair, pulling me closer to him. I moistened my lips, opened my mouth and took him in. Slowly. Inch by inch. It had been too long and I was savoring this moment as I imagined I was sucking on my favorite, a chocolate Tootsie Pop. I felt him trying to fuck my mouth. But I was in control. I pulled him out and began licking all over his dick. And then I put him back into my mouth and started sucking him hard. He now had both hands on my head and was grinding his dick against my throat.

"Goddamn, you a bad bitch!" I heard him mumble.

The deeper he tried to push, the harder I sucked. This nigga was gonna say my name. I sucked and licked that sensitive spot under the head with no mercy.

"Meaaahh," he finally groaned.

The way he was grabbing on my hair had Miss Kitty purring. He must have felt it because he stopped me.

"Let's take it to the bed," he said out of breath.

We stepped out of the shower, soaking wet and rushed into the bedroom. I lay back onto the bed and spread my legs. He remained standing on the side of the bed and pulled me up to the edge. Since my mattress was so high he put each of my legs up on his shoulders and eased inside me. I know I was a little tight because no other nigga had been hittin' this. He grunted.

"See what you've been missing," I seductively teased him as I matched his every stroke.

"Fuck!" he grunted again.

"See what good, tight and hot pussy you've been missing?" I wanted to burn that shit into his mind. "You've been missing out on this hot pussy."

BRIGGEN

Yeah, I packed a bag of my shit and left Shan to figure out what she wanted to do. I don't know who the fuck she thinks she is or what the fuck got into her. When a nigga comes home from jail, his woman is supposed to be there waiting for him, mouth open and pussy hot, just the way Mia was.

I knew that when she saw me and I didn't say why I was at her house, she didn't know what to think. Bottom line, I was stressing, needed to get away from Shan, needed to clear my head and I definitely needed to be up inside some hot, wet, tight pussy.

After that A-1 head job Mia gave me in the shower, I *had* to bless her with some dick. Niggas and bitches had been telling me that Mia don't be fucking around, and if I didn't believe it then, I believed it now because her pussy was tight as fuck. I was fighting not to scream like a bitch as I drove into her hot, tight juiciness. I went deeper and faster while Mia matched my every stroke. Our rhythm was synchronized. As far as I was concerned, that was still my pussy.

"Briggen . . . I'm nev . . . er . . . go . . . ing to . . . stop . . . lo . . . loving you," she moaned.

I gripped her hips and tried to knock her bottom out. Her pussy was hot and, at that point, all I could do was explode. *Fuck! I didn't cover up my dick.*

SHAN

After I heard Briggen start his car, I unlocked my bedroom door and ran down the stairs.

"No, this nigga did not leave me!" I snatched open the back door as he was backing out of the driveway. I was ready to hurt something. I slammed the door and the walls shook.

I called Keeta. I needed to talk to somebody. She wasn't at home, and she didn't show up until after I had bathed Anthony and put him to bed.

"I'm starving, Shan," she said as she ravaged my cabinets. "Listen, don't tell Briggen. I think I might be pregnant," she announced.

"What? By who?"

"That's a whole 'nother story. I couldn't wait for you to bring your ass back so I could tell you." I sat down on one of the stools at the counter. Keeta went into the refrigerator and began pulling out leftovers and tossing the food out. She rolled her eyes at me. "This is nasty, Shan."

"What do you expect? I haven't been home for a week."

"Speaking of which, how you gonna go to Vegas and not take me? I am so mad at you! You selfish bitch!"

"I needed that alone time, Keeta. Time away from everything and everybody. Something that your family does not seem to understand."

"My family?"

"Yes, you know you are down with whatever Briggen says."

"That's what you think? I got my own mind, Shan."

"Mmmmmhmm," I mumbled.

"So what epiphanies did you get in Sin City? Did you cheat on Brig? Come on, Shan, you can tell me." She started laughing.

"You laughing, but it's true. I did have an epiphany. Number one, I'm gonna start doing me. I'm going to be living for me and do me."

"Shan, please. If you lose your man you sure will be doing you." She started laughing at her own joke, but then she saw the seriousness on my face. "Alright, damn. What do you want to do? What do you have time to do?"

"Oh, don't worry. I got my shit all planned out. I'm getting ready to be a promoter."

"A promoter? A promoter of what?"

"Of shows. Entertainment. Bringing talent here to the 'D'. That's what."

Keeta finally decided to make us a turkey and cheese sandwich. She examined the date on the turkey slices closely and away to the trash the slices went. "Damn, y'all. Why don't somebody clean out the refrigerator? And just like I tossed that bad lunch meat, you need to toss that bad idea about being a promoter. First off, you don't know shit about doing that shit. Second, you got a baby and you're pregnant. Third, you already got businesses to run. You got the day care, the hotel, the—"

I cut her off. "Keeta, I don't know why I expected more support from you when you don't do shit. Hell, you ain't even got a job."

"What do I need a job for when I got a rack of niggas with money? Including Briggen?"

"Keeta, what happens to you when that rack of niggas gets locked up? And here your ass is depending on these niggas for your livelihood. You see what happened to Sharia. She put all of her faith, hopes and dreams in Briggen's hands. She built that club from the ground up and poof! It was gone just like that." I snapped my fingers.

"You can't talk, Shan. You running Briggen's day care and hotel. That shit ain't yours, technically."

"Ain't mines? That shit is in my name, why you playin'?"

"But it's still his, and just like he did with Sharia, he can take it. You only the front person he got runnin' it."

"Not anymore, I ain't running his shit. And we are married, so technically, it is mine. However, I'm doing my own thing from here on out. I've been putting other people first for way too long."

"How you gonna run a party-throwing business with a baby on your hip and one in your belly?"

"For starters, Briggen is getting ready to do his part, that's how. Just sit back and watch me."

"How are you gonna get him to do that?"

"He's gonna keep his son. Shit, he's able. He don't got no nine to five."

"Where is his ass?" Keeta snapped.

I looked at my watch. It was almost 11:30. I grabbed my cell and called him. *No answer.*

"Alright, Miss Big-Time Party Throwing P. Diddy promoter. I'm outta here"

"You'll see, bitch. And don't come asking me for a job neither," I teased her.

"Whatever!" She kissed me on the cheek and left.

As soon as I locked her out I called Briggen again. He answered the phone, sounding as if he was already asleep. The blood in my veins started to boil. Here I was stressing over his ass, and he's resting up in some other bitch's bed.

"Where are you?" I gritted.

"What?"

"Where are you, Briggen? You heard me."

"What do you mean where am I? You put me out, remember."

"I know you don't think that I'ma just stay a good little girl and allow you to sleep in another bitch's bed, do you?"

"You put me out, Shan. Now what do you want?"

I couldn't speak. My tongue turned thick, and my damn throat was dry. I ended the call and headed upstairs. I packed Anthony a bag of clothes, went downstairs and packed up some food, wrapped him up and headed over to Mia's. I didn't care that it was almost midnight. If he was at the bitch's house, he was in a position to keep his son. I had an agenda and could move around more freely without the baby. He'd be just fine with his daddy.

When I pulled up in front of her house and saw Briggen's car, I lost it. I started laying on the horn. When I got tired of doing that I called him. When he answered, I said, "I'm out front. Come and get your son." I hung up. I got out of the car and took the clothes and food bags out of the car and placed them on the front porch and rang the bell. I went back to the car, beeped the horn some more and then unfastened Anthony's car seat. I grabbed Anthony and his car seat and marched back to the front porch. I lay on that damn doorbell.

Briggen finally came to the door. "What the fuck is wrong with you?"

"You want to play house with this bitch? Here's a baby to make it real." I shoved the car seat with Anthony still strapped to it into his arms, turned and walked off the porch.

CHAPTER TWELVE

DARK

Cisco and I had just come from Oak Ridge, Tennessee. I saw why he wanted me to move and set up shop down there. I had to admit, the town was wide open. After a week and with the help of his two young cousins Dana and Wes, our shit was on swole. But I didn't give a fuck how much money was to be made. I wasn't moving way across the country to some dammed Oak Ridge, Tennessee.

"Yo, Dark, I know you ready to rock Oak Ridge to sleep, ain't you?" Cisco asked me. He was all hyped up.

"Naw, man. It's aiight, but I think you should have Rob or Mac run that shop. Them two niggas together will set it off. For real, it's too slow for me. I need to be around the action. And the 'D' got the action. We right in the middle of it. I'll be too restless down there."

"What? Nigga, you trippin'. I thought you was all about your paper." He gave me a dirty look. "Man, y'all muthafuckas kill me. Always talking about y'all ready to eat. Here I am serving you a plate where you can eat, all you can possibly eat, and you talking about you ain't hungry."

"Nigga, go 'head with that," I told him.

"What you want to do? Stay up here under me like you my bitch or something?" He paused and stared at me. "Aiight, then. Case closed."

"Your bitch? Fuck you!" I replied. I was now ready to body this nigga. It took everything in me not to shoot this faggot.

"Like I said, case closed, nigga. It's your loss. Hey, Rob, pull over. Let me holla at these hoes."

At that point, I wanted to crack the nigga's jaw. I was breathing fire as Rob pulled over, and Cisco rolled down his window. There were two chicks standing in front of the barbershop talking. When I looked closer I could see why Cisco said pull over. These chicks were all body, and one in particular kept my gaze, and when I realized that it was Lisha, I forgot all about crushing Cisco's jaw who was in Mac mode. He jumped out of the car, and I was right on his heels.

"Ladies, how y'all doin'?" he asked.

"What's up?" the one with the short blonde haircut answered. Lisha didn't say anything. She just looked at me and smiled. I pulled her to the side.

"Can I talk to you for a minute?" I asked her. "You owe me an explanation."

She twisted her face all up. "I don't owe you anything, Dark. You've been gone for seven years. What the hell I look like explaining something to you?"

"You said I was his father. I didn't know that. And you sure didn't tell me. How come you never said anything? Explain that."

She sucked her teeth and rolled her eyes. "Dark, you probably got mad kids running around here and ain't claiming any of them, and you don't have to claim this one. My son is fine. He has a daddy. I don't need you to start messing things up."

"Messing things up? Oh, so you want to ride my dick, but you don't want me to be a father to my son?" I wanted to punch this bitch in the mouth.

"Good-bye, Dark."

She turned and walked into the barbershop. I started to go after her, but then I thought about my son and froze. Was he in there? If he was, what would I say to him? Was the nigga playing daddy to my son in there?

I glanced over at Cisco, and he was engaged in conversation with the chick with the short blonde fade. She had tits and ass for days, a pretty dimpled smile and nice thick lips. I wondered if she and Lisha were bumping pussies, and if so, who was the man?

I turned my attention to the barbershop window and tried to see inside. It was crowded in there, and I didn't see Lisha. Upper Cuts stayed packed. I'm Seven Mile all day, but I would never get my cut on that hot ass strip.

"Dark, let's bounce," Cisco ordered, obviously trying to flex his muscle for the lady.

I was still looking in the window. When I spotted Lisha she was digging in her purse. A little man was standing next to her, trying to get her attention. He then held his head down, and it looked like he was playing a video game. Li'l Man was undoubtedly mines. Now that I was seeing him for the first time, I didn't know how to take it. I heard Maury's voice loud and clear: "When it comes to eight-year-old Damon, you are the father!"

"Nigga, I saw you drooling all over her!" Cisco shouted, fucking up my concentration. "They both was fine, wasn't they? But check this out. Tomorrow night, they having an all-white party out at P's. We rollin' up in there. I told ol' girl I would meet her there. And I'm thinking about throwing you a going away party."

I didn't know why this nigga couldn't get it through his thick skull that I wasn't going nowhere. But fuck it. I could show him better than I could tell him. I turned my attention back to the window. I wanted to roll up in the shop, but she had a point. I had been gone for seven years, and didn't know her situation. So I decided to respect her wishes, for now. But we definitely had to have a sit-down.

THE FOLLOWING NIGHT AROUND eleven we headed for the club. I had on a simple white tee, white Brioni slacks, and white-on-white Gucci tennis shoes. Cisco was rockin' a white-on-white Armani suit, white gators, with ice on his wrists, fingers and around his neck, draped like lights on a Christmas tree. To put the icing on the cake, we were gliding in a white-on-white stretch Mercedes limo. Cisco called the chick who he met in front of the barbershop whose name was Princess and told her to be outside. I was hoping that Lisha would be with her.

When we pulled up, I got excited when I spotted her and Lisha. There were so many honeys out and about, that if Princess wouldn't have had that short blonde fade they would have been lost in the crowd. Niggas and bitches were everywhere. I knew they were wondering who was up in here flossin' like this in the ride because everyone stopped what they were doing and all eyes were on the stretch Benz.

"Aiight, my niggas. It's showtime!" Cisco announced. It was me, him, Rob, Mac, Mook, Darnell and Dread chillin' in the limo.

The driver looked around, trying to find a park. "Yo, don't pull up in the parking space. Stop in the middle of the street and let us out," Cisco commanded.

The limo driver obeyed and did just that. Big Darnell and Dread got out first, since them niggas was supposed to be security. I was trying not to laugh. They had on dark glasses, black suits and earpieces. They were rubbing their burners as if they were nervous. The rest of us got out, and Cisco waited until last. By the time he stepped out of the cocaine white Benz, the crowd was right up on us.

I spotted Lisha and Princess in the crowd and waved them over.

Both were sexy as hell, wearing skimpy white dresses leaving very little to the imagination and strutting in stilettos that made my dick jump. Lisha looked me up and down, and her silence said it all. I knew I looked good enough to eat.

"You rollin' with me or what?" I put my arm out, Lisha grabbed it and Princess grabbed Cisco's. Then out of nowhere some more dimepieces came out of the woodwork on some groupie shit. Cisco let them roll too, and we ended up with an entourage of about fifteen deep. The VIP Section was already shut down, but Cisco dropped enough dough and they made us a VIP Section. Security roped off the section, and waitresses damn near half-naked quickly filled the area with bottles of expensive champagne and drinks. Our night had officially begun.

The females that had latched onto us outside were all competing for first place. I just sat back and scoped these bitches setting themselves up to end up getting drunk as hell and then tricked by the end of the night. I relaxed and watched the whole shit unfold as I rested my hand on Lisha's leg and threw back a glass of Bacardi Dark. After a few drinks, Lisha was loosening up. Back at the barbershop she had her nose turned up, but now she was whispering in my ear telling me about the bullshit plans she had for us.

Cisco immediately announced that he had the next round for everybody in the VIP Section. He was determined to floss harder than any other nigga up in there. And there were some niggas who could go hard. I saw Wiz Khalifa, Amber Rose, several Pistons players enjoying themselves, Dwele, and of course, the haters who were always on deck, mean muggin' Cisco. I had to pull Rob and Mook to the side and point out some niggas that they needed to keep an eye on.

Once Lisha got drunk, her lips got loose and she began telling me all about my son who I knew nothing about, Damon Mills Rashawn. He played football, had dry skin and may need braces. He loved hot dogs and potato salad, just like me. He called her last boyfriend and his fake daddy, Christopher. She told me that the nigga had been in his life since he was three years old.

She then went on to tell me that she and the chick she was living with had been together for a little over a year, and after I left her days earlier they had a knock down drag out fight. I didn't like the idea of her and that bitch doing that dyke shit around my son. It had to stop.

"Dark, the dick was soooo good. I'd take an ass whipping over that dick anytime. I hadn't been dicked down in sooo long." She was hanging over me and rubbing all over my chest as she yelled over "Black and Yellow."

I couldn't give her all of my attention because I was watching Cisco make it rain on four chicks, including the one he had dancing on his lap. He was talking mad shit about how he runs this city and if anybody needed a job to come see him. Niggas was watching him and whispering. I told Lisha to get her little girlfriend and leave because we were getting ready to go.

"We just got here," she whined. "I didn't even get a chance to dance with my baby daddy." She laughed and continued to touch all over me. "You can't be ready to go." She was whispering in my ear and nibbling on my earlobe and then she slid her hand between my legs. Under any other circumstances I would have found me a spot to get my dick wet, but I felt some shit was about to jump off so I had to shut that shit down.

I moved Lisha's hand and stood up. "I'll catch up with you later, Lisha. Yo, Cisco. Let's get out of here, man," I yelled as I got up on him.

"Dark, all this pussy up in here and you talkin' about let's go? Fuck wrong with you, nigga?" Cisco was drunk as hell, stumbling and yelling and shit.

Rob must have been feeling me because he said, "Niggas in here saying that you ain't nobody and you all up in their spot flossin' and shit."

"Fuck they mean I ain't nobody? I'm the fucking King of the 'D'." Cisco stood there getting louder, bottle in one hand, glass in the other, and spilling shit on everybody.

"Let's get out of here before shit start gettin' crazy. You know the drunker these niggas get the froggier they gonna feel. I can't enjoy myself knowing that shit 'bout to go down. You see them niggas behind you?" I asked Cisco.

"Man, fuck them niggas! How I'm gonna be flossin' too much? This is my city!" He turned around, put his cup on the table, reached in his pocket and threw up a stack of dollars at the niggas behind him, makin' it rain on them broke muthafuckas.

"Come on, man. I need to talk to you outside." This nigga was drunk and acting stupid, and I figured that would at least get him moving. Everybody else was already up and waiting on Cisco.

He stood in the middle of the floor and the four niggas that were sitting behind him got up. Cisco announced, "My name is Cisco, and I run this city, muthafuckas! Drinks on me, niggas!"

Everybody started cheering except for me and the haters. I didn't see shit funny because I had watched them all night watch Cisco and none of them muthafuckas had cracked a smile. I paid for the drinks, and finally we were on our way out of there. As we made our way out of the club Cisco was shaking niggas' hands and kissing bitches on the cheek, as if he was running for president. Then I noticed the same niggas that were watching us all night had strategically spread out and were following us. My senses immediately shifted to high alert. As we reached the door, the one with the front tooth missing bumped into me.

"Fuck you doin'?" I asked the nigga.

"Nigga, fuck you. Y'all pussies been up in here trying to floss all night." He scowled.

"Trying?" I laughed. "That's why your pussy-ass is so mad, 'cause we was trying?"

"Y'all ain't shit!" he spat, spit flying.

"Nigga, fuck outta here with that bullshit," I spat back, causing the bouncer's attention to divert our way.

"Break that shit up and take it outside!" the big Tiny Zeus Lister-looking bouncer growled out as he put his arms between us. I continued to stare this nigga down, refusing to be the first to back down. Realizing he wasn't fucking with no slouch, he scrunched up his ugly-ass face and slowly backed up. I turned around and Cisco was standing behind me like I was his mother and the other bitches on his team had the look of fear pouring from their eye sockets.

"These niggas gonna be a problem. Let's get the fuck outta here," I said as I turned to walk out the door.

"Man, fuck them niggas! We out having a good time," Cisco said in his drunken slur as we headed for the stretch Benz.

I turned and looked at him as I thought to myself, *How this silly muthafucka get to be in charge?* I picked up my pace, anticipating the opportunity to rock my burner. Just as I turned back around, a gray Dodge Charger with tinted windows and 22-inch rims pulled up alongside us. The back window slowly rolled down and a pump shotgun emerged from the crack. Then two cats from the ride jumped out. One from the front-passenger side and one from the back-passenger's side. I gripped my piece tight, bracing myself for whatever. The other niggas on Cisco's team looked as if they were about to shit on themselves.

"So what the fuck is this?" Cisco asked, standing firm in his spot like his ass was bulletproof.

"Nigga, you know what this is. Y'all bitch-ass niggas in our world. Come up off y'all shit," Snaggletooth yelled out.

Cisco chuckled and barked, "Nigga, suck my dick!"

"You hear this nigga?" Snaggletooth turned and looked at his boy while pointing at Cisco.

The next thing I heard was the clicking of the shotgun. I gripped my gun tight at my side and before I could blink my eye, a shot hit Darnell in the leg. He doubled over in pain. The roar from the shot caused the partying crowd to start screaming and ducking, giving me the diversion I needed, so I pushed Cisco to the side, grabbed Darnell up and used him as a human shield so I could bust off some shots.

Snaggletooth jumped over the hood and took cover, as shots rang out from the backseat. Cisco was crouched down on the side of the car leaning on the door breathing heavy. The other niggas scattered like roaches. I fell back on the ground and let off until my shit was empty, hitting the cat in the backseat as his head fell up against the glass. I heard the car go into gear and then speed off. Cisco rolled over, then jumped up shooting causing the back window to shatter. They sped up and were gone.

I looked around to check the damage. Darnell was dead with a hole the size of a baseball in his chest, and the other niggas were emerging from behind parked cars as sirens blared in the background.

"Let's go, nigga," I yelled out as we all piled in our ride and pulled off.

As we assessed everyone we realized that Mook was also hit. He had a small hole in his side. The rest of them niggas were scared and trembling.

Cisco, on the other hand, wanted to say a prayer for Darnell. After that he wouldn't shut up. "See, that's the shit there

I'm talking about! Y'all niggas need to take a lesson. Y'all 'sposed to be the muscle, and y'all muthafuckas froze up," Cisco kept repeating. Nigga's faces were tight, and the smell of fear leaked from their pores.

"Y'all niggas is pussy," I stated with venom dripping from my vocals. I looked at my hand. My knuckles were bloody from falling to the ground. I looked out the window thinking to myself as the driver raced through the streets, *Time to get rid of this dead weight.*

CHAPTER THIRTEEN

MIA

That bitch Shan! I could just fuck her up. That was just plain trifling! How you gonna drop your baby off at midnight? I was pissed yes, because I wanted to have Briggen all to myself. On the flip side, it was crazy and cute seeing him in the daddy role with his son. I had never seen that side of him. He still hadn't shared with me what happened that caused him to pack a bag and come running to my house. When I hinted at it, he just nixed me off.

I was willing to bet that, just like with myself, Sharia and Tami, once he felt that he got all that he could get from you and he's a little bored, good ol' Briggen was quick to toss a bitch to the side.

He and the baby had been at my home for three days. His son was beginning to cramp my style. I wasn't used to having a baby roaming around on my white suede carpet. I had to cover it up with plastic runners real quick.

"Look at how you are acting. You don't even come off as the mommy type," Briggen had the nerve to say to me.

"He's not *my* child, Briggen. Don't you think that has a little something to do with it?"

He laughed, "That's a lame excuse. If you are supposed to be my woman and I come to the table with kids, you are supposed to be able to step into the mommy role."

It was my turn to laugh. "Your woman? You got jokes. I haven't been looked at by you as your woman for a long time. I never gave up thinking that there was a chance for us. And there will always be a place in my heart for you. Plus, you know I was trying to have your baby, but you made sure that never happened."

"I'm going to my man's funeral, and then I have to take care of something. Can I count on you to watch my son or not?" he asked me, not even acknowledging my feelings that I had just shared with him.

"Of course you can. I've had your back from day one, more than all of those other bitches you had in your corner, and you know that."

"Mia, I'm not talking about having my back more than other bitches. I just need a babysitter."

SHAN

I had the house for four days all to myself and I had enjoyed every minute of it. I missed Li'l Anthony and was surprised that his daddy didn't come bringing him back. I guessed from here on out it would be a battle of the wills.

I started my business plan, and my first event was a month

away. I had noticed that there were a lot of old heads who liked to get their party on. So, for my first event I was bringing in Frankie Beverly and Maze, Cameo and Charlie Wilson to add that flava. I had booked the venue and had hired a street team to pass out flyers at all the salons, barbershops, bars and local mom-and-pops. I even paid for some ads on the radio stations during prime time.

But then I had this brainstorm. It said, "Go for it!" Since Halloween was coming up I was going to do something for the young heads. I needed to get some rap artists to come through and perform. I was on the phone for days making calls, only to learn that people didn't want to deal with you if they didn't know you. But the good thing was that money is a universal language and I was speaking it fluently. Before I knew it, I had an all-star lineup. Shit, I was geeked, and I was feeling myself.

BRIGGEN

If it wasn't for the fact that I was enjoying the time taking care of my son, I would have already taken him back to Shan and put my foot in her ass.

And Mia? That bitch had been talking about how she'd been down with me for years, how much she loved me and how she was the only one that got my back, but the bitch was jealous of my son. What kind of shit is that?

I had my boys' company come and put up surveillance cameras in her crib. I left her to babysit because I needed to see how she was going to treat my son and couldn't wait to play the tape back. It didn't make sense to drag him out to a funeral. I wish I would have thought about surveillance cameras and had them installed in my own damn house. The first chance I get I'ma make that happen. But the business at hand was after Melky's funeral I had to sit down with his cousin Wise. Just like me, he had beef with Choppa's family and wanted to talk to me about it.

Me and Wise left the funeral together and went to this hole-in-the-wall bar and grill on Rosemont called Scotty's. We grabbed a seat at the bar, and Wise brought a bottle of Hennessey.

"Dude, you really tryna get fucked up, ain't you?" I teased him.

Wise poured both of us a shot and tossed his back. He then poured himself another one, leaving me out.

"That's fucked up, man. That beef was supposed to be squashed," Wise complained. "If them muthafuckas think for one minute that I'ma let that shit go, then they obviously don't know about me." He threw another shot back.

"I feel your pain, but to take a head you gotta be ready to give one. And them niggas you planning on going after, they ain't no lightweights." I had to remind the nigga what he was up against.

"So what are you saying, Brig?" Wise threw another one back. "Just let the shit go?"

"I'm just saying, be ready to die, that's all. Ain't no way in hell you gonna fuck with them niggas and stay alive," I reminded him.

"So what? Act like shit ain't happen? You already know I can't do that."

"Just don't throw caution to the wind on this one, man.

Not having a plan, my nigga, is a death wish in itself. You need to have a plan. Me personally? I'm sick of all this shit. I got a son, one on the way. You got how many kids? It's a suicide mission, and Melky was my man, but it ain't nothing I can do." I said what I had to say and got up to leave.

"It's like that?" he asked, still on the defense.

"Nigga, I ain't got nothing to do with it."

"Aiight, then, cool." He held out his fist and I bumped it. "Just stay out of the way," he warned.

I left and headed to my house.

JANAY

Marquis and I were driving around the city. I was going down Northwestern one day and stumbled on this restaurant called Beans and Cornbread. They served a Louisiana gumbo that was to die for. We were just here two days earlier, and now we were back. Nick was meeting us for lunch. I was hesitant about bringing Marquis, but he kept begging to hang out with his mommy.

"What's up, boss lady?" Nick snuck up behind us and kissed my cheek. He grabbed the seat across from me. "I didn't know you were bringing a guest." He held out his hand for Marquis to shake. "I'm Nick."

Marquis extended his hand. "I'm Marquis. Nice to meet you," he stated proudly.

"Likewise." Nick turned to me. "I'm not going to order anything because I have another engagement. I was hoping that Boomer would be here. Should I wait? I really wanted to speak with him."

"Look, Nick, get over it. You are looking at the decision maker. Just say what you got to say," I told this chauvinistic nigga.

"Alright then. Because of who you represent I will. I'm musclin' Mr. G out. I am monopolizing the game. I wanted Boomer to be the first to know out of respect. All prices are going up twenty percent. But for your family, ten percent. Everybody else, twenty percent. Even with the increase I'm still damn near twenty-five percent lower than Mr. G. If you don't have any questions I'm going to excuse myself. Oh, and Melky's people said for you to watch your back."

I sat there watching this nigga leave. What does he mean by, "monopolize the game"? He's not holding like that. And muscle? I know he can't go up against a triple International OG like Mr. G! I mean, he got work, but shit, so does half the city. What is he talking about?

SHARIA

I couldn't believe my luck. This was un-fuckin'-believable. I kept putting it off, but Dark wouldn't let up. I could kiss him right smack in the mouth for that! He was determined to find the owner of the license plate that I had tossed into my garage. And bingo! Who did it belong to? The ol' bitch! Briggen's baby mama. I was ecstatic. That bitch was finally getting ready to go down, and I wanted a front row seat so I could watch it happen.

JANAY

I couldn't wait to get back so I could fill Boomer in on Nick's announcement. Boomer would have gone to breakfast with me, but he wasn't feeling well. I was beginning to worry about his health. When Marquis and I walked into the living room, Boomer was in his easy chair knocked out.

"Go play, Marquis. I need to talk to uncle Boomer."

"Mom, can I go next door to Shawn's?"

"No. Stay on the porch."

"Let that boy go next door, Nay. Why he gotta stay on the porch?" Boomer said, not opening his eyes.

"I thought you were asleep?"

"Just because my eyes closed don't mean I was asleep. Go on next door, Marquis."

"Y'all got that boy spoiled."

My son took off running. I sat down on the sofa. "You ready to hear this?"

"What?"

"I saw Nick this morning, and he said that Mr. G is out. He said that he was going to monopolize the game and that we all should be buying from him. All prices are up twenty percent, but for our family, ten percent. And he said that's outta respect. But at the same time he bragged that he was still coming in twenty-five percent lower than Mr. G." I sat back and waited to hear what my uncle had to say. He closed his eyes and didn't say a word. After several minutes, I got up to go get something to drink. I came back with a glass of sweet tea.

"You want something to drink?" I broke the silence.

"Your father always called him the 'spook who sat by the door,' and he called it right. He works quietly and strategically. I told you that boy was a damn genius."

"Genius or not, Mr. G's shit is five times better. Nick's is five times cheaper. If he muscles G out, how long will his prices be so low? What happened to Mr. G? Why didn't he call a meeting to let everyone know that he was out and Nick was replacing him?"

"Because that's probably not what happened."

"What do you mean that's probably not what happened? He can't just muscle Mr. G out. And what? Are we going to sit back and let him do it? What is everyone in The Consortium going to think?"

"Baby girl, that's up to you. If you would have been in this business as long as I have, you would have seen and heard of a lot of things. And you would know that anything is possible. But you are in charge of this family now. If a nigga is hungry enough, he can move mountains. If my hunch is right, this youngin just cornered the market."

"Greasy muthafucka," I laughed. "I can't be too mad at him because I would do the same damn thing if I could have. But I will tell you this, if he gets too greedy, some changes are going to have to be made."

"Calm down Nay. Don't think with your emotions. Mr. G most likely will be asking for a sit down. Once you hear what he's got to say, then you move from there."

"I hear you, Boom, but damn. This Nick character is rubbing me the wrong way. And before I forget, he told me that Melky's camp said for me to watch my back."

Boomer let out a sigh. "That's how this game is played. I really don't want to go to war right now, but we will do what we gotta do to protect our family. But we got a man over at his camp. If and when they make a move, we will be ready."

CHAPTER FOURTEEN

DARK

Shit was starting to unravel at a very fast pace. I had heard that the police had been questioning witnesses about the two niggas I dropped at the club. They were a couple of nobodies, so I knew that shit wasn't going anywhere. I actually did the city and its good citizens a favor. At the same time, by eliminating those crumbs, I had earned more respect from Cisco. And now he was sending them two scary security guards to Oak Ridge along with Rob and Mac. Cisco was still telling everybody how they froze up the minute it was time to do battle.

We were all sitting in Cisco's smoke shop, and once again, I was the man of the hour. I had the info on the license plate of the dude that snatched up Cisco's dope and money. Cisco's goons were piled in two cars and on their way over to this idiot's house when somebody told Cisco it was a chick . . . Briggen's chick.

"I don't give a fuck whose chick it is!" Cisco ranted. "Go and bring back my money and my dope right now or there's gonna be more than just one dead body lying around! And I mean, right now!"

"Hold up, boss man. Let me talk to you in private." I pulled him to the side. He was still crying about this loss and I was tired of hearing about it. Taking an "L" every now and then was a part of the game. But now that he knew who had got him, he was amped, when at first he had placed a lot of the blame on Dreamer, who wasn't even there.

"What? Can't you see that I'm in the middle of rallying the troops? We need to make a move now. Waiting around is only going to show weakness."

"I think you are going about this the wrong way. Let me handle it, boss man."

"The wrong way? Nigga, what the fuck you on telling me how I'm handling my business?"

"I'm just saying, think about what you doing for a minute. You getting ready to send two carloads full of niggas, in broad daylight, after a woman. Not only that, we gotta think about who we are dealing with. From what you told me about Briggen and from what I've learned, dude ain't no lightweight. We gotta be ready for him. And you know them niggas you sendin' are gonna fuck shit up. So let me handle dude. Ain't no rush. You know your money is spent. The dope is sold. If we do this right, we will come off with more than just some payback."

Cisco scratched his head, looked at me and started pacing back and forth. He looked at me again and started to speak, but I stopped him.

"I got you boss man. Let me handle this," I assured him.

He walked away from me and went outside. I assumed that was a yes.

SHARIA

"Dark, what the hell is going on? Why is that nappy-headed ho still breathing? I'm sick of seeing the bitch! I see the bitch in my dreams I'm so sick." And I meant that shit. She took my man and was flaunting her bastard child around as well as a big belly. I hated both of them. Just like I was going to take Briggen down, and since she was with him, I was taking her down too.

"Seeing her? What, you stalking her? That jealousy is eating your ass up," his simple ass had the nerve to say to me.

"Hell no, I ain't stalking her. Her face is plastered on all of these damn posters all over the city. Tell me you ain't see 'em." I unfolded a poster and showed it to him. "Instead of the bitch hiding or being dead, she around here playing fuckin' Don King! Promoter of the Year and shit. The bitch got a new car, she rockin' muthafuckin' Red Bottoms, the heifer dripping with ice, and I heard that when she go out she be giving her waiters $500 tips . . . This is some bullshit!"

"Damn, girl! How you know all of this?" Dark started laughing as if the shit was funny. I was dead serious. "My cousin is jealous!" he teased as he squeezed my cheek.

"I ain't jealous. It's just that I played my part in our agreement. When are you going to play yours? You had the bitch's info for over a week now. I know Cisco ain't going for this bullshit!" I spat, hoping to get him to pay my rage a little more attention.

"Sharia, chill the fuck out. She'll get handled when the time is right. If you ain't willing to put the work in yourself, then I suggest you sit the fuck down and shut the fuck up. I got this."

"I can't tell." At that moment I knew what I was going to do. I was going to see Cisco. I grabbed my purse and keys. "Fuck you, Dark! You black bitch!"

"Fuck you, too! Jealous bitch!"

DARK

My cousin is a nut. When she told me who that mystery license plate belonged to, I was skeptical because she hated Briggen and was mad jealous of his bottom bitch. Now she wants me to stop what I'm doing, run over there and take the girl out. Just like that. She had me fucked up and was talking shit while she was all up in my house, when I told her not to be coming over here. Cisco still didn't know that we were cousins, and I didn't want him to find out.

I was on my way to pick him up. The only thing he told me was he wanted me to make a run with him. I was on my way to meet Lisha when I got his text. I was wondering why she still hadn't introduced me to my son yet. That was the first thing we were going to discuss when I saw her.

When I pulled up in front of the smoke shop, Cisco obviously was looking out the window because the nigga came right out.

"Damn. You miss me?" I teased him.

"Nigga, I'm hungry. Let's go to the Subway or some shit like that," he said as he jumped into the car.

No, this nigga didn't get me way over here on an urgent text to take him to get something to eat! What the fuck is wrong with him? "Nigga, I'm on my way to get some pussy and you talking about going to Subway? Get somebody else to take you."

"Man, you know them niggas is rowdy around the way. I need to get in and handle my shit and get out. Who else I'm gonna take that's gonna have my back? Plus, I got something to show you."

"What you gotta show me?"

"Let's go pick up the sandwiches first." He sat back and got comfortable in my front seat. I could only shake my head and pull off.

I took him over to the Subway on Piedmont. The spot was clean, and he fucked with this chick named Jamilla who worked there. Every player I knew had that one hood bitch that they would smash whenever they got the chance.

I parked across the street, and we got out. I saw Cisco looking around to see if he saw her car. She drove a small, grey Toyota. It was parked on the corner across the street. She must have had the bomb-ass pussy because Cisco couldn't leave her alone, and plus, he gave her small packages to get rid of just so she could have some extra money.

This particular Subway stayed packed. It wasn't run by the Indians or Arabs. Nah, niggas owned this spot. Mr. Charles, who used to run a gambling spot back in the day ran it with his two sons. Bottom line, the nigga took pride in his restaurant.

When we walked in, Jamilla was propped up on a stool behind the register as if she was the queen bitch sitting on her throne. We gave a few niggas fist bumps and got in line. Jamilla didn't see us at first because she was barking orders at the Mexican lady working the sandwich bar to put more meat on the sandwich that she was making. The Mexican lady mumbled something in Spanish, and Jamilla mumbled something right back. And then she said in English, "You ain't the only one who knows that shit," and she rolled her eyes.

Cisco and I moved up to the counter and she rolled her eyes at Cisco. "Hey, Dark, what's up with you?"

"Shit. What's happening with you, Lady Jamilla?" She liked it when I called her that. "How are you? Long time no see."

"Tell me about it."

"Oh, so Dark is the only nigga you see up in here? You better get your fine ass down off that stool and come make Big Daddy a sandwich. You know I don't have these other hoes working up in here making my shit," Cisco announced.

She rolled her eyes, but got her ass down off her perch. She went and washed her hands, put on some gloves and came over to make our sandwiches. "Quita, come sit at the register for me," she called out. "What kind of sandwich do you want, Dark?"

"Oh, it's like that?" Cisco teased her. They did this same shit every time we came there. The nigga only came by once or twice a month. You would think that she would be used to it.

I said, "Fix me a meatball sub on a white roll."

"That's it?"

"That's it."

She got busy making my sandwich. "Dark, I ain't know you was my girl Stephanie's baby daddy. Let me call her. I told her you stop by here every once in a blue moon. I'ma call her as soon as I make your sandwich."

"Jamilla, don't play me like that. I ain't her damn baby daddy. She wish. I don't fuck with her like that. You can call her but wait until I leave this bitch."

"Y'all niggas ain't right. Be all in a bitch's shit and riding bareback, then when we say baby, y'all onto the next one." She twisted her lips and shook her head in disgust.

"Bitches ain't right either. Y'all be giving the pussy up wholesale, and then when the nigga don't want no more, y'all try to throw salt in the game. Going around talking about I'm her baby daddy. She on some bullshit."

"Dark, the boy look just like you."

"I don't give a fuck who he look like. He ain't my kid. Sheeit. You look like me, too. Am I yo daddy?"

Cisco thought my comment was funny.

"Hell no, you ain't my damn daddy!"

"Well then. Just give me my damn sandwich." She took my sandwich out of the microwave, wrapped it up and gave it to Quita who was now perched up on the stool and grinning at me as if I was fresh meat. It was obvious that Jamilla told her all about me and Cisco, because Quita was ready to be down with whatever. I turned my attention to her as Cisco placed his order and flirted with Jamilla.

"Would you like something to drink with this?"

"Yeah, give me a Sprite and three chocolate chip cookies. I gotta sweet tooth." She got off the stool and went to get my drink. I looked her up and down. She had on her little Subway outfit, improvised with a short-ass miniskirt. She had some thick legs and a phat ass that was trying to bust out of the skirt. She looked to be no more than eighteen. "Your name Quita?" I read off her little name tag scoping those C cups.

"My friends call me Q."

"How old are you?"

"I'm old enough. And that will be nine forty-seven."

I passed her a twenty. "Keep the change."

"Thank you." She got her change and stuck it in her pocket.

"Thank you, Q," Jamilla interrupted, walking over to the register with Cisco's sandwich in her hand. She was ready to get her throne back.

"Naw, Quita, stay right there. I need to talk to Jamilla. Jamilla, let's go outside," Cisco commanded.

Quita smirked because she knew what was up.

"Can you take your break, too?" I asked Q. I was trying to figure out how I could get in between those thick thighs.

"Maybe," she said in a sexy tone.

"You old enough, right?"

"That's what I said."

"Jamilla, can Lucy hold it down for a few minutes while I take my break?"

"Lucy!" Cisco yelled out as if he was their supervisor. "We need you to watch the register," he told her before Jamilla could say anything. "Come on, Jamilla. I need to talk to you. I'll be waiting for you out front."

As soon as we stepped outside, Cisco said, "Yo, Dark, let me use your ride for a minute."

"Hell no, nigga. I'm on my way to pick up Lisha. My shit can't be smelling like pussy and cum."

"I'm only going to get her to suck my dick."

"Then use *her* car."

"Nigga, you trippin'. It ain't like you driving a Maybach or some shit," Cisco snapped as he grabbed Jamilla by her hand and headed toward her car.

"So what's up?" Q asked me as she exited the store coming my way. She stood with her arms folded across her chest looking like she was down for breakin' a nigga off. "You ready to spend some dough?"

My phone vibrated. I looked down and saw it was Lisha. "Hold up. Let me get this." I turned my back to Q.

"Dark, where are you?"

"I'm taking care of something with my dude right now. Give me a couple of hours. I'll be there."

"A couple of hours? Tiffany will be back by then. See how you done messed shit up. Bad as I wanted some dick," she snapped.

"Well, if you wanted it that bad, you would tell that bitch to kick rocks. Fuck that bitch! I can't be on her fuckin' schedule." I was losing patience. And it didn't help that the quickie we had the last time I saw her had a nigga wanting to run back and put in some real work. Just like she wanted the dick, I wanted the pussy but I wasn't gonna sweat her. "You want me to come or not?" I turned and looked at Q. I was ready to talk shit, because I had some pussy standing at arm's length.

Lisha started spazzing out and then she finally said, "Fuck you, Dark!" and hung up. I laughed and threw my shit on vibrate.

I turned my attention back to Q. "So what's up?"

"What you driving?" Q asked.

I pointed to the pimped out Porsche Panamera Turbo S with the tinted windows across the street. This was the ride that Sharia put me up on.

"Is that good enough for you?"

"It is if you spending."

Oh, so shorty was a ho.

"If you got it like that then why you working at Subway?"

"That's for me to know and for you to find out," she snapped.

"Sheeit . . . Show me."

She came down off the steps and started walking to my car. I followed. She knew what she was doing, switching that big ass, causing me to rub my dick before I even got to my ride. I hit the locks, and she got in the backseat and I followed.

"You got a condom?" She wasted no time.

"Yeah, I got one."

"Good." She leaned over and unzipped my jeans. Wasn't nothing shy about Q. She blew hot air on my dick, and then it disappeared into her mouth. In a matter of seconds, my dick was harder than Chinese arithmetic. She took it out of her mouth.

"Why the fuck did you do that?" I panted.

"Put the condom on."

I guess I was moving too slow for her. She pulled one out of her pocket, tore it open and rolled it on me. She turned around straddled my legs like a pro and put her back into my chest.

"I like it up the ass," she purred.

"What?"

She had my dick trying to put it in her asshole. "I like it up the ass. Come on. I gotta get back to work."

"Naw, Shorty. I don't get down like that."

"How you gonna knock something you ain't tried before?"

"I don't get down like that!" I grabbed my dick and put it at her pussy.

This slick bitch let the head go in, pops up and I'm back at her asshole.

"Come on, nigga, it's hot and wet, just like the pussy," she said as she slid down on my dick. I was stunned. Q was right. The ass was tight and it was wet just like a pussy. I had never felt anything like it. She was bouncing up and down squealing.

I was still in shock. "It's so wet," I grunted in disbelief as I grabbed her waist and began to fuck her in the ass.

"I told you," she screeched as her ass cheeks smashed against my thighs.

"Q! Q!" Somebody had the balls to be banging on my tinted windows. And it wasn't Cisco.

She stopped her bouncing and froze. "Oh shit! That's Baby Boy," she whispered, jumping off my dick and pulling her panties up.

"Who the fuck is Baby Boy?" I was getting agitated, wanting her to jump back on my dick.

"My boyfriend. Well, my ex. Fix yourself up and give me the money. I'ma tell him you my cousin. His dumb ass will go for it."

"What?" I was fixing my jeans and ready to jump out and crack this nigga's dome. That ass was feeling good and I hadn't even busted my nut. And because of that, I wasn't paying her shit.

Q was already unlocking the door and getting out.

"Q, what the fuck you doing in this car? Why you ain't in there working?"

"I was talking to my cousin, Dark."

"Your cousin? Bitch who the fuck you think you bullshit-tin'? The way the car was jumping up and down, somebody was fuckin' not talking." And this little nigga went to kick-ing my freshly detailed ride. "Get the fuck out, whoever you are!"

"Baby Boy, calm down. You don't know this nigga. Stop making a scene. This ain't even necessary. Plus, I have to get back to work," Q told him.

But instead of the nigga listening to his girl, he started kicking my car again. I grabbed my burner, cocked it and got out.

"Kick my car again, little nigga," I dared him.

"*Little* nigga? You ain't the only one packin'." Li'l dude's voice wasn't even deep yet.

Dude was tall, but he was skinny as a rail with a mouth full of platinum. He had to be about eighteen. I guess Q was even younger than that.

"Come on, Baby Boy. I told you he's my cousin." She pulled on his arm in an attempt to dead the situation.

Cisco and Jamilla were now rushing over to where we were. When I looked at them Baby Boy rushed me and knocked me up against my car. I hauled off and hit him in the head with my burner. I hit him so hard he fell backwards and onto the ground. But that didn't stop the fool from getting up and pulling his burner out. He gritted, "You fucked up now, nigga. I was gonna let you walk away." But he hesitated, and that was the wrong thing to do. I began pistol-whipping him like that dude in *Goodfellas*. Blood was starting to fly everywhere. Cisco finally pulled me off him. I had to do it.

I couldn't help it. I shot him. Everybody started scattering and yelling.

"Didn't I tell you these Westside niggas get rowdy?" Cisco reminded me.

Cisco and I jumped into my ride and pulled off.

CHAPTER FIFTEEN

SHAN

I couldn't figure out where to hide my money, but I definitely wasn't putting my cash in nobody's bank. I remember overhearing Briggen talking about this dude named Silk, the God of Trap Cars. Why he had to be called the God, I didn't know. It sounded corny to me. Why couldn't he simply be the Trap Car Specialist? I did my research and with some serious digging I found his shop. At first he acted as if he didn't know what I was talking about until I told him who my man was. He then immediately changed his tune, but he still wouldn't deal with me. He suggested that I get a safe. I didn't want what was the obvious, a safe. I wanted my riches at my disposal and with me at all times. So what better place for it than my car? I told the Trap God, "Fine. You ain't the only shop in this town."

In my digging for that punk Silk, I came across this other shop. What I liked most about the owner was that she didn't ask questions. All she wanted to know was, how many traps did I need added to the car and what size? She was my kind of girl. I paid her, and she went to work. No questions asked. Three days later I went back and she gave me a lesson on how to open and close them all. I was amped as I left in my trapped up Mercedes GL450 and headed back home. I couldn't wait to stash my shit. When I got home I was going to fill my new bitch up . . . with dough.

I kept looking at my phone. Briggen had been blowing it up, but I didn't care. The only thing on my mind was getting my shit stashed. And I must say . . . I was feeling myself. I had two shows coming up and a pocket full of dough.

When I arrived at the house I immediately caught an attitude. Briggen's truck was parked out front. And somehow, I knew that this wasn't a social visit, and I was willing to bet that he didn't have my son. It was strange because I didn't even miss my man. I went into the house and found him sitting in the den, smoking a blunt and watching TV.

"Why didn't you bring Anthony with you?" I asked him.

"Because I was already out."

"Then who's watching him?"

"Mia has him. Have a seat." He motioned for the chair in front of him. I sat down. I knew that he wouldn't leave our son with her if he didn't trust her. He looked me over as if I was his child and I was about to be in trouble.

"She may have love for you but don't get it twisted. She has no love for our son, Briggen."

"Never mind that right now. So what's up with you?" he asked.

"I'm doing me. That's all."

"I see. So, is that where all of this money coming from? You doing you?"

"What money?" I tried to act aloof.

"The money it takes to *do you*. Throwing shows and parties ain't cheap. You got the venue, you've got insurance, you've got the entertainment, you've got your street team. Not only are you promoting shows, you bought a car. I see the dining-room set. You got shit upstairs that you haven't even popped the tags off of and you—" He held up his hand counting shit off on his fingers. I quickly cut him off.

"I know what I've got, Briggen."

"So? Where is this money coming from?"

"Between what I won in Vegas and what I borrowed from the bank that's what I've been using."

This nigga had the nerve to start grinning. "C'mon, Shan. You gonna sit here and actually lie to my face? What bank gave you a loan to put on a concert? The banks are holding on to their cash. So tell me what bank loaned you some money to throw a party?"

"First of all, Briggen. This is my business. Have I asked you for anything? No, so let me do me, okay?" I started to get up. "You know what? You got some nerve. You running around here pushing dope and fucking your star players and now you questioning me? Fuck you! I don't owe you any explanation. Go ask your bitch how she making her money," I smirked. "Oh, that's right, she makes her money by fucking you."

"I think you need your damn head examined."

"Yeah, you right, I do. I need it examined for fucking with you."

He stared at me, and then said, "You know what? You

keep this shit up if you want to. I'ma fix ya helmet for you my damn self."

"Briggen, leave me alone."

"You really think your ass is ready for the big leagues? You bringing all of this attention to yourself, and believe me, that shit is a double-edged sword. I hope you can handle it when shit hits the fan. And trust me, it is going to hit."

"What shit? It's my money. I can spend it however I want to."

"And what about this new behavior? I think this pregnancy is fucking with your head," he had the nerve to tell me.

"What?" I spat.

He stood up. "You heard me. I think you need to go see a doctor. You need to have yourself examined. You are not the same person I hooked up with and married."

Now it was my turn to grin. "But you are the same person?"

"The man you got with hasn't changed. No. I haven't started lying to you, hiding shit from you. Bringing bitches up in the house when you're not home."

"You're right. You haven't just started lying to me. Your ass has been lying to me all along. The only difference is when I got with you, you said you didn't hustle anymore. You told me your hands were clean and that they were going to stay clean, and I really believed that shit. But just recently you caught a case. Your ass been lying from day one. Now what else is up? I have a company to run."

"Come take a ride with me."

"A ride where? I got shit to do, Briggen." I just wanted his ass gone. Out of my sight, out of my house.

"To the doctor's office. Because you have officially lost your goddamn mind."

"A doctor?" Was this nigga fuckin' serious?

"You going through something, and you not telling me what and I don't know what it is, so I don't know how to fix it. I'm hoping that you will talk to a doctor. I'm worried about you, Shan."

"Of course I'm going through something. Here it is: For starters, I'm married to you! I got the FBI and shit running up in my house, I have a small child, I'm pregnant and my husband is not who I thought he was; therefore, I've been living a lie. Hell yeah, there's something wrong with me, but that something is you. So go! Get *your* ass checked out." I paused and looked at him. All I wanted to do was count and stash my newfound wealth.

He had two phones on him and both started ringing. He glanced at one but didn't answer. Both of them kept ringing and he answered one, which allowed me to dash up the stairs. I needed to make it to my bedroom and lock the door.

BRIGGEN

"Yeah, what's up?" I answered the phone.

"I need to put you up on something. Where are you? Can we hook up?"

I looked at my watch, looked around the house for Shan and went into the kitchen.

"Meet me at the bar on Passaic."

"Aiight. In twenty."

Lucky for Shan business was calling. Because I sure as hell was going to take her to see a shrink. Shan was hiding somewhere in the house. I was convinced that she was losing her mind. I had seen the same behavior patterns in my aunt Jill.

It seemed the first thing them crazy bitches did was cut their hair off. Then my aunt started taking baths in Evian water. She was buying all of these little-ass bottles and filling up the tub. Then she started wearing a whole bunch of makeup, painting her lips bright red. The next thing I knew, the police were throwing her ass in the back of the paddy wagon and she was stripping in front of them. They hauled her straight to the mental hospital. She let some no-good punk-ass man of hers drive her crazy. I was beginning to believe that for Shan, being pregnant again and missing her brother, was fucking with her mind. I didn't know. But nothing else made sense. She was an entirely different person.

I went upstairs and stood by the bedroom door. "Shan, I got to go, but I'm going to make you an appointment," I told her.

"Go to hell, Briggen! Take that bitch Mia to the doctor with you and leave me the fuck alone!" she yelled.

"I'll be back."

"I won't be here," she screamed.

I left.

WHEN I PULLED UP in front of Nipsey's, Nick was still sitting in his ride. I parked in back of him, and he got out and jumped into my truck.

"What's up?" I asked him.

"You got a problem," he told me.

"What kind of problem and with who?"

"Cisco. He got jacked for his last package. It was a nice one. But guess who got him?"

"Who?" I really didn't give a fuck and was wondering why he was telling me this shit.

"Word on the street is they found a license plate, ran it and it led them back to your house and Shan."

"Who?" I had to make sure I was hearing him right.

"Shan."

"Get the fuck outta here! Shan?" I was confused. I could see Mia or Sharia doing some shit like that but not Shan.

"Yeah, man. It leads back to her. And the streets are watching her too." Nick hopped out of the car and closed the door. He then tapped on the glass to say something else so I rolled the window down. "Oh! The other thing is that I'm tryna put this shit on lock. All prices are up twenty percent. I gotta run. I'm late. But I figured you needed to hear everything I just told you."

And just like that the nigga was gone. I sat there playing over what he had said.

For one thing, he did give me the missing piece that I was looking for. Still I wasn't one hundred up on why he was at my crib on two separate occasions. But I was now one hundred up on where Shan was getting this money from. But how did she get Cisco's package? That shit there had me foggy. And Nick talking about moving old man G out? What the fuck? Twenty percent? Where they do that at?

JANAY

It was a month too soon, but a meeting was called with all of the family heads. Shit was happening. Mr. G, the main connect, had beef because none of us were buying from him. Cisco's crew was dropping bodies as if that shit was legal. Briggen had caught a case and supposedly had robbed Cisco of a shipment, and now there were rumors of war between them.

Boomer and Born sat at the head of the table. We were in a conference room inside of Six-Nine's daddy's church, Antioch. Mr. G had everyone's attention. This was my first time seeing him in person. He had that rich olive complexion, like the majority of Italians do. His hair was dark brown and had a few grey streaks throughout it. It was slicked back. The one ring on his finger sparkled like a crystal chandelier. He wore an all black suit and a black silk tie with a red handkerchief in the right breast pocket. When he stood up, his two bodyguards stepped back.

"I am humbled by your presence but surprised by the shift and lack of respect for our business arrangements. We have made lots of money together, each and every one of you in this room. Some of you are old clients and a couple are new. I've always treated you fair. I've treated you all with respect. My fairly new clients, I didn't expect you to be one-hundred percent loyal, most of you are young and not familiar with protocol, so I figured that you would jump at the offer of a lower price even if the product was grade A bullshit! This I expected . . . but it hurt my heart to find out that my old clients, the same ones that I've helped establish from the beginning, have turned their backs on me.

"Mr. Six-Nine, remember when your whole shipment was stolen? And you traveled all the way to my home pleading for a replacement? I didn't go to war with you. I worked with you. Mr. Boomer, I've done business with you and Mr. Choppa for many, many years. I'm sure if my old friend Choppa was here he would not handle business this way, and I'm surprised that you would go for this. My product has always been of the highest quality. The best. It comes with my personal guarantee as well as with my protection.

"All of a sudden, each and every one of you has stopped patronizing me for some dumb street punk who couldn't tell pure cocaine from a pail of baking soda. It is total disrespect. I traveled all of this way just to tell you this personally."

Born spoke for every one there. "Mr. G., with all due respect, The Consortium has not banned against you. It's just an issue of supply and demand, profit and loss, and of course, staying competitive with the competition. It was never agreed or written in stone that we buy from you forever, regardless of the price or the quality. That was never the original agreement."

Mr. G then said some words in Italian to his bodyguards. One led the way, Mr. G. followed and the other one took up the rear. And they left.

After he disappeared, Born said, "I think that went well. But we will have to keep our eyes and ears open."

"No, that didn't go well. What he said in Italian was, 'After all of these years, they still don't know who I am.' You better believe that we have not heard the last of Mr. G," Boomer told us.

"I know it's not. But can we keep this meeting moving?" Briggen asked. Immediately he turned his attention to Cisco. Boomer gave him the floor.

"As far as me robbin' your shipment, that shit was impossible. Everyone knows that I was in jail. My mule got popped, gave my name up and I couldn't make bail because of some old shit I had in Miami from back in '03," Briggen explained to Cisco.

"Well, the license plate at the scene led to where you lay your head," Cisco countered.

"That don't mean shit! You can find a license plate in the street at any time. Like I said, I was locked up. And my wife is pregnant and got a baby on her hip, so if she could jack your boys . . . then they some pussy muthafuckas and they needed to be got."

Everyone started laughing which only made Cisco madder. He and his henchman Dark sat there mean muggin' everybody, neither of them cracking a smile.

"I want my shit, man. I'm showing you respect by bringing it out right here, right now, to the table," Cisco said as he pounded the table. "No talkin' shit or making threats behind your back. I'm talkin' right here, right now."

"Shit, you ain't saying nothing. That's how a real G 'sposed to do it. But like I just explained to you, I don't have your shit. Now if you had some proof, that would be another story."

"The proof is the license plate!" Cisco stood up. I could tell that in his little mind he was convinced that Briggen had his package.

"Alright! Alright!" I cut in. "The man said he was in jail. We all know that he was in jail. Without a witness, who is to say who has your package? In this business, you win some and you lose some. So until you get more evidence, I make a motion that there is no issue."

Born interrupted me, "Is everyone in agreement with that?"

Everybody said yes.

"What's pressing is Mr. G and all the bodies being dropped around here as if we in Iraq somewhere," Boomer said. "Cisco, you need to tone it down. Is there a problem we need to know about?"

"Naw, it ain't no problem. Not anymore. But y'all so busy monitoring what I'm doing, and in the meantime, my packages are being robbed, and this nigga Nick been raping us all. I'm not paying no damn twenty percent extra. That's some bullshit. How come none of y'all niggas complaining? What's the purpose of The Consortium?" Cisco snapped. "I'm taking my business elsewhere. Fuck that nigga and his twenty percent. Who else is with me?"

Six-Nine said, "Who you got that's cheaper?"

"Yeah who? Put me on that nigga," Born said. "We all know that even upping his shit twenty percent is cheaper than anybody else."

"If I can get us lower prices are y'all ready to buy from me?" Cisco asked. "This nigga, Nick, we gonna just sit back and let him muscle us?"

"If you get something lower, same quality or better, let us know. We can purchase together as The Consortium, not buy from you. Those days are over," I said. This was the first time I gave my input at a meeting and I meant it.

CHAPTER SIXTEEN

SHAN

I was appalled at the thought of Briggen wanting me to go
see some damn shrink. I mean, get real! He's the one who
needed the damn shrink, not me. I was simply trying to get
paid. My old-school show was almost sold out and I was
promoting heavy for the Halloween party, and I had stashed
all of my cash in my new trapped out truck. I was lovin' life!
And on top of that, Nick paid for five of the keys, and he
owed me for three more. I was going to get my hair dyed
red for my photo shoot and was now official. I named my
company Redbone Entertainment. My new name was now
Redbone.

It had been a long day and I couldn't wait to soak in a tub
of hot water. As my tub water was running, I got undressed. It
was an indescribable freedom to have the house all to myself,
and I was loving every damn second of it.

No sooner than I stepped into my plumeria bubble bath,

I heard footsteps coming up the stairs. Briggen burst into the bathroom. *Damn. I should have locked the door.*

"Briggen, please. Not tonight. It's late, and I'm tired. Ain't no shrinks open this time of night so what the fuck do you *want*?" I was too exhausted to fight with him.

"I *want* to put my foot in your ass. That's what the fuck I *want*. Get outta the tub, Shan!"

"What?" I couldn't believe what I was hearing.

"Now! Get your lyin' ass out of the tub, right now!" he yelled.

Oh shit. Looking at his eyebrows furrowed and the scowl on his face, I knew he was pissed off about something. I didn't know what happened, but Briggen had steam coming out of his ears. I stood up. "Pass me a towel, please."

He snatched one off the hook and threw it at me. "Get out."

He left the bathroom. I wrapped the towel around myself and got out. When I walked into our bedroom he was pacing back and forth.

"Sit down, Shan."

"Can I put—"

"Sit yo' ass the fuck down! Tell me about you losing the license plate to your car." My heart rate sped up. *Was I busted?* "What? I don't know what you're ta—"

Before I could finish the sentence he had come over to me and slammed me on the love seat next to the bed. For a moment I couldn't breathe.

"I'm not playing with you, Shan. Now, let's start again. How did you lose the license plate to your car?" He went back to pacing back and forth.

"A car rear-ended me, and it fell off." That's all of the information I gave him because I didn't know how much he knew. Even though he had me shook, that was *my* money and I wasn't giving it back.

"And what happened after that?" He lowered his voice.

"I guess that's when it fell off."

Briggen rushed over to me and wrapped his hand around my throat and lifted me off the sofa. "Bitch, this ain't no time for spittin' game. Niggas done put a hit out on you, and my hands are tied." He let me go and stepped back. He was breathing like a pit bull.

If I wasn't before, now I was scared shitless. He was looking crazy, and did I hear him say that they put out a hit on me?

"You know what? My son is safe, and you're here by yourself. You be the damn sittin' duck. Fuck it! You want to keep lying? Then go right ahead. I'm outta here! They can shoot the place up with you here. Shoot you up into little pieces for all I care." He turned to leave.

"Briggen, wait!" I begged, but he kept going. I jumped up and grabbed his arm. "No. Please. Okay. Okay. I'll tell you everything." He snatched away from me and went downstairs. I followed behind him crying and pleading with him to listen. "Briggen, for real. I thought I could get away with it. No one saw me."

"You're lying, Shan. Somebody saw you." He kept moving toward the front door and didn't look back.

"No, I'm not," I sniveled.

"Then tell me what happened." He turned to face me.

Damn. How did he find out? "There was a police chase

the day I went to see Mia. I pulled over to let them pass. When I started back driving, they didn't have the sirens on so I couldn't tell which way they were coming from. When I pulled out again and turned the corner, they were coming down the street, and that's when the car hit me."

"What car? The police car or their car?" he interrupted me.

"Not the police car. One of the vehicles the police were chasing. I think it was two. But right after it hit me, somebody jumped out of the car and started hopping away. And then the car doors flew open and a guy was bleeding. He was lying there. Blood was coming out of his mouth, and he was trying to talk. That's when I saw the first bag. I grabbed it and saw another one. I didn't second-guess it. I took both bags and threw them in my ride and drove off. I swear to you, that's what happened." I was now doing some serious boo-hooing.

"What was in the bags, Shan?"

"One had money and the other one had drugs."

"Ain't this some shit!" Briggen grabbed his head. Then he followed up with, "What the fuck!" And he punched the wall.

"Fuck!" He paced back and forth. "How much dope?"

"There were ten big bundles."

"How much money?"

"A lot. Nothing but one hundred dollar bills. I didn't even count it. I just started spending it. The truck I just bought. I paid for it in cash, and I still got a lot left."

"Where's the dope, Shan?"

I swallowed, scared to tell him this part.

"Where's the fuckin' dope?" he yelled. "You still don't understand how serious this is, do you?"

"I gave it to Nick," I mumbled.

"You what?" He came over to the love seat and stood over me.

"I gave it to Nick!" I said out loud. "That's why I called him over here."

"That pussy muthafucka! He never even told me that part." He spoke under his breath, but I still heard him.

"That's because I made him promise not to. Don't get him mixed up in our business."

"What do you mean you made him promise? What y'all got going on? Why are you protecting this nigga? You don't even know him like that. How stupid could you be to call a nigga over that you don't even know and give him ten bricks? Shan, what the fuck have you been smoking?" He was dead-ass serious.

"Leave him out of this, Briggen."

"Leave him out of this?" He laughed. "Who the fuck is this nigga to you? Why are you being so overprotective with this nigga? What, you fuckin' him?"

"Of course not." My tongue was getting thick. I was so nervous I could hardly swallow.

"Then what is it? Go ahead and tell me the truth. You fuckin' this nigga, right?"

I didn't know if I should come clean about me and Nick. I mean, for me, that would be like opening up a can of worms.

"The truth, Shan! Or are you just a stupid bitch?"

"Bitch? You calling me bitch now, Briggen? I'm not stupid! I've known Nick since I was in high school. He was my brother's best friend."

BRIGGEN

No, this bitch didn't just sit here and tell me she has known my connect for years. I mean, how shiesty could that be? When I first introduced them to each other in the backyard, them muthafuckas acted as if they didn't know each other. I mean, what the fuck was that all about? How long have they been sneaking around socializing and shit behind my back?

"You know what, Shan? This is a little too much information for me to digest right now." This bitch had thrown me for a loop. My mind was all over the place. Ain't nothing worse than a man having to wonder if his woman is getting dick behind his back. And with the connect?

"Briggen, it's not what you're thinking." She had the audacity to say to me with a straight face.

"How the fuck do you know what I'm thinking? You guilty?" I spat.

"I can tell by the look on your face what you are thinking. But no, trust me when I tell you that we are not fucking. He's like family to me. He's like a brother," Shan had the nerve to tell me.

"Yeah, right! You fuckin' the nigga."

"No. I'm not."

"You lyin' bitch! Yeah, you fuckin' him."

"I'm not lyin'. I did but—"

"You did?" I grabbed her by her hair.

"When we were in school, Briggen. A long time ago. He got me pregnant and I got an abortion. I was only sixteen. That was the last time."

"You bitch! Why the fuckin' secrets? You could have told me this shit a long time ago." He shoved my head back.

"Bitch?" she asked with squinted eyes and taking deep breaths. "It's like that? I don't deserve being called a bitch." She looked at me with tear-filled eyes.

"And I don't deserve the bullshit you've taken me through. So now we even." I started to walk away but quickly turned back around.

"Why didn't you tell me you knew him? Where is your fuckin' loyalty, Shan? I can understand and don't expect any loyalty from him, but you are supposed to be my wife. You know what? I'm out of here. Y'all deserve each other."

"Briggen, wait!" She tried to grab me.

"Don't touch me Shan." I got the hell out of there as fast as I could before I found myself putting a hurting on her. Everything was clear to me now except for the real relationship between her and Nick. That was a calculated move on both of their parts to not tell me that they knew each other. And to not know why had me spooked.

SHAN

I felt relieved for having to tell Briggen about me and Nick. It wasn't as if we were fucking; like I told him, I was only sixteen. I just needed him to take care of the business for me. On the other hand, it felt good to get the shit out in the open about the abortion. I needed to tell that to somebody.

I had been blowing up Nick's phone, but he never answered. He probably thought that I was calling to ask about the rest of my money, but I wanted to put him on notice that the gig was up. Briggen knew everything. Plus, I wanted to let him know that the people whose package I ended up with knew that I had it. Strangely enough, I wasn't worried. Between the two of them niggas, they needed to handle it. They were my protectors. Nick, because he sold the dope off, so the dirt was on his hands. And as far as Briggen goes, I knew regardless of how angry he might be, he would never let anything happen to me.

I got back into the tub and took the hot bath that I needed. I had a long day ahead of me. I had to get my new hairstyle for the photo shoot, and my first show was Friday night. And I couldn't forget the Halloween party was the following weekend.

The minute my body calmed down and relaxed in the hot, soothing, bubbly water, the doorbell rang. Now I had to jump out of the tub, grab a towel and run downstairs. It probably was Keeta. Briggen must have stopped by and told her all of our business.

When I peeked out of the door, to my surprise, it was Nick. I rushed to open it up.

"What's up? You've been blowing up my phone." I closed the door, and he gave me a hug. "Are you okay?" he asked with concern in his voice.

We stood there hugging as I spoke into his chest. "Briggen just left. He came over to tell me that I was on my own. They found my tag, they know their stash ended up at this house, and . . ." I took a deep breath, "I had to tell him about you. He now knows that me and you go way back."

Nick remained quiet as we stood there rocking each other. It felt good being in his arms, and I could have been mistaken but it felt like he was getting a hard-on.

He finally spoke, "I'm just glad you are okay. And I knew

it was only a matter of time before he would find out. Hell, we were the ones who made him suspicious."

"Suspicious?" I asked as I leaned back and looked up at his face. And when I leaned back, yes, I felt it. Nick's dick was hard. And the scary part was, I didn't care. I remained right there pressed up against it.

"Yeah, suspicious. Brig is sharp, Shan. He didn't get to where he is by being a slouch."

"I know that, but we didn't give him anything to be suspicious about."

"I came over here twice while he was locked up. That did it. But there ain't shit we can do about that now. I'm just glad that you are alright."

His hand slid down to my ass and pulled me closer. I was already pressing up against him. But now I was up on it. He leaned in and kissed my forehead and then my cheek. I could feel a little juice oozing out of my pussy. Rocking up against his dick was feeling nice. His dick was getting harder, and my pussy was getting wetter.

"Give me a kiss, Shan," he ordered. I froze. He was rubbing and squeezing my ass. "Give me a kiss," he said again, but this time with a little more force.

I glanced up at him and he kissed me and I kissed him back. I found myself wrapping my arms around his neck. He lifted me up and took me to my new marble dining room table and sat me on top of it. We kept kissing like we were in high school. He unloosened my towel, and it fell off me. He started playing with my nipples. I was on fire. He took my hand and placed it on his hard on. I squeezed and rubbed it. It was on. I thought about how the curve felt when it was up in my pussy and went to unloosening his belt and unzipping his pants. He wouldn't stop kissing me and teasing my nipples, so I pulled his dick out and started rubbing it up and down my pussy. I hadn't had any dick in months. I put the head to my opening, and Nick did the rest. He stopped kissing me and grabbed my ass and eased inside of me. We started fucking each other right there on my brand-new dining room table. That little curve in his dick was still there. I spread my legs wider, encouraging him to fuck me deeper and harder.

"This pussy always belonged to me. Make sure you tell Briggen that. Now bring it on to daddy."

I grabbed his ass and got my fuck on. Yes, I had done the unforgiveable. I thought about pushing him off me, but it was too late. I had already gone too far, and plus, it was feeling . . . "mmmmm," I moaned. Too good to stop it if I wanted to.

My eyes popped open. I was frantic and shivering. I was still in the tub. The water was cold. I had dozed off.

CHAPTER SEVENTEEN

SHARIA

I was curled up in Cisco's arms as we lay on the bed watching Kevin Hart's *Laugh at My Pain.*

"Baby, I heard that the bitch who jacked your package is running around here promoting shows. She's acting as if she did nothing wrong," I purred those words and snuggled closer to him.

"Yeah, well, don't worry about her. Her days are numbered," he said as if he knew something I didn't. But it still wasn't good enough for me. I wanted that bitch dead . . . and I wanted it yesterday.

"I'm just saying. She flossin' hard." I pressed the issue.

"I got this, baby girl. She'll be handled. Trust and believe that."

I wasn't convinced. Number one, the bitch was still breathing, and number two, they didn't know Briggen the way I knew him. I gave them the intel on her over a month and a half ago. I pushed Cisco's arms off me and crawled out of the bed.

"I'll catch you later," I snapped, unable to mask my attitude.

"What's the matter with you? I thought you was going to hang with me tonight. We ain't even fuck yet." He pushed the satin sheets off him and got out of bed.

"I got something to do. I'll catch you later." I was disgusted and didn't want to be around him, not right now. He stood there baffled as I threw on my clothes and rushed out of there.

SHAN

That dream I had about Nick and me gettin' busy was creepy. But the matter at hand and what was pressing was for me to move. Nick felt that it wasn't safe for me to stay there and suggested that I come over to his place until things blew over. I wasn't about to put myself in that position, because my dream would have become a reality, and I wasn't ready for that.

So, I declined and told him I would get my own place and I did. I found a nice condo inside a brand new subdivision out in Farmington Hills. Far away from the city and about an hour from where we lived. It was brand new, three bedrooms, two and a half baths, full basement, den, living room and dining room. It would do for the moment. Me and three guys from the moving company stuffed the truck with everything we could. I had them bring over my dining room set and Anthony's bedroom set. The rest of that shit was Briggen's. I gave Keeta ten stacks to go pick out and pay for my living-room and bedroom furniture. I got the receipts and arranged for the delivery. I didn't tell her where I lived. Like I said, it was only temporary and plus, she loved to shop. I wasn't going back to our house. I had what I needed and what I didn't have I could buy.

I had to finish getting ready for my first sold-out show. I couldn't have cared less that there was a bounty on my head. Wasn't shit gonna spoil this for me.

DARK

All of a sudden Cisco was sweating me about taking out Briggen. I told him I would, when the time was right. I almost had my plan airtight when I got word that my cousin Sharia was in Cisco's ear and now he was sending niggas after him where he rested.

"Man, what are you doing? I told you I got this. Let me do my job." I was trying to get him to back off.

"You taking too long," he said.

"According to who?" I almost blurted out Sharia's name.

"According to the streets. The streets talking about I'm soft. You know when that happens, more niggas think they can chump me," he rationalized.

"The streets ain't saying shit, Cisco. You gonna fuck up my plan," I warned him.

"No, I ain't! I'm just sending a message, that's all."

"By who?" This nigga was really starting to irk me. "What kind of message and by who?"

"I got them niggas going over there later on."

"Awww, man. We talked about this, Cisco."

"Nigga, if you feel that they are gonna fuck the mission up, ride wit' 'em. As a matter of fact, I *want* you to go with them."

"Naw, man. I do my dirt all by my lonely. That way if something goes wrong, it's on me. I'm not taking a fall for some other nigga's stupidity. You go ahead and send a bunch of trigger-happy punks and watch how they gonna fuck it up." This fool had me pacing back and forth.

Cisco stood up. "I'm not *telling* you, man! I'm *ordering* you to go with them."

"And I'm *telling* you, no! I'm advising you to fall back." We were now toe to toe.

"Dark, you forgettin' who your superior is. Don't forget who put you on." He spat in my face.

"And you don't forget who got these niggas fearin' you." I spat back at his and then turned and left.

AND JUST LIKE I told him, them dummies would fuck up . . . they did. They went by the house, sprayed it with bullets, and no one was home. There was only one casualty, and that was the neighbor's poodle. That shit was all over the local news stations. The only plus I saw was that the media gave up all they had on the residents. The report went like this:

> "We now have breaking news. This is Alexis Wiley live for Fox 2 News on the scene of what appeared to be an attempted drive-by in this usually quiet community. Eyewitnesses report hearing numerous gunshots around the home of a Mrs. Shan McGhee, a show promoter and

owner of RedBone Entertainment, who recently moved from the residence just days ago according to an eyewitness.

"Mrs. McGhee moved like two days ago. She was a nice woman and good neighbor. I just don't understand who could do something like this. I just thank the Lord no one was home, but my condolences go out to Mrs. Petty. It's a shame what they did to that dog. What is the world coming to?"

We contacted RedBone Entertainment but have received no comment. We will keep you posted as the story develops. This is Alexis Wiley reporting live from Fox 2."

The media gave me the info that I needed. I still wasn't all the way clear on how she walked away with the dope and the money, not without having some help.

SHAN

"Girl, turn on channel nine, Keeta yelled into the phone. "Hurry up!" she screeched.

"Hold up. My TV ain't even turned on." I had a new flat screen that I didn't even know how to work. I was still unpacking boxes of clothes and dishes. The place was still unorganized.

"Girl, you too slow. You missed it," she snapped.

"I got it on now. What's up?"

"It will come on again. They had your house on TV," Keeta said excitedly.

"My house? Why?"

"They showed your neighbor, the short, black, pudgy lady. They killed her dog, and they sprayed your house all up. You lucky bitch, you moved out in the nick of time."

"Who sprayed it up?" I didn't want to believe what Keeta was telling me even though Briggen had already told me that there was a hit out on me.

"They didn't say all of that. But they did tell all of your business. You probably need to call the police. You know they said it was all drug related."

"You spoke to Briggen?" I could hear him saying it now, "I tried to tell your ass!"

"He didn't answer his phone. Girl, somebody is mad at y'all. I'm so glad y'all weren't home. Niggas be hatin' when they see somebody else doing good. They interviewed the neighbor lady and she said y'all are such a nice and quiet couple, she didn't understand why anyone would want to shoot up the house. They also said that Briggen is out on bond in connection with a drug-trafficking case. So all of y'alls business is out in the open. And oh, you got some free advertisement! They said your company's name. When did you call it Redbone?"

I didn't have time for Keeta's jokes. My company's name? I was really an open target now. I hung up with her and called Briggen.

"Oh, so your ass wanna call me now? See what you got us into, Shan? And you around here flossin' with new rides and promoting shows and shit, like you untouchable. This ain't no game. What if we would have been at home with our son?" he spat. "And I've been trying to reach you. Why haven't you been answering your phone?"

"Because I have a new one for my business, and I left the other one by mistake."

"Are you back at the house?"

"Of course not. I moved out," I told him.

"You moved out?" He sounded surprised.

"I sure did."

"To where?"

I clammed up. I didn't know if I should trust him or not.

"Shan, you know what? Fuck it! It ain't me you should be worrying about. But remember, when the heat gets turned up, don't call me." He hung up sounding mad, of course. That was the story of our lives.

I called Nick. He still owed me for three keys. For real, I wasn't worried about them. "Nick, you heard the news?" I asked him as soon as he picked up.

"Yeah, I heard. It's a good thing you left when you did. You alright? What did Brigg have to say?"

"I'm fine, and he said what I expected him to say. When are you going to have the rest of that for me?"

"I'll let you know. Where are you?"

"I'll let you know," I told him and hung up.

MIA

Shit was getting crazy. And I'm not talking only about Briggen's house getting shot up and Shan moving and not telling him where she lived. Anthony was starting to grow on me. Briggen had been running the streets around the clock leaving me here to babysit. I wasn't used to being cooped up in the house all day. So I would get his car seat, strap him up, and we would be gone. What really went to my head was when my mother told me that he could pass for my son. That was the icing on the cake. From that point on, I was mommy.

I had just hung up with my mom who said they were on their way over to pick me up. It was my stepdad's birthday, and we were taking him out. I had been babysitting Li'l Anthony all week, and Briggen didn't come in last night. So that meant Anthony had to go. I had been blowing up his phone, worried sick about him. He never bothered to call me back, so I finally called Shan.

"Hello, Shan, this is Mia. Have you heard from Briggen?"

There was a moment of silence on the other end. Then she finally said, "I thought he was laying up in your bed every night? You haven't heard from him?" The bitch's words dripped with sarcasm.

"If I had I wouldn't be calling you."

"Well, no, I have not spoken to him in a few days."

Click.

This crazy ho had the nerve to hang up on me. I called her right back. I got comfortable because it was me who held the trump card.

"I can't believe how silly you are acting. Your behavior is old and tired. When you got hooked up with Briggen, you knew he was fucking me, Sharia, and damn near everybody else. So get over it. He's with me now." I wanted her to understand that.

"I can't tell. If he was with you, why are you calling me looking for him?"

"That's because I have *your* son. I'm getting ready to go out, so you need to come pick him up, or I need to drop him off."

"You what?" I could hear the panic in her voice.

"I have your son and I can't reach Briggen, so come get him or I can drop him off."

"I am on my way to the Marquis for the show. I have to oversee everything. Tonight is my entertainment company's debut. Oh my God! How am I going to make sure everything goes right with a baby on my hip?"

"That's not my problem." It was my turn to be sarcastic.

"Where's his father?"

"I told you I didn't know."

"Oh my God. I don't believe this. Let me see who I can call and I'll call you right back."

"No, Shan. Come get him now or tell me where to meet you. This ain't my child."

"I'ma have Keeta come and get him. Please. Give me five minutes. I'll call you right back."

"Mmmhmm." The bitch changed that stank-high-and-mighty attitude real quick.

SHAN

Un-fuckin'-believable! Here Briggen done left my son with that bitch. I couldn't wait to talk to him so I could cuss his ass out. I called him and got his voicemail. Then I called Keeta, and when she didn't pick up I started to panic.

Here it was my big night and I couldn't get a babysitter. I called Mia back and as her phone rang I swallowed my pride. My stomach was starting to cramp.

"Mia, I can't reach anyone . . . at all."

"No problem. I'll just bring him to where you are."

"Mia, can you please keep him for me?" I had to get humble.

Here I had to call the bitch that my husband was fucking, begging for help.

Mia burst out laughing. "You know this is every bitch's dream, right? Oh, so now you *need* me to do something for you? I'm sure this is a tragic turn of events for you."

"Mia, I'll pay you a grand. Just keep him for the night." I had my fingers crossed.

"A grand?" she scoffed. "I can get that from Briggen for just lying on my back."

"Two grand," I told her. I knew she heard the desperation in my voice. "And as soon as I reach Briggen or Keeta I'll have them come and get him."

"Make it twenty-five hundred and enjoy your show. Smooches."

The phone went dead. *Bitch.*

CHAPTER EIGHTEEN

SHARIA

Oh my God, this nigga is a beast. He had been fucking me crazy for the last three hours. He had me in a full buck in the middle of the bed hitting it from the back like he still owned it. All I could do was bite down into the pillow and clinch the sheets tight. His powerful push buckled my knees with every thrust. Just when I thought I couldn't take no more he began to slowly slide in and out of my wetness at just the right angle, teasing my spot.

"How this feel?" His deep voice sent chills up and down my spine as his strong hands held me firmly in place.

"Yeees . . . ohhhh . . . yesss," was all I could release from my mouth as a gut-wrenching orgasm threatened to take over my entire body. I moaned louder, and he stroked faster until we both exploded. He remained inside me as he fed his ego.

"Still can't handle all this big dick, huh?"

"And this is still the best pussy you ever slid up in," I managed to reply still out of breath.

"Hell, yeah. And it's all mine," he shot back, smacked me on the ass, then pulled out slow. I fell forward on the bed and just lay there as I watched him walk that sexy, glistening body to the bathroom. When I heard the shower come on I pulled the sheet over me and dozed off. About thirty minutes later he was sitting next to me rubbing my leg. I opened my eyes and smiled. He was fully dressed and smiling back.

"You straight with the plan?" he asked me.

"I told you I got you," I responded, my voice full of confidence.

"We about to fuck all these niggas. I just need another week or two."

"Don't worry about me. I'll be fine. Just hurry up." Just as the words left my mouth he leaned in and kissed me.

"Love you." He whispered.

"I love you, too." As I watched him get his stuff together, I took a deep breath and scoffed at the plan that he put together. This shit was going to be sweet. I was going out with a bang.

DARK

I had got Cisco white-boy wasted. He told me that he was so drunk he couldn't see straight and that he hadn't got this drunk in a long time. That was just the way I wanted him.

I pulled into an alley on First Street. He said he had to piss. Before I could stop the car good he opened the door, stumbled out and began to hurl into a trash can. I popped the trunk and got out. In the back I had some Spanish wire, also known as a garrote. I grabbed it and waited for Cisco to stop hurling. I didn't want to get that shit all over my gators and the tailor-made slacks I wore.

"Aww, shit!" he grumbled, as he hugged the garbage can.

I leaned up against the car, waiting patiently for him to finish hurling. It seemed as if he would never stop. When he finally straightened up, pulled out his dick to piss, I eased up behind him and wrapped the wire around his neck. I pulled and tightened. He struggled to loosen the wire from around his neck, I'm sure surprise and uncertainty were running through his mind. I didn't let go of the wire until his tongue stuck out and his body went limp at the same time. I had planned this for weeks.

Immediately I began to drag him to my trunk, heels scraping the ground, dick sticking out and all, as I tossed him in and slammed it shut. I had to get him to the casket I made for him in an abandoned junkyard filled with a bunch of cars. I had lined the trunk of an old Cadillac hearse with lime and lye. All I had to do was put Cisco in it. If and when somebody came across him, it would be too late.

SHAN

If I didn't know what being on cloud nine was before, I was well acquainted with it now. My first show was a blowout! I had at least seven offers on my voicemail from individuals and organizations that wanted to pay me to do exactly what I did for me. With the bar, I cleared about forty grand. Not bad for my first show in an economy that screamed recession. I paid almost nine grand for security and two personal bodyguards that were on me every second.

I rang Mia's bell and looked around and noticed that there were no cars parked anywhere. That was weird. It was only eight thirty in the morning. I took out my cell and phoned her. She picked up on the first ring. "Mia, I'm out front. I'm here to pick up Li'l Anthony. Thank you so much and I have your money."

"We are out having breakfast. Why didn't you call me first?"

"I was just trying to get him off your hands. Last night you sounded as if you had to get rid of him and as if he was such a burden. And I apologize for that. I was under the impression that his father had him."

"His father still hasn't shown up. And oh, there's some ladies here talking about the show. They're going on about how good it was and how they had not had a good time like that in a while."

I started grinning from ear to ear. I knew my shit was on point. "It was the bomb. You had to have been there," I told her.

"Now my mother is sitting here talking about letting her know where the next one is going to be and wants you to bring Ron Isley to town."

"Tell her I will get right on that." I was pumped.

"Look, we just ordered our breakfast. If you want, you can call me later on and you can come and get him. If his father gets back I'll have him call you. Open my screen door and slide my money under the second door," Mia instructed.

"Okay." I was shocked. This ho was actually being nice to me. "Thank you, Mia." I meant that.

She hung up.

Damn! That bitch must have bumped her head. Either that or Briggen's dick done fucked it up. He can do that. But right now, it didn't even matter. I did as she asked me, slid the envelope with the stacks under the door. I couldn't wait to get home, take a nice hot bath, hop in my bed and crawl under the covers. I didn't miss Briggen, but I missed my baby. I would get him as soon as I had two more events.

My body was dog tired, and it ached. My stomach was beginning to tighten up again. I was praying that it wasn't contractions. I was going on six months. It was way too soon for that.

JANAY

Murder, murder and more murder was all I was hearing about and now thinking about as I sat in my usual spot on the couch talking to uncle Boomer.

"Why don't we just take Nick out? And then we can deal with the connect?"

"If it was that simple, it would be done like that all of the time. Only a fool gives up their connect. Remember how you used to like that movie *Blow*? Once he gave up his connect, his 'partner' had no more use for 'em. So you gotta have a well thought out plan," my uncle reminded me.

"But we all know about Mr. G," I reasoned.

"Yeah, so now you're saying you want to go back to paying G's high prices? You gotta think these things through. If you take him out without getting a commitment from his connect first, then that defeats the purpose. Think about it. I mean Mr. G may not even want to fuck with us like that anymore. So then what?"

"Oh, he would. Money talks Boomer." This nigga Nick was getting under my skin. He seemed to be making moves while I was remaining still, and I didn't like that.

"I tell you what, Unc, let me set up a meeting with Mr. G."

"How do you plan on doing that and on what grounds?"

"The grounds of getting rid of Nick. I have a plan. I'ma put somebody on Nick." I wasn't giving up that easy. How the hell did my daddy want me to take over without making any power moves? Right now it seemed that I was just his daughter keeping his seat warm. I went over to my uncle Boomer, kissed him on the cheek, and I left. I was on a mission. I was going to visit Tiny.

SHARIA

Dark was sitting in my living room listening to me plead my case to hold up with taking Shan out. I had something to show that bitch.

"What aren't you telling me, Sharia? I ain't stupid. You was just hell-bent on gettin' her popped; now you want us to spare her? I don't think so."

"Dark, trust me on this. Just wait for me to give the go-ahead."

"Wait for you to say go-ahead? Who the fuck are you?"

"Dark, remember we in this shit together. It's because of me that you are where you are."

"Bullshit. It's because of how I get down that I am where I am."

"You know what? I'll talk to Cisco myself. I'll tell him to hold up."

"Well, you are going to have to send that nigga a post-card 'cause Cisco is on vacation, and while he's gone, I'm in charge. And when I'm ready to move on this bitch, I will. Case closed."

"He's on vacation?" I had to think about what Dark was telling me. And then it hit me. "Dark, don't tell me you did him. So soon? That wasn't the plan." I lowered my voice.

"I said he's on vacation. He'll be back."

My crazy cousin assured me, he'd be back, but the look on his face said the total opposite.

DARK

My next move was me calling a meeting with all of Cisco's crew. I told them that it was mandatory, and whoever didn't show was out. The meeting took place in a hall at a secluded location. I stood at the head of the table dressed in all-black, feeling like Nino Brown in *New Jack City*. I could see the skepticism on everybody's faces when I showed up alone.

Before I could say a word, loudmouth Dread, who I met that day in the shop, yelled out, "Where's Cisco? How we gonna start this meeting without the boss?"

I glared at this muthafucka, and the room was silent. "Did I ask you to speak, nigga? If you shut the fuck up, I will tell your loud ass why y'all are here." I had beef with him since that day he told me to eat the floor.

Dread snarled and gritted his teeth as I continued to speak. "Listen up, 'cause I'm only gonna say this once. Cisco is out of state on business. He found a new connect in NY, and if things go as planned, we all will be making nearly double over what we've been making. He'll be back as soon as the deal is done, but until he returns, I am in charge.

"Everyone is to report to me about everything. If you're on the block and you gotta take a piss, you call me first. Anybody that needs to talk to Cisco has to come through me. Give me the message and I'll give it to him. He don't want y'all niggas calling him every time a feen comes up short. The man is out on business and is only accepting calls from me until he gets back. If any muthafucka in here don't like what I just said, there is a fresh body bag with your name on it. Any mutherfuckin' questions?"

The room was silent as each of these niggas processed what I had just told them. Of course Dread had to open his big mouth. He felt he was the closest to Cisco, not me. "Get the fuck outta here with that bullshit, man! I know Cisco longer than you, and that Hollywood shit you talking ain't making no kinda sense. Put the nigga on the phone, if he's only answering your calls! Call him and let him say this shit himself!"

I gave Dread a stone-faced stare. He obviously had some pretty big balls to challenge me in front of everyone the way he was. Especially since I knew he understood what kind of work I put in.

I walked down to the end of the table to where he was. "Look, y'all, I'm in charge, and whoever has a problem with that can take it up with Cisco when he gets back. But in the meantime, it's my way, the highway or the dead way." And to make my point I swiftly grabbed this Dread's head, pulled it back and sliced his throat . . . right there in front of everybody.

"Oh shit!" Reggie, who was sitting on Dread's right yelled out as he jumped up, knocking his chair backwards.

Tank, who was on his left yelled out, "Yo, you got blood on my tee!" He jumped up as well.

I heard a couple of nigga's mumble, "Crazy muthafucka." But I didn't care. I stood there behind Dread and asked, "Anybody else got something to say?"

NOW, SHARIA? SHE WAS up to something with this Shan chick. I just couldn't figure out what. In the meantime I had all my shit lining up just right. The only thing I messed up with was the police protection. The Po-Po who Cisco was in good with didn't make himself known to me, and Cisco was careful to keep that piece of the puzzle under wraps. Now I had to go and ask The Consortium for help. I didn't want to do that this soon because I wanted to set a few more things up first. I was caught between a rock and a hard place.

JANAY

I left Tiny feeling better about this Nick situation. She understood that I needed to move fast, and she was up for the task. She needed to turn this muthafucka out.

As I was driving, I noticed a black Escalade about two cars back. It was making every turn that I was making. I cursed myself for not knowing when it picked me up.

I dialed Boomer as I stayed on the highway. "Unc," I said when he picked up, "I'm being followed."

"Damn it, Nay, I told you to have Eddie go with you."

I didn't say anything in my defense because I knew I was dead wrong but I liked traveling alone.

"Where are you?" he asked me. His voice was calm. I'm sure he was hoping to keep me calm.

"On 96th."

"Let me get Eddie on the other line. Don't hang up."

"Unc, whoever it is, is trying to pull up beside me."

"Don't let that happen. Because if you do, they damn sure are going to shoot you."

"Shit, Unc! I think they are trying to run me off the road!" I gripped the steering wheel tighter as I sped up and changed lanes again. Everything I did, the Escalade did.

"Eddie said to try and bring them to that warehouse on Piedmont," Boom instructed me.

"I'll do my best," I told him as I tried not to panic.

"That's your only option unless you can lose 'em or pull over when you see a state trooper."

"Fuck! It don't look like I can lose him. Ow!" I screamed out. "They rear-ended me!" My heart was now racing. I had never been in a car chase before.

"Are you okay, Nay?"

"Oow! They hit me again, Boomer. I gotta get away from them! These niggas are trying to run me off the road! Damn it, and they doing this shit in broad daylight!" They hit me again, and I jerked forward skidding against the divider, and just like that, the Escalade sped up and disappeared. But my heart rate did not slow down.

"Nay, what's happening?" I heard Boomer yell.

"They're gone, Boomer." I breathed a sigh of relief. "I guess they wanted to scare me or send me a warning. It was most likely Melky's people. My car is fucked up. But I'm alright, just a little shaken."

"Take your ass straight to Eddie's. Do it now, Nay," Boomer ordered, not giving me a choice in the matter.

"I am."

CHAPTER NINETEEN

SHOKKAH

I sat on my prison bunk mad as hell. I had tried calling this nigga like forty times and got no answer. Even his bitch was ducking my calls. I knew I should have never trusted this nigga. Here it was I who saved this nigga from an ass rape by them Aryan muthafuckas, and he crosses me. I sat contemplating how I should handle this shit, making sure I was legit in my gripe. Then the thought came to call this nigga one more time. I pulled my burner from the stash and hit speed dial. After the fourth ring, this nigga finally decides to pick up.

"Speak," I hear this nigga say into the phone like I'm his bitch.

"Speak? Nigga, where's my get-right?" I was speaking of the $100,000 this nigga owed me for all the support we were giving him, plus protection. Shit, when I ate he ate, when I smoked he smoked, and I put my reputation on the line to keep this nigga safe for two years.

"Nigga, I don't owe you shit."

"Fuck you mean you don't owe me shit?"

"Like I said, you put your shit out there; now it's on you. When I left the jail I left all that shit in there, including you. Don't call my fucking phone no more." *Click.*

"Did this muthafucka hang up on me?" I said out loud. This nigga think I'm pussy. I know the fact that I got a life bid makes this nigga think he can talk to me sideways. I sat for a minute in hope of calming down but no such luck. The more I thought about it, the angrier I became. I knew there was only one person I could depend on to handle this shit in a way that would give me some peace.

DARK

I was driving along bumpin' *Watch the Throne* and smoking a blunt, contemplating how I was going to handle all the obstacles that was before me, not to mention my money was getting funny, since I was stashing every dime to re-up and re-up big. I needed to hurry up and come up on one of these niggas. My cell went off. I looked and saw an out of the area on the caller ID. I started not to answer it but went ahead.

"Hello."

"What's up, patna?"

"Oh shit. A voice for sore ears. What it do, nigga?" I yelled in the phone, happy to hear the voice on the other end.

"Nigga, I can't call it. How's the outside treating you?" Shokkah asked and laughed his sinister laugh that I would share with him when we sat up smoking that sour in our cell at night.

"Maaan . . . Some days are a blast, others are a fucking hassle." I told him the truth.

"I hear that. But it beats the hell outta being in this muthafucka," he reminded me. "But listen up. You know I don't bullshit around so let me be straight. I need some chicken fried, and I need it greasy. You can take it over to my wife's house because I know my son will enjoy it." I heard him loud and clear. This conversation was all code to kill a nigga with severe prejudice and wifey would tell me who.

"I got you. I'll get it to her tomorrow. What time is best?"

"Eight o'clock is good for her."

"Aiight."

"My son been saving his allowance. It might be hard to get it from him, but I'm sure once you start tickling him he'll give it up." Then he started laughing again. I said to myself so this muthafucka owe him money and I need to put the screws to his ass and collect. I was down like a muthafucka.

"I got you."

"All a man got is his word," my man Shokkah got real serious.

"You sacrificed one of your men for me, and I owe you my life. When I say I got you, I got you." And that was my word.

He wasn't going to have to worry about me. Killing was my favorite pastime and there was money involved. Just the diversion I needed.

NICK

I was sitting in the back of Mo's Bar when I looked up from my Corona as this sexy pair of legs passed my table. *"Damn"* was all I could say to myself as I watched that ass swish in her short skirt as she headed to the counter to conduct her business. I watched her command the room as she wheeled and dealed. After I sat watching for a few minutes, I made my move. Shit, I might as well. Because the one woman I want is married with children.

"I'll get that for you," I said and slid several yards to the hostess.

"You'll get that for me," she gave me this funky attitude and slid my money back. Her little display didn't faze me. It actually turned me on.

"It's like that? You too sexy to be so mean." I flashed her a sexy smile.

"And you need to try pulling that shit on one of these bubble-headed ladies up in here. That shit don't impress me." She turned back to the woman at the counter who had a smirk on her face and continued to handle her business.

"Can you join me?" I interrupted her.

"Join you? I don't even know you."

"Pleease." I held my hands together and gave her the puppy-dog eyes. She was trying to play hard, but I managed to get a smile out of her.

"Is this how you get dates?"

"Nah. This is how I get what I want." I looked her up and down, then settled on her eyes. Old girl was fine as hell. She stood at 5'4, about 120 pounds, all curves. That skirt was resting midthigh showing off her sexy caramel legs. She gave me a little smile as she puckered her glossy lips.

"So what if I say I don't want to join you?"

"Have dinner with me instead?"

"I would say I'll think about it."

"That's all I ask. I'm Nick." I extended my hand, and she placed hers in mine.

"I'm Tiny," she replied.

I knew I had her. She agreed to meet me later, and we became inseparable from that day onward.

TINY

Damn, this nigga is sexy. There we were, after a couple of weeks of dating, sitting in a restaurant. The hunger in this nigga's eyes to get between my legs was getting me wet. Tonight just might be his lucky night. I had been teasing him like crazy, had him begging. I had him just where I wanted him. Too bad this was only business for me. The business that Janay was paying me for.

"You gonna spend the night with me tonight?" he asked, then leaned in and kissed my collarbone.

"Maybe," I shot back, as his hand roamed back and forth up my leg.

"You know you need to let me handle this," he said, looking into my eyes as his hand slid up my inner thigh resting his fingers on my zipper. He then slid his fingers up and down the lips of my coochie. I had to admit, this nigga was definitely fuckable. But I wasn't trying to give it up this quick. I was trying to make him crave it.

"You act like you ain't never had no pussy before." I grabbed his wrist stopping his little finger tease.

"And you act like you scared."

"Scared of what?" I gave him that *nigga, please* look.

"Of him." He grabbed my hand and placed it in his lap.

His dick was on swoll—long, hard and thick. Now, that's how you convince a bitch because if I wasn't ready to fuck him before I was damn sure ready to fuck him after that.

"That don't scare me."

"Well, let him talk to you for a little while." He gave me that irresistible smile. I nodded yes, then he flagged down the waitress for our check.

NICK

As I opened the door to my apartment I was devising all of the positions I was getting ready to have little mama in. I clicked the light switch and walked in. She came in behind me, and I locked the door.

"This is nice," she said, looking all around.

"It's aiight. Just a little somethin'. Have a seat." I headed to the kitchen and grabbed a bottle of wine and two glasses. When I returned she was sitting on the couch with her shoes off. I sat down next to her, popped the cork and poured us both a glass.

"I've been having a real good time with you these past couple of weeks," she said as she raised the glass to her lips.

"Me, too," I said as I placed my hand on her thigh. "Can I get that kiss you've been promising me all night?" She gave me the okay, then it was on. I leaned in and placed my lips on hers. After I slipped my tongue in her mouth there was no turning back.

TINY

Damn, this nigga was official. He was kissing and touching me in all the right places. Within minutes, he had my shirt off and a mouth full of nipple sucking it just right. I squirmed in my seat as his hands and mouth put my body on fire. I could feel the wetness forming in my coochie as he began kissing his way to my zipper. He unzipped my jeans and slid them open, placing gentle kisses at the top of my panties while pulling at the side of my jeans.

"Can I taste you?" he whispered. I didn't hesitate. I pushed his face to the place. He pulled my jeans all the way off, then stared at my pussy like it was a juicy steak. He pulled off his shirt and then his pants and sat back on the couch.

"I thought you wanted to taste me?"

"I do. But I like my meals brought to me." He pulled me by the hand causing me to stand in front of him. Then he slowly slid my panties down until they hit the floor. Pulling me toward him he leaned in and inhaled my scent. "Mmmm . . ." he moaned, then lifted me up so I could stand over him. There I stood, legs wide open and pussy fully exposed. I lowered myself into position, and his tongue took over. He began slowly tickling my clit with the tip of his tongue, then he let his tongue glide between my wet lips.

"Mmmm . . ." The work he was putting in was feeling so good. My knees were getting weak. I think he sensed it because he grabbed my legs one by one and placed them over his shoulders sitting me right on his face, palming my ass just right. He then ate my pussy like it was his last meal.

NICK

I knew she couldn't hang talking all that shit. I had her ass hollering and crying and begging for mercy. After she came for the third time I eased her down and slid her right onto my dick. Damn her pussy was tight as hell. She was so small I could move her any way I wanted her. She held me tighter as I bounced her faster and faster. Her moans were intoxicating. When I hit that spot she took over. She pushed me back and began nibbling and sucking my neck. She planted her feet firm in the couch and came up and down on my shit just right. Her pussy muscles clinched tighter with every thrust. The room was now filled with both of our moans.

"Make him talk to me," she whispered in my ear as she continued to work her show. I grabbed her ass and pushed her down hard every time she came up. "That's what I'm talking about" was all I heard as she moved faster and I pushed harder.

"Oh shit," I yelled out as I felt myself about to release.

"Gimmie this dick, boy," she said through clinched teeth.

"Mmm . . . shit," I moaned. Her muscles were squeezing tighter, and the pussy was getting wetter with every stroke. I hung in there for a few more strokes, but she pushed down on me causing me to enter her deeper and as I exploded, it was over for me. I held her tight in my arms and kissed her lips.

TINY

The next morning I knew I had to put my signature on this nigga if I wanted him to act right. Just as he turned over I saw what I needed to see. He had that early-morning hard-on. I put my head under the covers and went to work. As I began to suck I felt his dick get harder in my mouth, then I felt his hand rest on the back of my head. As I slowly pulled him in and out of my tight jaws I could hear him begin to moan. I moved the cover from my head and picked up the pace. Rotating the sucking of his dick and running my tongue up the line between his balls made him open his legs a little wider. I had all the access I needed. I ran the tip of my tongue down the line and flicked it slowly over his asshole. When I felt him jump, I knew I had him.

Quickly I went back to working that pole, sucking harder and faster. I looked up and his head was buried deep in the pillow, and when I felt his leg shake, I knew he was close. I took him to the back of my throat and tightened my jaws. The sound of my slurps caused him to moan louder. He was on the brink. He grabbed a handful of my hair and tried to go deeper in my throat. Good thing a bitch got skills. His breathing picked up, and he began to grunt. I moved faster and faster and just as he was about to come I slid my finger in his ass and stroked. That nigga screamed like a bitch as his whole body shook. He released into the back of my throat hard and long, and I swallowed every drop. I slowly removed my finger and sucked my way to the top of his dick. I watched as his stomach heaved in and out and a smile spread across my lips.

"I fucked you royally, huh?" I asked. But that nigga couldn't even talk. I got up and headed to the bathroom. Mission accomplished. That muthafucka was now putty in my hands.

NICK

I ain't 'bout no gay shit, but had to admit that shit felt good as hell. I ain't never come like that before. Then to have a bitch suck you like that then talk shit and walk out the room. Fuck what you heard. That's grounds for marriage. I lay there basking in that nut that I just busted and couldn't say shit. I was fucked up laying there staring up at the ceiling, then I dozed off.

DARK

I sat in my car, crouched down, waiting for this nigga, Sig, to come home. Just when I thought I was about to get real restless I see this penny ante hustler pull up in a gold Hummer. I watched him dead his engine and step out of his ride. He was staggering a little and fumbling with his keys and phone. I eased out of the car and ducked behind a car when his cell phone rang. I slid behind the tall bush on the side of his house and pulled down my mask.

"You better be here in a hour. And wear that sexy shit I like." He was talking to what appeared to be a female. When he got to the door he again fumbled with his keys and dropped them on the porch. When he came up, I was right on him and busted him over the head with a blackjack. He fell to the floor like a sack of potatoes. I scooped that nigga up and carried him to my ride and threw him in the trunk and drove off.

SIG

When I woke up I was buck naked and hanging in the middle of a room. I looked up through the blood dripping in my eyes and saw that I was handcuffed to some chains that hung from a beam in the ceiling. I looked around the room and noticed that I was in an abandoned building. I tried to pull on the chains to see if I could free myself, but I couldn't. I wiggled around for a few minutes, then I heard footsteps coming from behind.

DARK

I walked up on that nigga and burned him with my cigar. He screamed as he tried to turn to see what was going on. I walked in front of him and started my interrogation.

"Do you know why you're here?" I stated in a calm voice and took a seat.

"Nigga, I don't know you," he tried to sound real hard.

"Do you know Shokkah?" His eyes grew bigger by the second.

"Look, that nigga is crazy. I don't owe him shit."

"I didn't ask you anything about owing him. You guilty nigga," I said, then kicked him, causing him to swing back and forth.

"Where is my partner's money? And I don't plan on being here all night."

"I'm telling you, I don't owe that nigga shit. You let me go now and I can make it worth your while."

"Muthafucka, your word is shit. Why you think I'm here? 'Cause you ain't keep your word." I got up and walked to the table and removed the lid from a barrel of fluid under Sig's feet, then I grabbed the control box and sat back down and took a long drag on my Cuban. "So you gonna take my nigga's kindness for a weakness?"

"I told you I paid my debt," he yelled, breathing heavy and struggling with the chains in another attempt to free himself. I pushed the green button which slowly lowered Sig toward the barrel of hydrochloric acid. I got off on offing muthafuckas with chemicals.

"What the fuck?" this nigga yelled and started squirming. "Hold up." But it was too late. I lowered him until his feet hit the acid first. I heard the sizzle, then I heard this nigga release a bloodcurdling scream. When I saw his eyes roll back in his head I pulled him up. His feet had shriveled up and looked as if it was burned on a grill. He was shaking and gasping for air. I stood up and grabbed the needle full of epinephrine and hit his vein. I didn't want this nigga passing out on me.

"So, where's my man's get-right?"

"Fuck him," he mumbled.

"Oh, you a tough guy, huh? Okay." I sat back down and hit my button again, causing him to dip right to his calves. I was planning on draggin' this shit out as long as I could. Again he hollered and jerked. Spit bubbles formed on his lips. He had flesh and muscle hanging and now the bones on his feet were totally exposed. He was tough.

My phone rang and I picked it up. "How his wife feel?" I asked Mook who was about to take her on the date of her life. I hit the speaker button and she was screaming in the background.

"No, pleeeease." He released another scream and I knew his wife's voice was getting to him.

"Wait, hold up. I think Luther ready to sing." I turned my attention back to Sig. "And you were saying?"

"Tell her to give it to you. Please, just don't hurt her," he pleaded with tears in his eyes.

I relayed the message to my man, who then said he'd call me back. About ten minutes later, my cell rang. Mook said that his girl had led him to the stash spot and my, my, my, at least that nigga had at least a quarter million dollars in cash and jewelry. My man quickly bagged that shit up, then put two in his girl's head. My motto has always been *No witness, no case.*

"See how easy that was?" I kicked him and he swung back and forth. "You could have saved us all some time." I took another pull and blew the smoke in his face. He was shaking and crying as the acid ate away at his skin. I yelled out, "All a man got is his word." Then I walked to my seat, sat back, and lowered the rest of him into the barrel. He screamed and twitched as the acid bubbled up. Blood was coming from his eyes and ears. He jerked, gurgled and gagged on spit. Right before the acid ate its way to his chest his head fell back and he was dead. I watched as his body was slowly lowered until there was nothing left but handcuffs and chains. Once his head went under, I released the cuffs, let them fall in the barrel and put the lid on.

"Two down, one to go." I walked off in anticipation of counting my riches.

NYLA

"Goddammit!" I yelled as I threw my bags, purse and dry cleaning on the couch. I had hit my toe on my way through the door. I limped back to the door, closed and locked it. I then bent over to examine my toe to see if I had fucked up my nail polish.

As I stood to walk back over to the couch, my cell phone started ringing. I searched through the pile and found it.

"Hello," I said into the phone.

"Tiny?" It was Nick.

"Hey, what's up loverman?"

"I'll be running a little late. So instead of 8:00 I'll be there by 9."

"Okay. I'll be ready. Looking forward to it."

"Me too." He hung up.

I tossed the phone onto the couch. Walking to my bedroom I went straight to the closet and hung up the two dresses, and then went to retrieve the three pairs of shoes and accessories. I still hadn't decided what I wanted to wear. After I laid everything out, I wrapped my hair and jumped in the shower. As I went over in my head my mission at hand, I had to keep reminding myself that this shit was multipurpose. Not only was I after Nick, I was also after Briggen. There was one thing for sure and two things for certain: my promise to make Briggen pay for Forever was true, and that nigga was getting ready to pay with his life.

DARK

I parked on the corner of the very spot where I got my start. I shot a man here, and I met Cisco here. Now it was burning down to the ground. The blaze appeared to be spreading to nearby businesses. I watched the firefighters, ambulances and police cars around the smoke-filled building. The firefighters fought the blaze as the flames roared out of control, destroying everything they touched. Shit, it reminded me of myself and the situations at hand. Shit was about to get real out of hand, and I was gonna destroy everyone and everything that tried to touch me.

I had got word that it was the local feens who torched our spot, because they were mad that we upped our prices. But I knew better. This had Briggen's name all over it. This was payback. But this was good 'cause I had special plans for Forever's big brother.

"Yo, you called Cisco? I think he needs to know about this," Mook was standing at the driver's side of my car. He was the one who would probably end up being my right-hand man. He was down with whatever moves I made and proved his loyalty repeatedly.

"Yeah, I told him." I rolled my car window up, and then rolled it back down. "If you need something let me know. I gotta check on something."

"You want me to go with you?" he asked me.

"Nah, I'm good."

I cranked up my ride and pressed play on my iPod. "Hustlin'" by Rick Ross blasted through my speakers as I sped off. I lit up a blunt and tried to decide which trap I would stop by first. My cell rang. I looked down and didn't recognize the 757 number. I was curious and didn't remember a chick from the 757 area that I fucked with, and then thought that maybe it was some business so I answered it. All I heard was crying.

"Hello. Yo! Hello?" I asked. Some chick on the other end

was crying loud as shit, fucking my swag straight up. "Who da fuck is this?"

"Joy," the crying chick answered.

"Joy? Who is Joy?" I wanted to know.

"I apologize, is this Dark?" I heard the ho blow her nose.

Okay. Now she had me going. First off, I didn't know a Joy, and how did she get my number? "What can I do for you?"

"Charles," she sobbed. "He gave me your number . . . to call . . . if some*thing happen*ed to him." She cried harder.

"Hold up. Who is Charles?"

"I think you guys called him Cisco!" she sobbed.

You guys? "And who are you?" Cisco never told me about no one named Joy.

"This is Joy. I'm Charles's wife, and he gave me your number as the number to call if I didn't hear from him. Have you talked to him in the last week?"

"No. He told me he was going on vacation," I lied. I was still trying to digest the fact that he had a wife and he gave her my number.

"My husband didn't go on a vacation, damn it!" she screamed.

"What do you mean he didn't go on a vacation? That's what *he to*ld me."

"My husband would never take a vaca*tion* without taking me and our two baby girls. That's how I know."

Whoa. She just dropped another bomb on me. A wife and kids?

"So let me get this straight," she challenged. "You haven't heard from my husband, and you don't know where he is? Is that what you are telling me?" She was frantic.

I had to get off the phone with this bitch. And fast.

"Yes, ma'am. That's exactly what I'm telling you," I found myself saying. This Joy person didn't sound like your average hood rat. And she sounded like someone who demanded respect. "However, he never told me he had a wife."

"That's because that was none of your business."

"Well, I don't believe you are who you're saying you are."

"Your name is Mills and you're at the top of the list. They call you Dark. And you just got released from federal custody in April. Since my husband gave me your number to call and you haven't heard from him, I'm going to the police. You can mark my words."

Now I was convinced.

BRIGGEN

Yeah, that nigga Cisco was getting ready to feel my wrath. I don't know how the fuck he imagined himself muscling me in my own damn city. And then shoot up the spot where I rested my head? He got the game twisted.

To let him know I ain't the one to be fucked with, I had one of his hot spots burned down to the ground, and I was getting ready to have another one of their spots turned to ashes. I knew this nigga didn't live in the area, and he's lucky he didn't because just like he sprayed my house, I would have sprayed his. The only difference was I would be sure that him and his family would be home.

As far as Nick was concerned, that nigga was dead to me. I just hadn't decided on how I was going to handle him. For one, I wasn't too twisted over the fact that he went to my crib while I was gone to help out. Because when a nigga is in your corner and you get knocked, it's his duty to check on your family. But he lied. She lied. Here these two sneaky muthafuckas knew each other all along, used to fuck and lied about it. I still haven't figured out what's the deal with them two. Because I am sure there is more to their story.

Now for Shan's dick-eating ass. I'm cutting her ass clean off. She'll see. When I showed up on her doorstep with Li'l Peanut, the surprised look on her face said she was about to faint.

SHAN

I had just sat down at my computer when my doorbell rang. I shoved away from the desk to see who was at my door. I almost died when I saw Briggen standing there with my baby. When my baby saw that it was his mommy under all this dyed red hair, he started bouncing up and down, squirming to get out of his daddy's arms.

"Anthony! Look at you!" I cooed as I took him out of his arms and started raining kisses all over his face. "Mommy's booga bear is getting so big. I miss you." I turned my back to Briggen as he came in and shut the door. Then it dawned on me that I didn't tell this nigga where I lived. I turned and asked him, "How did you find me?"

"Don't worry about it," he snapped, as his eyes darted all around my new condo. I didn't have much furniture, but it was still nice. "What did you do to your hair?" he had the nerve to ask me.

"Don't worry about it."

BRIGGEN

Her hair was bright red as if she was on some Nicki Minaj, Lil' Kim shit. She had on red stilettos, a black miniskirt and a black top hugging her big belly. I couldn't believe what I was staring at. Anthony started crying.

"Is he hungry?" She began examining all over our son's body as if he she was looking for signs of abuse or some shit.

"No. It's his nap time. We've been out all morning."

"Let me take him to his room and lay him down."

I followed her upstairs into Anthony's bedroom where she laid him down onto his bed. It wasn't decorated yet, but it had all of his things from the last house. As she tended to our son I took the opportunity to do a walk-through of her hideaway. The first stop was, naturally, the bedroom. I swore that if I saw any signs of any nigga's shit other than mine in there I was going to put my foot all up in her ass. But there was no sign of any man's gear . . . not even mine. The bitch obviously left my shit at the other house.

I then went to the other bedroom which had nothing but new clothes spread all around. I inspected the hall bathroom and went downstairs into the kitchen. I opened the door to the backyard, looked out and stepped out onto her patio. I stayed there until she finally came downstairs.

"He was sleepy. Thanks for bringing him by. But seriously, how did you find me? I told no one where I was, not even Keeta."

I remained standing on the patio with my back to her.

"Briggen, I asked you a question!"

"I'ma ask you some questions. Where's my shit? You left all of my shit at the other house?" I turned around and faced her, "Why are you so worried about how I found you? You got more shit to hide?" I waited for a response. "And how are you going to just up and move and not tell me? Look at your hair. And why are you walking around the house dressed in stilettos and shit like you on TV? When was the last time you looked at yourself in the mirror?"

"I am not your child, Briggen, or any of them other bitches you got cast under your spell. Remember, it was your secret lifestyle that caused our home to get shot up. You should be glad I left when I did. And how are you going to leave my child with Mia? She said you were gone for days and you didn't even check on him."

"Where was his mother? Where were you, Shan? Let me answer that. My son's mama was out running the streets, shopping, throwing parties and robbing dope dealers. You like your new lifestyle, don't you? You done turned into Miss Real Housewife of the Streets all of a sudden. You need to come back down to earth. You have a baby, you're pregnant and you're not street-smart. Those streets are going to kill you, Shan."

"Don't be leaving my son with strangers, Briggen."

"Then you keep him. I don't know what the fuck is wrong with that head of yours. I'm out of here."

"I have a show tomorrow night. You have to take Anthony with you." She was following me to the front door.

"No, you got so much mouth. You keep him, since you are so worried about who I'm leaving him with." She grabbed my arm, and I pushed her back. She came at me swinging.

"I hate you!" she screamed.

I was ducking her blows until I grabbed both of her arms and held them behind her back.

SHAN

"What in the hell has gotten into you?" my husband screamed in my face. "What did *I* do to you? Not a damn thing," he ranted, and he was right, for the most part. He held my arms behind my back. I was trying to break loose. I had to go get Anthony. He was not leaving this house without taking him. I had a show to promote.

"I'm not turning you loose until you tell me what your problem is. I will admit you into the mental hospital if you don't tell me something that makes sense."

By the tone in his voice I could tell he was worried about me. And right then I broke down and started crying. "I'm not crazy, Briggen. Is that what you think? I have to be crazy to get your attention? That's why I hate you."

"Why do you hate me, Shan? You are not making any damn sense."

"Because."

"Because what? You got my full attention, talk to me."

"I don't want to talk. Let me go."

"Not until you tell me why you hate me. Because I damn sure don't hate you. I love you more than anything."

"No, you don't, Briggen, and you know it. Don't insult me like that."

"Yes, I do. And you know it. Why do you think I tried my best to give up everything for you? The hustle, the bitches . . ."

"Don't even try it!" I screamed. I didn't want to hear that.

"That's why you acting like I have to take some of the responsibility because you know it's true." He kissed me on the neck.

"Don't kiss me like that."

"Like what?" He tried kissing me again. "Like this?" He kissed and sucked on my neck and just like that, my dumb ass was beginning to melt.

"Stop it." He let my arms go, and I used the opportunity to push him away. He grabbed me, walking me to the couch. "Get off of me! Stop it! You lied to me!"

I kicked his leg, broke away and headed for the stairs.

"Shan!" I heard him yell, then he was right behind me. I don't know why I was trying to get away from him. I ran the best I could in stilettos. When I reached the top of the stairs I ran right into my bedroom, out of breath and damn near lost my balance. I tried to close the door, but he pushed it open so hard, I almost hit the floor.

"Briggen! What are you doing? Stop it." He grabbed me and threw me onto the bed and got on top of me. "You're messing up my clothes, mooove . . . Brig! I have clients to go meet." I squirmed under him.

"Be still. I'm getting me some of this pussy today."

"I don't think so! You better go fuck the ho you just left."

"Uh-uh. I want to fuck this ho right here." His hot breath met my neck as his soft lips followed. He was wearing me down.

"I'm not a ho! You are the ho." He had my legs open and his dick out. There was nothing else needed to be said. The next thing I heard was my panties ripping. I squirmed a little bit, and then welcomed him inside me. "Daddy," I moaned, enjoying his deep strokes.

"What? Didn't I tell you I was going to fuck you today?" he asked as his dick slipped in and out of my wetness.

I didn't respond. I closed my eyes. As the sounds of our

moans filled the room, I was overcome by the emotions of both love and hate.

"I miss this pussy," he whispered between the soft kisses he was placing on my lips.

"I miss this dick. I still hate you though," I responded while sucking his lips.

"Why?" He plunged deeper.

"Ahhh . . . Because I still love you." At that moment I was like, fuck it! His dick was speaking loud and clear, and my pussy was listening.

"Brig—oh shit! I still love you," I told him again.

"Of course you do."

Bastard.

CHAPTER TWENTY

DARK

Sharia had called me over to her crib to share some news with me. She told me this was definitely something that she had to tell me face-to-face.

"Aiight. You got me here, so what's up?"

"Nigga, please. Don't act like I just want you here to be all up in your face. Sit down." She pushed me onto the sofa. "That number you gave me to look up? The Joy girl? She is Cisco's wife of seven years. I knew something was strange about that nigga, but I couldn't put my finger on it. That nigga lived a double life." She hit her palm with her fist, pacing back and forth.

"Seven years?" I blurted.

"Seven, cousin. But that ain't the clincher. The bitch works for a Congressman Duffy. So if she wants to make trouble, she can. And from the way you said she sounded, she probably already started."

"Man, fuck that bitch! I'm the one who can make trouble," I reminded Sharia.

"Cuz, listen to me. That nigga Cisco kept a list and she has it."

"What kind of list?"

"Nigga, you know damn well what kind of list, and if she has it, that shit could get in the wrong hands. My gut is telling me that we can't take this bitch lightly." It was obvious this new bitch had Sharia shook, but I wasn't beat.

"Maaan, fuck that bitch and her list! Shit, I got a list too, and she on it. And from what I see, her name is coming up next," I said, then smiled.

"Look, you do what you got to do. I told you, so my hands are clean. This shit ain't no game, Dark." She looked at me with concern in her eyes. "I'ma catch up with you later. I have an errand to run so make sure you lock up before you leave out."

She left me sitting there looking at the walls and listening to my thoughts. I had several loose ends to tie up before I met with The Consortium. But one thing I was sure about: the shit she just revealed confirmed that all my shit was coming together.

SHAN

I was so excited. Tonight was going to be another huge success to add to the entertainment portion of my résumé. It was Halloween, and I had rented this mansion outside of the city. It was supposed to be a Halloween costume bash but it looked more like a Pimp-of-the-Year contest. So many niggas came dressed as pimps, and bitches came dressed as hoes. Where was the originality? I mean, after all, it was 2011. Pimps didn't even dress like that anymore. Standing at the front door, I saw several Nefertitis and there was a Little Bo Peep. I mean, who wants to dress up like a sheepherder? Speaking of which, I saw an Italian couple dressed like Snooki and Pauly D from the *Jersey Shore,* Otis the security guard from *Martin,* Hoda, Spider-Man, Steve Jobs, Kanye West, Jay-Z and Lil Wayne. There were twenty niggas dressed like The Mack, Lady Gaga, Prince, the Dali Lama and about five Foxy Browns, four Nicki Minajs and for myself, I kept it simple. I was a Catholic schoolgirl, with two pigtails, barrettes, and Mary Janes. My main concern was that everybody looked as if they were having a good time. Local TV and several magazines were present, snapping pictures and conducting a few interviews. I was in my moment, that was until I saw Briggen and Mia heading up the walkway without wearing costumes. The smile I had been wearing up to that point instantly dropped from my face. My nostrils flared as hot flashes surged through my body. I started to say something, but instead, I turned and disappeared into the house real quick.

BRIGGEN

I was surprised when Mia and I pulled up in front of this haunted mansion. There was valet parking, and cars were everywhere. As I stepped over dead bodies to get to the front door, I saw that the spot was packed. I couldn't front. I was somewhat impressed.

"Damn, baby, she is serious about this party stuff," Mia said.

I spotted Shan standing there with a big smile plastered on her face. But when she saw me and Mia, she frowned, turned and walked away.

"Mia, let me talk to Shan. We are not staying long, so don't get lost," I warned her.

I'm sure she saw the lust in my eyes. That's why she gave me a look that would kill a nigga, but I didn't give a fuck.

I headed to where I hoped Shan was going. When I spotted her, I was into her little Catholic schoolgirl persona. She wore the short skirt, little socks, patent leather Mary Jane shoes and two cute and sexy little curly pigtails. I was turned on.

"Shan! Shan!" I called her. When she turned around I saw her breasts threatening to burst out of the blouse she had on. Her two red pigtails with red ribbons tied around them swung as her head snapped back. She waved me off and kept on walking. I followed her through the crowd and into the kitchen. Then I grabbed her hand.

"Hey, young lady, what's your name?" I asked her.

"What are you doing here with your bitch?" she asked dryly.

"Why are you giving me a hard time, as if we didn't just fuck the other day? Plus, it's a costume party, and I bought a ticket just like everybody else."

"Then where is your costume?"

"I just came to check things out. I don't need a costume for that," I said as I massaged her hand.

"Mmmhmmm. What's up, Briggen? I know you are not here to just check things out. So what's up?" She was all skeptical and shit, but I ignored that and tried to get my mack on.

"They say that you little Catholic girls are fast. Look at you all pregnant and shit. You ever been out with a hustler before?"

She stood there looking me up and down as if she was trying to figure me out. Then she said, "Been there and done that. You see my belly, don't you?" She played along pulling her hand away from mine as she grabbed a green lollipop out of the candy dish sitting on the kitchen counter. She unwrapped it, keeping her eyes on me and began to suck it seductively. "Now what can I do for you . . . Mr.? What did you say your name was?"

"The name is Mr. Thompson. And yours?"

"I'm Shan. Is that your girlfriend you were with?"

"Don't worry about that. How old are you?"

"Don't worry about that," she shot back.

The way she made her lips wrap around that lollipop reminded me of how she sucked my dick. "Can I take you for a ride in my car?"

"Depends on what you're driving. And why we gotta go for a ride? What do you want from me?"

"I'm driving an Aston. You ever rode in one of them before?"

"An Aston? That would make the girls at my school very, very jealous."

"It sure would. So come on. Let me show it to you." I grabbed her hand again, ready to take her to my ride to get my joint waxed.

"Slow down, playboy. I'm not *that* concerned with what you are driving. I'm more concerned with what you're working with. If you ain't working with the right size stick, I will be disappointed."

I took her hand and guided it up and down my stick. "Is my stick big enough for you to handle?"

She wouldn't turn it loose. "Yeah, I can call you Big Daddy. But damn, I don't think I can make it to your ride." She had that fuck-me-right-now look on her face that I knew so well. She grabbed my waist and pulled me closer. "Show me this Aston," she teased.

"Hold up, Shorty. I need to make sure you are ready for me." It was my turn to play hard. "You sure you can handle all of this?"

"What do you mean by that?" She pretended she didn't know what I was referring to.

I placed my hand on her thigh and slid it up that short miniskirt she was wearing so well. To my surprise she didn't have on any panties. "Oh, you *are* a fast one." Her juices were already sticking to her thigh. I slid two fingers up in her pussy as she unzipped my pants. I took my fingers out and sat her on top of a stool. "Why the fuck you ain't got no panties on?" Our game was over. I was done playing. I had an attitude, but my dick was still hard as hell, and I needed to get some relief.

"Because I knew Big Daddy was coming to see me," she purred as she grabbed my dick and placed it at her hot wet opening.

"Bullshit, Shan." Just as I plunged my dick up in her, Mia barged into the kitchen.

"Brig—"

"I'll be right there, Mia," I snapped.

Shan wrapped her legs around my waist and started riding my dick.

Mia looked at me up in Shan's pussy and lost it, "Fuck you, Briggen!" she screamed. "You and this bitch deserve each

other! I hope your black ass got a ride home! I'm outta here."
She hawked and spit on the floor.

I wanted to give a fuck, but I couldn't. Shan was fucking
me only as Shan could do.

"Oooh, Big Daddy," Shan moaned, as if Mia had not just
thrown a temper tantrum. "I'm lovin' what you working with."

"Shan, answer me. Why the fuck you ain't got no panties
on? What nigga up in here were you planning on giving my
pussy to?" I was still on that shit as I slid in and out of her
pussy, fucking her harder.

"Nigga, please," Shan mumbled. "We barely fucked twice
in the last four or five months, and you gonna choose now
to be on some macho bullshit? Shut up and fuck me!"

"You ain't got no panties on, and your pussy was all wet.
What the fuck am I supposed to think?" I was mad, but the
pussy was feeling too good for me to pull out. Instead, I
started fucking her faster.

"I don't give a fuck what you think. Somebody was gonna
fuck this pussy tonight, it just happened to be you." At that
moment Shan started cumming. I was so mad, I tried to
pull out to keep her from enjoying herself, but her legs were
locked around the back of my legs, and she had both hands
squeezing my ass. I couldn't move if I wanted to. I was stuck
there watching her facial expression as she skeeted all over
my dick.

"What the fuck you mean, somebody was gonna fuck this
pussy?" I asked all out of breath.

"Let me find out, my baby is jealous," she said releasing
me from her grip. "Shit, I needed that," she said, continuing
to ignore my bitching. Her blouse had popped open, and I

couldn't help but lean over and angrily suck her tits and bite at her nipples. The shit was good. I had forgotten what I was missing. What the fuck was I thinking? Pregnant pussy was the best.

Even though I was still hard, I stood back and tucked my dick away. "I'm not going to ask you again." At that moment, I thought I heard gunfire but wasn't sure because there was so much commotion mixed with the loud music.

Shan pushed me back. "Did you hear that?" she asked, confirming what I knew I had heard. She got down off the stool and fixed her clothes. "I know these niggas ain't crashing my party! I know they not crashing it!" She started yelling and looking as if she was about to spazz out over her damn party. "They're coming after me, Briggen."

"Something's going on. That was gunfire." I grabbed her. "Stay your ass back here. Stay, Shan."

"I'm not a dog, Briggen. You stay!" she said still trying to pull her clothes together.

When she saw me pull out my gat, she knew it was no longer a game.

JOY

I sat there conflicted and afraid, waiting on the person that Cisco instructed me to turn this list over to. I looked over it a million times, and I still couldn't believe that he was involved with these people. His list was getting ready to change my whole life. Not only was my husband's killer going to come to justice, I stood to receive millions of dollars. Cisco was going to keep his promise to me from the grave that I would never have to worry about how me and the kids were going to eat.

DETECTIVE SHERMAN

"Hello, Mrs. Whittaker," I said as I approached the table in the conference room of the DEA's office. She turned around with glossy eyes, and her nerves seemed to be frazzled as she stood up to shake my hand.

"Please, call me Joy."

I gave her a quick shake, and then sat down.

"I just want all of this to be over," she stated as she slid the paper across the table.

"Don't worry. I made a promise to your husband that I would take care of this for him."

"So when do I get my money?"

"It will be deposited in your account by midnight," I said as I opened the folded paper. When I saw the names on it I could have choked on my own saliva.

"Have you found my husband's body?"

"Not yet. But we are on it."

As Joy got up from the table she looked me in the eyes and said, "I may be a widow in pain, but trust and believe, I am not a fool. That list has been duplicated several times, along with the names of cops, informants and witnesses. Don't fuck with me, detective. And I want my husband's body. He deserves a decent funeral," she threatened before walking away.

CHAPTER TWENTY-ONE

SHAN

I heard all of the commotion, and it felt as if my bones were shaking. I didn't know if I wanted to stay in the kitchen or run out the back door. But I did know that my party was ruined. That's why I hated these Detroit niggas. They never just come out and have a good time. Just as I decided to run out of the back door, the kitchen door swung open and this big dude wearing black sweatpants and a hoodie came barging in. His baseball cap was down low on his face.

"Your name Redbone, right?" he asked me. I was so scared, I couldn't part my lips. When I wouldn't answer, he asked, "You the one on the posters, right? Yeah, you her." He pulled out a gun and came toward me. I started screaming.

"Don't scream now, bitch! I didn't hear yo' ass scream when you jacked Cisco's package. Look at me, bitch." He took off his hat. "Do I look familiar?" My eyes grew as I thought back to the day I saw him. "Yeah, you do remember me, bitch.

You looked me dead in the face when you reached over me and took those bags. That was a major loss for me." He put the gun to my head.

"I got your money. I got your dope," I stammered, scared for my life as well as the one life of my unborn child.

"Where is it?"

"It's at my house. Please don't shoot me."

"Bitch, the only thing I want is your life." I heard him release one into the chamber.

The kitchen door flew open. Talk about captain-save-a-ho. Briggen was right on time. I had never been so happy to see my husband. I was having one of them life-flashing-across-your-eyes moments that people say you have right before you die. Brianna, Peanut, my baby and the one in my stomach.

The sound of gunfire snapped me out of my trance. Tears immediately started to run down my cheeks. Briggen had stepped in, arm raised like it was nothing and let one off. The nigga's arm flew up, and his gun went off, hitting the ceiling. He could have shot me, I thought. This lame's blood splattered all over me before I dropped to the floor, screaming again. But this time, I couldn't hear myself, and then everything went black.

JANAY

Me and Boomer were sitting in Tiny's living room. To think I was ever considering giving Nick some play. He let Tiny turn him out just like that. She was able to be all in his phone and gave us Nick's connect number. His name was Bronson. Boomer and I were going to take a trip to Canada to see him.

I gave her an envelope filled with ten stacks and stood up. "Thanks, girl. Your work is done."

"Aww, are you sure?" she pouted. "I'm practically living with the nigga. You want anything else? I mean, name it, because I could get it."

"Nope. That will do it for now." I gave her a hug and we left.

I was tripping because he told her that Briggen's wife did stumble on Cisco's package and money. He said the girl kept all of the money but gave him the dope. He had sold it all but only gave her half the money and he used the other half to put toward what he needed to establish himself with this new connect. So, in my mind, I didn't see no other way to deal with him but to take him out. He also shared with her his plan to take over and to get everyone warring with each other. *Damn*. I would have never pegged this nigga for the type to get pussy whipped . . . But pillow talk? He really ain't a "G" after all. Boomer said I needed to be in his spot. Pulling moves like that, the nigga had to know that his days were numbered. It was time to put all this shit out on the table. And because of that I had called for an immediate sit-down, and everybody had showed up except for Cisco.

"Your boss don't have the respect to show up at an emergency meeting?" Boomer asked Dark.

"Like I said, he ain't my boss, and he's on vacation," Dark answered snidely.

"Janay, this better be good. I left the golf course to come here," Born said causing everyone else to start bitching and screech, "Golf?"

"Yeah, muthafuckas, *golf*," he shot back.

"If it wasn't urgent I wouldn't have called everyone," I snapped.

Everyone sat down and got situated. After I called the meeting to order, to my surprise, in walked Nick.

"This muthafucka," I heard Six-Nine mumble.

"Y'all called a meeting to discuss me, and I wasn't invited? *Tsk. Tsk.* Shame on all of you." He took his time looking at everyone in the room. He had the floor, and he knew it.

"What the fuck you mean, shame on you? You're the one who ain't playing fair," I told him.

"Fair? Girl, this is *The Game*. And you do whatever it takes to win. It's about winning."

"We will see about that. This meeting is for us to do a little housecleaning. Have a seat, Nick," I replied nice and calm as I waited for him to sit down. I looked around the room and focused on Dark. "Didn't your boss get the memo? We needed him here. Like Boomer said, the meeting is mandatory."

Dark looked around the room at everyone. Then he said, "I'm glad this meeting was called because I have an update. Cisco is no longer in charge of this family."

"You know the rules, youngin'. Cisco has to appoint you, and he should have been here to do that," Boomer told him.

"Cisco is gone. He won't be coming back. Everyone here should be able to read between the lines." He shut up so we could digest what he had just said. "But that ain't the issue at hand." He leaned in and sipped on his drink.

"Then what is the issue?" Six-Nine asked him. "I told him he needed to keep a close eye on you. It's obvious that he didn't listen."

"He obviously didn't," Dark said to Six-Nine. "The issue is, apparently before he left us, he made a list with all of our names on it. The nigga gave the list to his wife and told her if she didn't hear from him within a particular amount of time to get the list to the appropriate people."

"Appropriate people, meaning who?" I asked.

Dark peered over at me and smirked as if to say, "You dumb bitch."

"Appropriate people, as in law enforcement," Born answered my question.

What? I ain't going back to prison, I thought, trying my best to keep my game face on in front of The Consortium. "And why would he do that?"

"He obviously did listen to you, Six," Boomer said.

"A list? Are you sure?" I didn't want to believe what I was hearing. "How do we know your informant ain't on no snake shit?"

"I spoke to her. That informant is his wife. She called my cell phone and told me. She was distraught, and I can only suspect the worst from her," Dark said. "Also she works for this congressman named Duffy."

Well, I'll be damned. Cisco was married to some disgruntled chick that has our names on some damn list, who works for a congressman who was trying to move up. And to make shit worse, the list would be an asset to this congressman's career and whoever else could benefit from it politically, I was sure. But I still couldn't figure out how the fuck we let something as crucial as that slip right past us.

"Anybody else have something to share with us before we discuss why I called you all here?" I had to get back to the issue that was at the top of my list, and that was Nick.

Briggen let out a chuckle. "So, that means that Cisco is gone, and you are the nigga responsible for sending dude to my wife's party? She's pregnant, man!" Just that quick Briggen looked as if he was foaming at the mouth. Dark was up and out of his seat, they had their guns drawn on each other. I never saw uncle Boomer move so fast in all my life.

"Not here, youngins! We are in a hotel. Y'all settle this on y'all's time!"

"You damn right, I'ma settle this shit." Briggen flashed a smile at Dark as he put his gun away.

A smile? That's a dangerous nigga in my book. Even though they both sat down, Boomer remained standing over where they were. I had gotten word that they were burning and shooting each other's shit down all over the city. For us to supposedly be working together on the same team, I couldn't see it. These niggas were all crazy.

"Anybody else got something?" I asked. And since no one spoke up, I said. "Okay, other than Melky's people trying to run me off the road I want everyone to know that Nick here has an announcement to make." I turned to Nick. "I'm glad you decided to join us, and I'm glad that you are willing to give us an update. The floor is yours."

Nick stood up and scanned the room. "Relax, everybody. What I'm about to say ain't all that bad. I've been serving you all for quite some time." He turned toward Dark. "Before Cisco left us, he made a failed attempt to do what I've managed to accomplish. You all didn't appear to be mad at him, so I expect the same cooperation." He paused. "I want to be the connect, the number one supplier. And I hope that business can continue as normal. I—"

"How can it continue as normal when you raised the price twenty percent? I think that's kind of steep," Born interrupted. "Don't y'all?"

Everyone started talking at the same time.

"Hold up. Hold up, everybody," Nick stated calmly. "I took the percentage into consideration. I did. And I've decided to cut it to fifteen percent," he said, and then sat down.

In my opinion, fifteen percent was being greedy. I couldn't wait to talk to this Bronson guy myself. Through all of this, I did notice that Briggen was shooting Nick daggers throughout the meeting. That was a surprise because I thought they are boys. There was more conversation between everyone, but I had blocked them all out. I felt as if my back was up against the wall. For this shit to be worth my while, I needed to be at the top of the food chain, which meant moving into dangerous territory by trying to undercut Nick and go to his connect. But once I did, there would be no turning back.

BRIGGEN

I was up and out of there shortly after Nick made his announcement. I couldn't wait to have a sit-down with Mr. G. He had assured me that whenever I was ready to make a move to let him know.

I had to go check on Shan. She was still very much shaken up so the little flashy party-promotin' girl wouldn't even leave the house. I tried to tell her that this shit wasn't no game. Now she seemed to understand. She was lucky she didn't lose her life. Even though four people were shot, no one died except for the one nigga I popped.

I pulled up in front of Mia's. She was standing in the doorway. I rolled the window down. "I gotta check on Shan, but I got your text to stop by. What's up?" She came to the car with an attitude, of course. I hadn't been back to her house since the Halloween fiasco.

"I received a message from your boy behind the wall."

"And?"

"He said that some nigga named Dark killed your brother. He said he's sure that you know him."

I sat there thinking about what she had just told me, and it all made sense. Dark was too smart for his own good. He got with Cisco, learned the ropes, got in with The Consortium, rubbed shoulders with the players and took Cisco out. But who had him do Forever? And why?" That was still unclear to me. And why was this nigga just telling me this. I rolled my window up and pulled out of the driveway. Too much shit was going on for me.

CHAPTER TWENTY-TWO

SHAN

I lay on the couch crying and had been in my bed for the last few days. I never had a gun to my head before and never wanted to experience that again. I was still waking up in cold sweats. What also devastated me was the fact that my party ended up being a total failure. Because of all of the drama that went down, the people who had hired me to do their events had pulled out. Every last one of them muthafuckas cancelled. As a promoter, I was finished before I ever got started.

I heard Briggen's truck pull into the driveway. He had been keeping a close eye on me. I was so glad that I had enough sense to not give the police my new address. Our next-door neighbor said that they had been coming by our other house every day. I couldn't have cared less.

"Shan, you awake?" I heard Brig's voice coming toward where I lay. "Hey, baby, I'm glad to see that you got out of that bed. But now you moved from the bed to the couch. That's progress," Briggen said to me as he leaned down and kissed me on the forehead.

"I spoke to Nick today." As soon as those words left my lips, I knew I had fucked up.

Briggen started breathing heavy. "Why in the fuck are you calling that nigga?" his mood going from sugar to shit.

"He owes me money, Briggen. We had a deal. I want my money, that's why."

"You want your money or do you just want to be in the nigga's face?" Briggen yelled.

"He owes me money. I just want my money!"

"Your money? That's why you are in this predicament now. And just so you know, you got all you gonna get out of that nigga. He done sold all of your dope as soon as you gave it to him. Don't you think if he was going to pay you he would have done so by now?"

I wasn't going to answer that because this was my business. Briggen could think whatever he wanted to think.

"Shan!" He interrupted my thoughts. "The nigga beat you for your money, so let it go. I don't want to hear about it no more. And I don't want you talking to him." Briggen sounded as if he was threatening me.

"He wouldn't beat me."

"Well, he did." Briggen looked at his cell, and then rushed into the kitchen and picked up the wall phone. He dialed and turned his back to me. I still didn't understand all of this gangsta and drug stuff. Are the money and drugs more important than your word to your family?

"Shan, I'ma need you to get yourself together." Briggen

burst out of the kitchen, urgency in his voice. "Start by getting up off that couch. I need you to do what you need to do to get back to your old self ASAP. I need you to go to Keeta's and get our son. I need to get y'all out of here. After you pick him up, I'm sending y'all away." After he said that his phone rang. He answered with a few one-liners, and then hung up.

"Away?" I tossed the blanket off me and sat up, feeling more fear than when I had a gun pointed at my head. "What do you mean away? Who was that on the phone?" He was making me nervous.

"Don't worry about that. Just concern yourself with getting everything together. I'll let you know more when I get back," he told me as he snatched the keys off the coffee table and rushed out the door.

BRIGGEN

I was ninety-nine percent sure that shit was about to hit the fan. I had just hung up the phone with my man. He said that a list was given to the Feds with the names, numbers and a few addresses of each member of The Consortium. Cisco's wife apparently had some serious connections up high and she was angry and determined to avenge her husband's death.

I was faced with the decision to walk away from all this shit or stay and fight, which I did before, and won. But at the same time you gottta know when to walk away. And the more I thought about it, the more my heart was telling me that it was time to walk away.

SHARIA

Things were moving at a rapid-fire pace. All of the news stations were running the same story meaning that our run was over. I kept the news on Channel 7.

> *"This is Michel Brant, live from Channel 7 News. I'm here in front of the Federal Court Building where officials just brought in reputed crime lord, Nicholas Powell. According to inside sources, there had been an ongoing investigation for the last four years of several drug rivals in the area. However, officials reveal that they never knew the mystery man behind it all, until now. And that mystery man is allegedly Mr. Vincent Garibaldi. Investigators say that Nicholas Powell has been the silent partner of drug kingpin, Mr. G. AKA Vincent Garibaldi.*
>
> *An anonymous tip came through and federal officials raided several warehouses allegedly owned by Mr. Powell, including some property in Palmer Park and one right here in the city. Officials also say they have confiscated nine million dollars in cash along with pounds of heroin and cocaine with a street value of seven million dollars. Investigators say that this is only the tip of the iceberg and are anxiously waiting to see what will unfold. Again, this is Michel Brant and I'm live here—"*

I turned the TV off and fumbled around for my cell. I had to get a hold of Dark. Our time had run out.

JANAY

I flipped from Channel 7 News. I was done with the game.
It was no longer the same. I used to only participate when
I felt it was necessary because my dad would handle everything. Me trying to run our family myself was not going
to happen. Doing those twenty or so months, believe it or
not, just about knocked all of the taste out of my mouth
for this shit. Niggas were more cutthroat than ever. Bronson wouldn't meet with us unless Nick was present so all
the work Tiny put in was for nothing. There was no honor
among thieves as it was back in the day.

Me and Boomer had a long talk last night. We were on
the same page. He said he wasn't up for going to war with
Mr. G and figured it was time to throw in the towel. I was so
relieved to hear him say that. He had no idea. I had planned
to move to Charlotte with him to run his three gas stations.
He told me that while he and my dad were on the run they
made millions stealing gas. Yes, gas! I had never even heard
of or would have thought up no shit like that. He said they
invested in one gas station and never paid for the gas. It didn't
matter who delivered it. They would resell it and never pay
for it. And they bought stolen gas trucks. After they made all
the money they could make and had a hand in putting The
Consortium together that's when my dad said it was time for
him to turn himself in and get us out.

So with the millions upon millions of dollars he had
stacked, why in the hell did my dad want me to be in the
drug game? Boomer said only my dad could answer that for
me. He said as for him, he didn't want that for me and he
and my dad argued about it often. But when it all boiled

down to it, I was my father's daughter. But I told Boomer that I could make my own decisions and I was deciding to get out, whether my father liked it or not.

These were critical times and except for Dark and Nick, we were all seated around Boomer's dining room table.

"I'm not going anywhere," Six-Nine said. "What proof is a damn list? Besides Nick, we don't even know who's on it. We could be running for nothing."

"I'm out," Briggen said backing up from the table as if the table was hot to the touch. "I'm not waiting on muthafuckas to run down on my ass. I've pimped this game for all I could, and I have no regrets."

"Looks like it will be more for us." Born looked over at Six-Nine. Then he looked at me. "Baby girl, if your daddy was here, he'd be looking at this as a challenge."

"Well, he ain't here, is he? Me and Boomer, we out. I wish y'all much success. Uncle Boomer, I gotta go pick up Marquis." I got up from the table and looked around at the faces of what was and what was to come. Then I walked out of that dining room feeling brand new. Grabbing my Gucci bag and keys I was ready for a new life. I didn't even feel this invigorated when I stepped out of the prison.

My car was parked up the street, and I felt so free I felt like skipping. That was, until I saw that same Escalade that ran me off the road. I turned around and started running for the house.

"Booooooom . . . er!" I screamed. "Booooooom . . . er!" I heard gunfire, and then I felt a burning sensation shoot through my whole body. I was forced flat down on the ground. I was hit. I was shot.

My uncle's door flew open, and I heard footsteps, cursing

and yelling go by me and more gunfire. The war had officially begun.

DARK

After four days we thought that we had finally found out where Joy lived. When I got the call that Nick had got popped . . . hearing that shit threw my concentration and focus on the job at hand. It appeared from the way that this nigga was moving around he was invincible, but now I begged to differ.

If Cisco gave this bitch the ins and outs of who everybody was, then she must really know some people. Either that, or Cisco was a fuckin' plant. The very thought of this nigga being a snitch or a cop began putting the whole picture into perspective. When you look at it, why, all of a sudden, was everything unfolding since his disappearance? Who was Cisco? If his wife was that high up, how could he be so deep in the dope game? The shit wasn't adding up for me and I knew this bitch had to go.

"What's up, boss man? You ready to do this or what?" Mook obviously sensed my sudden mood change.

"Let me think about it for a few minutes." As far as I knew, that bitch could have surveillance all around her. They could've been waiting for us to strike. For all I knew, they could have put her up to calling me. If Cisco was an undercover agent the whole time, then that bitch had more than names. We had been doing some real grimy shit for the last year, and my name was behind it all. I was stuck. What if I was being paranoid? What if I allowed it to stop me from removing a witness? I paused to listen to my gut. My gut instinct warned me not to move, but I wasn't listening. A dead witness couldn't tell any lies.

"Aiight. Let's do this," I said, putting on my gloves and opening the car door.

NICK

Damn. I sat on a hard-ass bench retracing all of the moves I had made in the last six months. I didn't see any mistakes other than Tiny. The same way I fell for Brianna, I did with her. Bitches always got me fucked. I thought about Tiny's actions and our own conversation. Hell, other than her, I was so very confident in the moves I was making that I didn't even have a lawyer. It had to be them Consortium niggas. Once I told them I was the man, they started plottin' and hatin'. They wanted me to get out of the way. But like I said in the beginning, when the smoke cleared, they would see who the real boss was.

CHAPTER TWENTY-THREE

MIA

"I am so sick of this, Briggen. Why do you do this to me? Why do I allow you to do this to me?" I asked for the thousandth time as I watched him pack his things. "We have this same conversation over and over again."

"Mia, this is not the same conversation. You obviously ain't heard a word I just said." He came over to me and grabbed my shoulders. "Listen to me. It's time to go. Shit is about to get real ugly. I'm out, and I'm not suggesting to you or asking you. I'm telling you. Just like you followed me from Memphis to Detroit, follow me to the next city if you want to. We done raped this city for all we could. Pack your shit and go. It's not like you have any ties here. You don't have any children or anything."

"Oh, I don't, huh?" I was now into my feelings and emotions. This was not supposed to go down like this. This was supposed to be the happiest moment of my life. "I'm pregnant, Briggen. I'm pregnant with your child. How do you think you can just come lay up in my bed whenever it's convenient for you, and then quickly walk out of my life? Not anymore. I'm having your child, and you are going to give me the same respect you give Shan."

Briggen continued to pack but at a much slower pace. Yes, I dropped a bomb on him, and I knew it. Mr. Careful finally got caught with his dick exposed.

"Like I said, you need to pack your shit and get the fuck outta here," he told me, not bothering to acknowledge the bombshell that I just dropped on him.

"So, you are simply going to ignore what I just shared with you?"

"Mia, baby, I'm not ignoring you. I just need you to understand that these are dangerous times—the clock is ticking—and you need to get outta here."

"You selfish . . . self-centered . . . son of a bitch! You don't care about me at all, do you, Briggen?"

"You know the answer to that, Mia. This is not the time to be acting all insecure and shit."

"Briggen, answer me with a yes or a no. Do you care about me?"

"Mia, you know I do."

"Then take me with you. Take me and our child with you." I went over to him and wrapped my arms around his neck.

"Mia, you need to pack your shit and go. I gotta stay behind and tie up a few loose ends." He removed my arms from around his neck.

I couldn't believe him. I mean, this was the straw that broke this bitch's back. "Where are you sending Shan?"

"I'm not sure yet."

"Then send me wherever it is you are sending her. Don't just discard me like I'm a piece of trash. That shit ain't fair." I was crushed.

"Life ain't fair, Mia. I got your number. Stick around if you want to, but don't say I didn't warn you. I'll be in touch."

Those words felt like a stab to my chest. I couldn't believe he was so nonchalant about the whole thing. Before I knew it, I ran to the kitchen and snatched my .45 from the cabinet. When I made it back into the living room he was already at the front door. "Briggen, stop."

He turned and said, "I'll call you." His gaze then dropped to the gun in my hand. I finally got his attention. He stopped dead in his tracks and dropped his bags as he walked toward me with a look in his eyes that I had never seen before. It wasn't anger or hate but a look of worry and defeat. As he walked closer to me I gripped the handle tighter. I wanted to let him know that I was mad as hell and I wasn't gonna take his shit anymore! He stood in front of me not saying a word as I held the pistol to his chest.

"I'm sick of your shit, Mia!" he said as he gritted his teeth. "You want to kill me now? You got the heart, so do it. You really think I give a fuck? What? Okay, you pregnant? Fine! So the fuck what! Go on TV and tell the world. You finally got what you wanted and look at you, your ass still ain't happy."

I gasped.

He rolled his eyes up into his head. "Mia, what? You gonna shoot me? I don't have time for the drama bullshit. Hell, you don't have time for it neither. I told you to pack yur shit and go."

I raised the gun and pointed it at my temple. Briggen laughed in my face.

"You's a dumb bitch. So now you want to kill yourself? You really think I care whether you live or die? You was just some convenient pussy." He smirked, then continued. "And pregnant? You should be thanking me for getting you pregnant. Probably the best thing that ever happened to you. You got a gun, what? You hard now? Then pull the fuckin' trigger, Mia."

Listening to those words, my whole world came to an end and I was completely crushed.

"Do it, Mia, pull the fuckin' trigger. Pull it, bitch!" he encouraged me.

Oh, this nigga thinks I'm playing. Well, I'ma show him.

I squeezed the trigger.

BRIGGEN

"Mia, nooooooo!" I found myself yelling for nothing. It was too late. She was already slumped onto the sofa. Her beautiful face torn in half, looking like something out of a horror movie. I stood over her frozen in place. The only thing moving were the tears rolling down my cheeks. "Mia, noo, damn it!" I looked at her stomach. Was she really carrying my seed this time? Or was she trying to threaten me into staying here with her? The one eye that was still in place was looking right at me. The gun dangled from her hand.

Did I love her? No. Did I have love for her? Of course. I backed slowly away from her.

SHAN

It was hard but because of the seriousness in Briggen's tone and urgency in his voice but I got myself together and went and picked up my son. I then sat up all night waiting for him to come home. By the time he walked through the front door, I had dozed off on the couch.

"Did you get Anthony?"

"Yeah, I got him. What's going on?" I jumped up and followed him. I was dying to hear what we had to say and was loving seeing him sweat like this.

"Good. I want y'all to head for Canada first thing in the morning."

"What are you talking about?"

"I want y'all gone first thing in the morning."

"Canada? You want me to go to Canada with a baby? Without you?" I was acting as if I was petrified at the thought of doing such a thing.

"I'll be right behind you. No more than 48–72 hours. Just like how you laid low here in the house, you can do that at a hotel."

"But, Briggen, we talking about Canada, not this house or some resort. And what if you don't come?" I found myself, to my surprise, tearing up.

"What do you mean, what if I don't come? I'ma be right behind you." I could tell he was getting agitated with my questions.

"I'm scared, Briggen. Can't I wait for you?" I was the damsel in distress and he was loving it.

"No, baby, I got some loose ends that gotta be tied up. I need to know that you and my son are safe."

"What about Keeta? Can I take her with me?" I flopped back down onto the couch, I was ready to accept my Academy Award.

"Shan, stop it. You can do this." He got up in my face yelling. "We don't have time, so stop whining and get the fuck off that couch and let's go." He grabbed my arm, and I stood up. He went outside to the car and was bringing boxes and suitcases inside.

Yes, I had a passport. But I had never used it before. I wanted him to believe that my main fear was—what if he never comes?

So I asked, "Well, what about Mia? Can she come with me?"

When I said her name, he froze and dropped the suitcases to the ground. He sat down on the porch and then he did something that I never saw him do. He broke down and started crying. I didn't know what to do or what to say. He caught me completely by surprise. I stood there, scared to move.

A few minutes later, as if it never happened, he stood up and said, "Don't worry about Mia. Just pack your shit and be ready to leave in the morning. Mia's dead."

What the fuck? The thoughts ran through my mind about all this gangsta, drugs, and bitch shit, it had finally gotten to be a little too much for me.

"So what you gonna do? You gonna stick around or get your ass outta here?"

Mia was dead. I got the point.

DARK

I had been going around making moves and life was sweet. I had just come back from Oak Ridge. Them niggas was down there grindin' for real. They were gonna make me filthy rich. They handed over the cash and didn't ask any questions. I assured them that I would recommend to Cisco that they all get a promotion.

As soon as I pulled up to my bachelor's pad, I noticed the black narcs' vehicle across the street and the white van parked on the corner. I pulled out my cell and dialed Sharia.

"Yo, I'm back. What's been up?"

"Everybody lookin' for you. That's what's up."

"Everybody like who?"

"Baby mama."

"Who, Lisha?" I got excited.

"Who is that?" I could picture Sharia frowning up her mug on the other end. "I'm talking about Stephanie. She—"

"Psst. I keep telling you, that ain't my seed." I cut her off.

"Then who is Lisha?"

"Who else been looking for me?"

"That's all who actually knocked on my damn door. Undercover cars have been parked on the block just about every day. They got me scared to go outside."

"That's all they been doing is parking?"

"That's it."

"Hell, they could be out there for anybody."

"That's true, but I'm still paranoid."

I hung up and sat there. I wasn't going back to anybody's prison. I'd hold court in the streets before that would happen. Just then someone banged on my window, startling the fuck out of me. I didn't even see the mutha-fucka ease up.

"Mr. Hayes." He flashed his badge. "I'm Detective Bennett.

Can I speak to you for a minute?"

I rolled down the window. "Do you have a warrant?"

"No, not yet."

"Then what makes you think I'ma talk to you?"

"Because I know you ain't got nothing to hide."

"You damn right I ain't got nothing to hide. As a matter of fact, hop in. We can take a ride."

His partner had eased up behind him, and the one that was trying to get into my car went to talk to him. I already knew what I had to do. I cranked the ignition, threw my ride into drive and pulled off. I glanced in my rearview mirror, and the fools were running down the street to jump into their car. I whizzed by the van parked on the corner. It didn't move, but the black car was moving.

I hit my cell. "Yo, tell everybody to strap up. I'm coming through with a white and black on my tail. Let these mutha-fuckas know what's up!" I was leading them to my stomping grounds where I had foot soldiers down for whatever. I was doing eighty when a cruiser cut me off. The last thing I remembered was flipping into the air.

SHARIA

I got the call around midnight that they had Dark in custody, but he was in the hospital with a brain concussion and some broken bones. He was trying to outrun the police. There was nothing that I could do for him because I was packing up, waiting on my phone call to get out of dodge. I was ecstatic! It was finally payback time. However, I was trying to decide if I wanted to take a chance and go over to Dark's apartment.

He had money at his spot and if I didn't get it the Feds would. It was a chance I had to take.

BRIGGEN

I saw Shan and my son off. Shan was a nervous wreck and was fighting me every step of the way. I told her that I would be driving her ride to Canada to meet her. Thanks to the cameras I had installed I knew where she had hid her cash.

I was in the waiting area of the Trap Spot and Lucy, the chick who installed Shan's traps, was showing me where all the spots were in her truck. After I left there I headed over to my crib and pulled up into the garage. I began opening all of the traps so that I could unload the cash that she had stashed away but was coming up empty. I must have spent damn near two hours tearing the truck apart. Finally, I came across an envelope and I opened it. The red sheet of paper said:

> Briggen, "This is payback, muthafucka!"
> Shan aka Redbone and Li'l Anthony.

And she had kissed it with red lipstick.

"You fuckin' bitch!" I spat.

I couldn't mull over that shit. I had much bigger fish to fry. I then went to the stash spots in my house to grab my three moneybags. I had shit under the floorboards under my carpet in the bedroom, in the walls in the basement and in the attic. After I did that I was ready to pick up Sharia and hit the road when the doorbell rang. I went to the window and peeked out. There was a big fat white undercover at the door. He was by himself.

"Mr. Thompson, I know you're in there. Why don't you open up the door? I need to ask you a few questions. My partner is at your back door so you might as well open up. If you want me to call for backup I can do that as well."

Game recognized game and this was turning out to be my lucky day. I cocked my .380-caliber Beretta, stood behind the door and said, "Come in."

Big fat whitey came through the door. I put the burner to his temple.

"Thompson, you can put that away. Sherman already told me you were okay."

"Then why didn't you say that when you first made yourself known?" I put the burner away. Sherman was my man on the force. "So what are you here for? Where's Sherm?"

"I figured you would make this your last stop before you made your attempt to flee. And I must say your timing is perfect. Your admirers at the FBI are hot on your ass."

I laughed. "I'm not attempting to flee, I am fleeing."

"We know that."

"We?"

"Yeah, we. And we came by for our good-bye present. I've been camped out in front of your house for days. I need to take a shit and a bath. So, if you want to make it outta here, pay your dues. I'm here for Sherman's share as well. And you got my partner at the back door."

I didn't trust this muthafucka as far as I could smell his funky ass. So I kept my guard up and raised my burner. "Get Sherm on the phone," I ordered.

"C'mon, now. Do you think I'm bullshittin'?"

"Get Sherm on the phone."

I waited as he pulled his phone out of his jacket pocket. He dialed Sherm and went to talking. "Put him on speaker," I instructed. He did.

"Sherm, what's up? Where you at? Who is this muthafucka you sent here?"

"I have a family, man. I can't be sitting around waiting on you to show up. The flunkies with no lives can do that." Sherm started laughing. "Go ahead and take care of them. And get the fuck outta here." The phone disconnected and just like that he was gone. Meeting him was one of the most solid moves I had made in this game.

"I told ya," Fatty said.

"Grab one of those gray bags over there on the steps." Fatty wobbled over there with a big-ass smile on his face. He opened the bag as soon as he touched it. I watched as he shuffled the stacks around and barked, "What the fuck is this shit?" He turned and looked at me.

"What the fuck you talkin' about? Take the shit and get the fuck out. Greedy muthafucka. That's more than enough. Look, call Sherm. I don't have time for this bullshit."

"Oh, this is more than enough?" Fat Boy asked. He turned the bag toward me, and when I focused on the contents, I almost lost it. I rushed over to where he was standing and stuck my hand in the bag and came up with nothing but a handful of Shan's cheesin'-ass, redhead-wearin' promotional flyers. I dumped the bag onto the floor in a panic. I went for the other two which were filled with the same bullshit. This ho had to have at least 5,000 of them shits in there.

Fat Boy wasted no time. He grabbed his radio and barked, "Carter, come in now."

Carter burst through my back door, weapon drawn. Fat Boy was already calling for backup. Next thing I knew, I was facedown on my living room floor getting iron bracelets on my wrists.

"Hold up, Fat Boy! Wait a minute. Let me think about this shit."

"You facing kingpin charges, so you'll be able to think about it for at least twenty to thirty."

CHAPTER TWENTY-FOUR

NYLA

Ding . . . Dong . . .

I heard the doorbell ring as I was helping Tameerah out of the bathtub. I quickly wrapped her in a towel and ran downstairs. When I opened the door a young UPS guy handed me a big brown box with the prison address as the return label. My heart sank as I thought about this being the last of Forever's things. I signed for the package, took the box and closed the door. I quickly sat on the couch and began to rip the tape off.

As I ruffled through the contents my hands started to shake. I took his shirt into my hands and put it to my nose as the tears welled up in my eyes. I thought of the last time I saw him and the pain on his face when he told me not to come back to see him. As the tears ran down my cheeks I could hear my daughter calling me.

"Mommy, I don't see my clothes."

"Here I come," I yelled back then stood up, throwing the shirt over my shoulder. As I started to walk away a piece of paper fell from his shirt pocket. I bent over and picked it up. I then began unfolding it. The words leapt off the page as my mind began to race. Here it was, I thought, I would never get to the bottom of all this shit, and now Forever Thompson was speaking from the grave.

The letter read:

> *My Dearest Nyla,*
>
> *Baby, if you are reading this note then things are going exactly as I predicted they would. I need you to do this for me: go into the basement. You know that old sofa you kept trying to get me to throw out? Give it to my baby girl and tell her Daddy loves her. And then that picture frame of that 2 dolla bill on the wall in the bedroom, open it. That's a gift from me to you.*

I was confused. I read the note again and again. This was not like Forever to leave his daughter some damn old ass sofa, and me a fuckin' $2 bill! I kept asking myself, is he serious?

I ran upstairs and my baby asked, "Are you okay, Mommy?" She smiled at me as I laid her clothes out and turned on the TV to the Disney Channel.

"Yes, I'm fine, baby," I replied as I walked out of her room and into my bedroom and ripped that picture frame off the wall. I then headed straight downstairs to the basement to destroy that fuckin' ugly ass sofa. I stormed down the basement stairs and there it was . . . an old dusty, raggedy red and black suede sofa, the one he refused to let me throw away.

"I am gonna get rid of this piece of junk tonight, so help me God!" I said out loud.

I began pulling and pushing that sofa across the basement floor, but for this to be a love seat it was really heavy. But that wasn't going to stop me. I yanked the cushions out one at a time throwing them across the floor with such force, causing one of the zippers to bust. I grabbed the box cutters and wanted to slice it to shreds. But that's when I saw it.

I ripped a hole large enough for me to see the stacks of bills strategically wrapped and stacked in plastic and couldn't believe my eyes. I tore a large hole in the back of the sofa and saw more stacks of money. That's when I fell to my knees and cried. "Damn, baby . . ." Now I had to think about the picture frame. I stood up and went to pick up the picture frame off the floor, took it apart and a key fell out. The key was to a safety deposit box and there was a card that had a bank address.

JANAY

"Nay! Nay! You understand where I'm coming from, don't you?"

I heard my dad and yes, I understood him clearly, but I kept walking away. The only reason I came to visit him was to hear him tell me face to face that he didn't want me out of the game. And he did, he said it was because the legacy of our family name was more important.

"Nay." My dad caught up with me. "Don't leave until the visit is over. Don't you want to hang out another hour or so with your old pops?"

"What for, Daddy? So you can try to convince me that the legacy of our family name should be upheld in the underworld? Daddy, we are not royalty. You talking about the dope game. Illegal activity. Activity that won't preserve the family name. Look at me! I'm all bandaged up because I was shot. They tried to kill me. If I remain in the game, I might as well just kill myself, Daddy.

"This has to stop somewhere. I will either end up dead or sent back to prison. Is that what you want for me? I don't want it for myself. My mind is made up. I'm leaving with Boomer."

"To do what, Nay? Sit behind some cash register? Is that what you want? You want to punch some damn 9–5 time clock? I see for you much more than that. You can have that whole city, Nay. All you gotta do is do like I tell you."

"Daddy, I don't want the whole city. I don't care what it takes. I don't want to go back to prison and leave my son out here for somebody else, or worse, for the streets to raise. I'm leaving, Daddy. I'm out."

My mind was made up. My daddy was one of them niggas that would die in prison or watch the entire family die first before letting the game alone. Well, this time, he would be dying by himself because I was gone, no longer a puppet at the end of a string.

BRIGGEN

As I was being led out of my half-million dollar colonial home, I was in shock. Them bastards had me in a box. If they had their way, I knew that I would never again see the light of day. As Fat Boy opened up the back door, I noticed Sharia's Porsche pulling up beside us. I didn't want her to see me like this so I tried to turn around. But Fat Boy had my arm and was talking to his partner. Sharia jumped out the car, ran up to me and spit in my face. She then stuffed two dollars in my pocket and dusted off her hands.

"Bitch, you cold." I thought I heard Demetria's voice but nixed it off.

"Ma'am, you have to move away," Fat Boy said in the direction of Sharia's car.

I heard laughter and looked over at the car. Nyla rolled down her window and said, "How does it feel to get fucked?"

Sharia rushed to her car, jumped in and pulled up so that the back passenger window came down. Demetria yelled out as she fanned herself with a stack of bills, "When they bending you over, just relax your muscles, nigga!"

I wished more than anything that I could snatch that bitch Demetria up and pull her snitching tongue out of her mouth. "Fuck you, bitch! You was a mule and always will be one!"

"At least I'm a free one muthafucka!" she yelled at me.

All three of them bitches burst into laughter, and then they pulled off.

DARK

I ended up back at Benny Thrillz, where it all began for me. I was sitting by myself thinking about how everything came together in my favor. I couldn't believe that all them OGs came to me one by one like I was the pope and each one of them confessed their sins and rolled over on the other one.

But the kicker was the chick. She came bearing gifts. This bitch actually had a connect. Big Choppa was no joke.

Crystal walked in and sat down across from me. She pulled out an Arturo Fuente and lit it. She obviously was feeling herself. "I told Big Choppa that I've been waiting a long time for this." She said and took a puff.

"Not longer than me." I told her, "I done killed me many muthafuckas to get in this spot."

"We could go back and forth all day about who fucked up for us to get where we at, however time doesn't afford it. This is business and I had to step up to the plate and think like a man."

"Whatever it takes," I told her. Her connect was the missing piece to my puzzle. Me and Crystal sat down last night over a couple of drinks. I knew of her but didn't know her. She said that her dad, Choppa and uncle Boomer didn't think she was capable of being in the game. But since Janay stepped down, her father was desperate and had no one else to turn to. She seemed ready. However, her being ready or not was of no consequence to me. I just needed her connect. I started to say something else but I looked up and saw the rest of the crew walking through the door. Six-Nine was in front trailed by Born and Tareek.

"Yo, I heard you got fucked up! Legs, arms broke all that shit," Born said.

I had a cast on my arm, but that was it. "Nah, niggas be exaggerating. My arm was fucked up that was about it."

"I heard you ain't get no bail," Tareek added.

"If I ain't have no bail, I wouldn't be here now, would I?"

Each one took a spot at the table, and we started handling the business at hand. It was now a new day in Detroit. After

about an hour we managed to restructure the whole organization and everybody was happy with their new position.
We called the waitress over and ordered a round of drinks to
celebrate our new partnership.

As we sat talking, drinking and laughing, my phone rang.
I noticed it was that same 757 area code from when Cisco's
wife had called me. What the fuck could she want? Curiosity
had me by the balls so I hit the answer button.

"Hello," I said with apparent agitation.

"I heard you were doing real well for yourself, so I wanted
to send you a gift."

"Bitch, don't call my fuckin' ph—" she abruptly hung up.
"Hello?"

Everyone looked at me as the whole atmosphere of the
room changed. Six-Nine and Born were grinning. Before I
could digest what had just happened, three gunmen holding
semiautomatic rifles burst through the door wearing black
masks and began lighting shit up.

SHAN

As the plane lifted off the ground I was caught up in mixed
emotions of both relief and regret. For the first time in my
life, I had made all of my own choices. As I looked down
at my son who had finally conked out, it confirmed that the
move I had just made was the right one. I was free. Calvin,
or Briggen, no longer had a hold on me. And ironically, I
managed to walk away with everything I worked for—and his
shit too. I wish I could have been there to see the look on his
face when he checked my car. And even more so, when he

went for his stash and found out that it was gone too. And his dumb ass thought I was the stupid one.

I took a deep breath. The pressure made my ears pop. I never could get used to that feeling. Once the seat belt sign went off, I unfastened myself and went to the bathroom. When I returned to my seat the flight attendant asked, "Would you like anything to drink?" as she grabbed a cup from the stack.

"Yes, I'll have a glass of cranberry juice with ice." The woman poured my drink and passed it to me. "Thank you." She nodded and moved on to the next passenger.

"Are you okay?" the deep voice comforted my ears as his hand rested on my stomach.

"I'm good, thanks," I said, smiling back at him as I rested my hand on top of his. I wished that the baby were his.

"Can we toast to this?" he asked as he raised his glass.

I grabbed mine and raised it to his. "To Shan and Nick." We clinked glasses.

"And to all the muthafuckas that didn't see this coming," Nick added.

We both laughed and took a sip.

I sat back and closed my eyes, reveling in the moment. "*Payback Ain't Enough,* but it sure is a muthafucka."

READING GROUP QUESTIONS

1. What do you think was the cause of Shan's unexplainable behavior? Or was it explainable?

2. What was it about Briggen that allowed him to have such control over the ladies in his life?

3. Do you think Nick showing up or Forever's death caused the wedge between Shan and Briggen?

4. Is Big Choppa crazy, delusional or power hungry to want his daughter to take over his seat in the drug game?

5. Who do you think that mystery man was who Sharia had sex with?

6. Did you like anything at all about Dark?

7. Did you foresee Shan tricking Briggen?

8. What was your reaction to Briggen's response when Mia told him she was pregnant? What was your reaction when she threatened to blow her own brains out?

9. What was your reaction in the end when Briggen was taken away in handcuffs? Or were you rooting for him to get away?

10. What was your reaction when Shan and Nick ended up on the plane together?

A Preview of

THUGS
PART 6

CHAPTER ONE

FAHEEM

"Fah, this place is going to be crawling in a minute, dawg," my cousin G told me again.

"My son, man. My son, G," I said.

"I understand, but 5-0 will be here. What you wanna do?"

"My son, G. They shot my son." I squeezed him tighter, wishing I could turn back the hands of time. I had just met my son and was so grateful to have him in my life. And just like that . . . he was gone. This bitch called life don't ever play fair.

"Believe me, man. I know how you feel. You already know I've been there," Snell said. "But we got two muthafuckas dead and my little cousin here. You hit, and we got all of these burners on us."

"Y'all go. I got this. Ain't no sense in all of us dealing with this shit. Leave me be."

"Can't do—"

"Snell! Y'all get the fuck away from here. Y'all played y'alls part. You and G, go. Just get a hold of Jaz and tell her I need her. Don't tell her what happened, just tell her I said to come back home. Make sure the burner Wali had is still on him. Take mine." I kicked it away and went back to hugging my son while getting my story together.

RICK

My heart beat a mile a minute as I picked Kyra up from the porch and took her to my car. It felt as if I was performing a kidnapping. My palms were sweaty; my adrenaline was high. Moving like I was on a real live mission, I lay her across the backseat. My cell rang. It was Nina.

"Shit!" I spat. Now I was feeling like I was caught cheating so I decided to take the call. "Nina, baby. I'm in the middle of something. Can I call you back? Is everybody okay?"

Silence lingered on the other end. Then she finally asked, "Is everything okay with you?" as if she knew something was up.

"Everything's fine. Let me call you later." I ended the call before she could say anything and rushed back to the front porch to get Kyra's bags. I tossed them inside the popped trunk and then jumped into the front seat. I cranked the engine and headed for my hotel.

KYRA

I was dreaming I was riding in a car. But how did I get there? The last thing I remembered was standing in front of Rick.

My head was pounding. It felt more like it was about to burst through my eye sockets. I moaned, "My head."

As soon as I did, the car stopped and jerked forward, damn near throwing me off the backseat. I wasn't dreaming because the next thing I knew, the back door opened and this beautiful specimen of a man leaned over and asked if I was all right and if he should take me to the hospital.

"No. No more hospitals! I just need something for my head. It's pounding." Just as quickly as he was in the backseat asking if I was all right, he was back up in the front seat and pulling off.

We drove for a few minutes before the car stopped. I pressed both hands to my forehead and squeezed. Rick jumped out, and after several minutes he came back with some milk and a bottle of Tylenol for migraines. He helped me sit up.

"You can't take these on an empty stomach." He opened the carton of milk and held it to my mouth as if I was an invalid. Rick then opened the pill bottle, shook two out into my hand. I swallowed them, drank some more milk and lay back down. I badly wanted this headache to go away. It hurt to even think. The car started moving again and my thoughts were moving even faster. I was remembering people, places and things. My baby. My baby daughter, Aisha Kaeerah. Where was she? Rick. I remembered creeping around with him while I was still loving Marvin. Marvin? I was struggling to breathe, gasping for air. Gun. Mook pressed a gun up against my temple. I screamed at Marvin to give this nigga the money and to stop haggling with him. Then Marvin shot Junie and told me to put the car in reverse. I did and I crashed into the car behind me. That was when Fish jumped out, shot Mook and then he shot me. The last thing I remembered was hearing my daughter saying, "Daddy, we can't leave Mommy." I started crying and then everything went black again.

TRAE

Satisfied, I went into his bathroom to wash the blood off my hands and my blade. Pulling the ski mask off, I stuffed it inside my pocket. I then took off the hoodie, turned it inside out and put it back on.

After slipping out of this nigga's room and bypassing the elevators, I entered the stairwell. I rushed down six flights to the second floor and decided to get on the elevator. Just as I anticipated, when the doors opened it was full. I stepped on and got off with the crowd and made my way out of the main lobby passing security.

Outside, I started walking down 168th Street, thinking how that last move was done purely on emotion. Never a good thing, but it sure had me on a high. I hopped a bus and rode for a few blocks, got off and flagged down a taxi. I had the driver drop me off down the street from my apartment.

Mission accomplished.

AFTER ENJOYING A LONG hot shower, I lit a blunt and sat on the couch. I wanted to soak in and enjoy the peace and quiet around me, especially since I knew it was only the lull before the storm. The storm that I had created. I was attached to this apartment because it held so much of where I came from and who I was. That's why I would never sell it. My thoughts drifted back to when I first brought Tasha here. Bringing females to the spot was a no-no. But I knew she was the one. I'll always remember getting out of the hospital and having Tasha nurse me back to health here. What used to be my bachelor pad, now had tampons under the sink and a bedroom with bunk beds and Transformer curtains. This apartment also held a lot of memories from my hustling days. Me and Kay would be grindin' non-stop, running the streets for weeks at a time, and I would come home for only a day or two before we would be gone again. I couldn't forget how glad I was to have snatched up Tasha right when we were on our way out of the game. I was ready to settle down with that special someone who'd make me feel as if all that grindin' was well worth it. Tasha stepped up to the plate and made me feel just right.

I dozed off, but was awakened by somebody banging on the door. When the knocking got louder, I sat up and in walked Kay. We still had keys to each other's cribs.

I knew he would be stopping by, which was one of the reasons I didn't retire to the bedroom. I got up and went to the bathroom to wash my face and brush my teeth. Wide awake, I was now ready to face the music.

I went back into the living room and glanced at the clock. 3:33 A.M. I sat down, relit the other half of the blunt, took a few tokes, and stood up and passed it to my main man.

"So, you heard," I said to Kay as I sat down. I looked over at him and he looked as if he had been through war and back. His eyes were bloodshot and he wore the same clothes from earlier.

"Of course, I heard. I'm just leaving the muthafuckin'

precinct, a place where I said I was never stepping foot in again. I was one of the last niggas to leave the hospital room, so you know the police had to question me," Kay paused. "You fucked up, dawg. You did that shit in a public place. You know they got cameras everywhere in a hospital."

"Who did you mention it to?" I was still elated with my deed and didn't care about some damn hospital cameras.

"You know me better than anybody. Who the fuck you think I mentioned it to? At the station I only answered what Harry told me to answer. But you know I had to tell Angel bits and—"

"Fuck, nigga! Why did you have to say shit to her? You know she gonna tell Tasha. Tasha needed to hear this shit from me first." Hearing that took some of the fun out of what I had done.

"Nigga, I told her not to tell anybody, especially Tasha. And what the fuck do you mean 'why did I have to say shit to her?' Who do you think answered the door when the police came by? Who do you think called the lawyer? You may think you did, but you ain't pull the perfect crime, nigga. Not this time. You may have fucked yourself, and my hands are tied."

I thought about what he said and finally realized he was right. So I said, "For what it's worth, I apologize for putting you in this situation. I owe you for this one."

"You owe me more than an apology!" Kay barked. "You really got me in a fucked up situation. Anybody else, we wouldn't be sitting here talking," my partner-in-crime said as we locked gazes. They don't make niggas like Kay anymore. Here I done killed his brother, but because of our history, the circumstances, and him respecting the game, we didn't have to go to war.

"So, what's everybody saying? What's Mama Santos saying? You and her were the only ones stopping me from totally wildin'."

Kay chuckled, "Man, stabbing my brother in the throat wasn't wildin'? Like I said, I'm trying to keep it quiet. But there was a blurb over the local news. I didn't tell Kendrick, and Angel and my moms is up at the hospital now. He's in critical condition. Hell, the lawyer said that's the only reason they let me go. But if he dies, Trae, you gonna have a hard time getting out of this one. You need to get your attorney on this ASAP. Harry is reppin' me so you can't use him."

Time felt like it stopped. What the fuck did he mean in critical condition? I was there when that pussy took his last breath. How the fuck can a nigga survive stabs to the throat? Hell, I know I cut the jugular vein. Critical condition? That's impossible.

"Trae! Trae! What the fuck is wrong with you?" Kay yelled. "Yo, you looked like you spaced out."

I leaned back into the sofa and shut my eyes. I was not gonna let this nigga tear my family to shreds.

Kay laughed again, "Oh, I know what your problem is. You thought you deaded him, didn't you? The higher power obviously ain't done with neither one of you niggas yet." My eyes popped open just as Kay stood up. "Not yet. But we'll see what happens. The next six hours the doctors say are the most crucial." His cell rang; he glanced at it. "This is Angel now. I'm outta here."

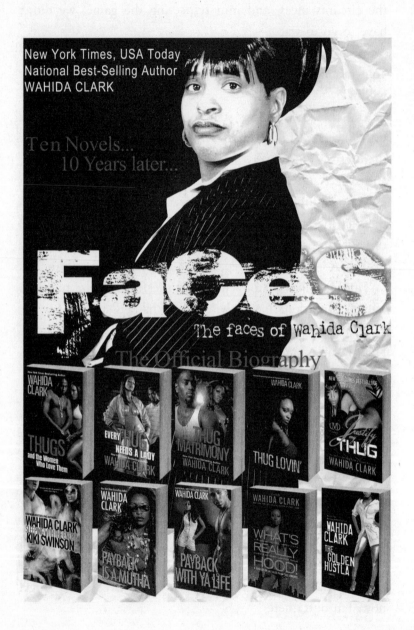

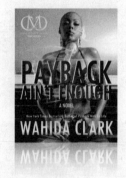

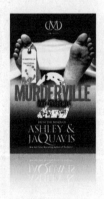
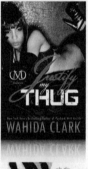
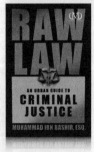
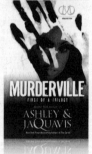